ESCAPE

THE SHORTEN CHRONICLES BOOK 2

ROSALIND TATE

Shorten Manor
Stables
Armoury
Servants' Hall
Office
Manor
Bower
Tennis Court
Greenhouses
Lucy's Cottage
Mrs Evan's Cottage
not to scale

Life is like a game of cards. The hand you are dealt is determinism; the way you play it is free will.
Jawaharlal Nehru

CHAPTER 1

Sophie Arundel leaned forward in her chair, nearer the flames in the cast-iron grate. Despite the merry fire, the bedroom was autumn-chilly. By her feet, a black retriever yawned, and beside him, Sophie's dog, Charlotte, gave a sleepy snore.

'*So* missing central heating,' Sophie said aloud, though she was alone apart from the dogs. 'But I miss slouching more.'

Sophie hadn't chosen to get stranded in an alternate 1925.

No flapper dresses here, or jolly parties, and slouching wasn't an option, wearing what Sophie called the full Monty: a corset made of whalebone, a thin chemise, and a long, teal-blue silk gown. The skirt narrowed below the knees, making walking difficult — and striding impossible. A plain round neckline contrasted with tight elbow-length sleeves, finished with scratchy lace.

A scent of old stone edged with lemon-sharp polish permeated the Manor, and distant doors closing and the pad of maids' footsteps outside Sophie's room were the soundtrack of her life.

Yet only three months ago, she'd been starting university in 2017, exploring a noisy, bustling campus. She'd walked into a lift, expecting to step out into a tower block corridor, but found herself in a country lane, part of a grand estate. And then the lift had vanished, apparently into thin air.

Sophie's four-poster bed had a canopy that cast most of the bedspread into shadow, but the morning sunlight, dappling through floor-to-ceiling French windows, was tawny-bright. Fine to read by.

She picked up *The Times* from a polished side table, folded it and squinted at the tiny dense print. Below adverts for face cream and dressmakers was a short news article:

Militia Routed in Manchester. After a reign of terror that left prominent citizens dead and injured, communist ringleaders are now safely behind bars. The whereabouts of other militia members remains unknown...

Grim men and women in a police line-up stared out of a sepia photo.

Manchester was a hundred miles away, wouldn't affect the Manor.

Sophie put the paper back on the table and glanced at an eye-catching, gaudy novel: *The Duchess Novelette: A Wild Love.* On the cover, a man dressed in black tie leered at a girl swooning on a couch.

Penny Dreadfuls were risqué, easy reads. Her maid, Maud Watkins, kept 'unsuitable' novels in Sophie's room to avoid them being confiscated by the housekeeper. Not a fan of servant-reading censorship, Sophie was happy to pretend *A Wild Love* was hers.

She opened a less exciting book, *Etiquette of Good Society,* but had hardly read a page when Maud came in.

Maud smoothed out a wrinkle on her black dress. 'Sorry, Miss. I thought you were in the library.' Her eyes were red-rimmed.

Sophie leapt to her feet. 'Maud?' Sophie used her maid's first name in private, but as Maud was a stickler for propriety, she refused to call Sophie by *her* first name. So Maud was 'Mrs Watkins' in public and Sophie was 'Miss' ... everywhere. 'Is it the baby?' Maud's sister had recently given birth, hadn't been well.

'The police telephoned the Manor... Mr Slater's died.'

Sophie thought she'd misheard, that Maud meant *Mrs* Slater. 'Your sister—'

'No, Miss. Her husband. Heart attack, they said.' Maud gulped. 'Very sudden. She's in a terrible state.'

Before she had time to consider what was appropriate or proper, Sophie hugged her and after a moment of embarrassment or panic, Maud gave in.

'You're not alone with this,' said Sophie. 'You need to sit down.' She gestured at the blue armchair by the fire.

Maud perched on the chair and Sophie rang a bellpull to get Maud a cup of tea. But Maud was here, not downstairs, in the servants' hall or somewhere in the house. She couldn't respond to the bell.

'You must go to her,' said Sophie.

'I'd have to take the afternoon off.'

'I can't promise but I'll see if Reynolds can take you.' Reynolds was one of the Manor's chauffeurs. 'If it would help, I'll come too.'

'I don't want a fuss, Miss.'

'No fuss.'

A maid appeared in the doorway.

'Could we have sandwiches and tea? And please prepare a food basket for a new mother.' The maid nodded. 'And can you ask the head gamekeeper if he can spare Miss Blackmore? She needs to mind the dogs.' Charlotte didn't need minding, but Jack did. He had cataracts, was nearly blind.

The maid scurried away.

'I'll clear this with Lady Lacey,' said Sophie.

When Sophie had arrived at the Manor from the twenty-first century, confused and frightened, Lady Anne Lacey had invited Sophie to stay on as a guest. Without that kindness, Sophie would have died in a ditch.

Anne agreed to Sophie taking the car, as Sophie expected she would.

Back in Sophie's room, the dogs' noses were too near dainty sandwiches and a silver tea service, and Maud was twisting her hands in her lap, ignoring the dogs and the food.

Miss Blackmore came in. Training to be a gamekeeper — a first for a girl here — her face was ruddy from working outside. 'How long am I minding the dogs, Miss?'

Sophie handed her the leads. 'Just the afternoon.'

Jack left with Miss Blackmore and after a mournful stare at the sandwiches, so did Charlotte.

Maud selected a day gown from a huge mahogany wardrobe. The dark blue skirt was fashionably shortened to above the ankles, and the matching hat was big and showy. Maud took out a navy cape. Floor-length, that was showy too.

'Shouldn't I wear mourning?' In the wardrobe was a veiled black hat and a funeral dress of corded silk and wool.

Maud shook her head, close to tears, so Sophie didn't ask why.

Once she'd changed, Sophie put on wrist-length, white linen gloves. When visiting, except when eating and drinking, ladies *always* wore gloves. One of an endless list of mad rules.

~

They set off in an open car with rain falling from a dull sky. Sophie's hat was soon sodden and heavy, and the leather-soft upholstery turned slick and slippery.

'Where's Slater's bakery?' Reynolds, short and thin and sporting a neat moustache, was a chauffeur, but wasn't like a taxi driver, familiar with every road.

'Halfway down the high street.' Maud twisted her hands.

'Is there anyone who could take over baking?' said Sophie, hoping to distract her.

'My sister will, Miss. And she's got Miss Kemble, her all-sorts maid.'

'Ladies can be bakers?'

'Mr Slater's mother started it, years ago.'

Counter-intuitive stuff. Women couldn't vote here, yet they ran businesses… 'What's the baby's name?'

'Rose.'

'Good name.' Rain dripped off Sophie's hat and she wiped water from the brim.

Small stores lined the road — butchers, greengrocers, dress shops — but being a Sunday, they were closed, and there was little traffic. They passed a police station, a few more shops, and stopped outside a three-storey, red-brick building. Above the door, BAKERY was carved in large letters, and on the door was a closed sign.

Sophie and Maud got out, Reynolds handed Maud the food basket from the boot, and gave her a sympathetic smile.

'Could you pick us up at three?' Sophie asked him.

He nodded.

Maud headed for a narrow alley. 'We can get in along here.'

Beyond the alley was a courtyard and the rear of the bakery. The back door opened into an industrial kitchen dominated by a blackened oven, set in a wall by a brick fireplace. Sturdy wooden cupboards lined the other walls and in the centre of the room a bare, workmanlike table was scrubbed clean.

Sophie sniffed, enjoying a warm bread smell. She took off her wet cape and gloves and put them on the table. Removing her hatpins, she laid them on the table too. A foot long and potentially lethal, they needed careful handling. She placed her soggy hat on top of the pins and stifled a sigh. Yes, she shouldn't have taken off the hat or the gloves, but surely in the circumstances, Maud wouldn't mind?

At the far end of the kitchen, Miss Kemble, the all-sorts maid, was making her way down a metal spiral staircase, cradling a baby. When she reached the bottom, she did a mini curtsey.

'Miss Kemble, this is Miss Arundel,' said Maud.

Sophie smiled at the maid, feeling awkward. Miss Kemble was a child, looked about twelve.

'Mrs Slater's in the front parlour,' said Miss Kemble, leading the way through a doorway.

Maud's sister lay on a ruby threadbare sofa in a loose dark dress, her eyes closed. Her hair was up in a messy bun, the exact auburn shade of Maud's, but Mrs Slater's face was more angular. A fire was lit in an inglenook that dwarfed the room, making the bread-scented air toasty warm.

'Mr Slater's in there.' Miss Kemble glanced at a shut door.

Maud put the basket on a chair. 'We've bought cake and meat and a nice pudding.'

Mrs Slater opened her eyes and registered Maud, saw Sophie and hastily sat up.

'How can we help?' said Sophie.

Mrs Slater patted her hair. 'Miss Kemble, tea.'

'Yes, Miss.'

Miss Kemble gave Maud the baby and hurried to the kitchen.

Rose started to wail and Maud rocked her, making

shushing noises. She sat beside her sister. 'Lizzie, you're going to be all right.'

'I'll help make tea,' said Sophie. She wasn't helping at all. Coming here had been a mistake.

Just as Sophie stepped into the kitchen, the back door crashed open.

Two men brandishing shotguns barged over the threshold, followed by a man and a woman, each waving a pistol.

CHAPTER 2

*B*ack in the summer, a footman had been arrested for attempted murder. That crime and its aftermath had sent shock waves through the Manor. Pending trial, Edmund Hunter had been remanded in custody.

But this was the man who was in front of Sophie now, wielding a shotgun. Edmund sported a new beard and moustache, but those striking dark eyes were unmistakable. Had he been tried and acquitted — or had he escaped?

Edmund stared at her, surprised. Sophie gave him a slight nod of recognition while her mind raced. What did he want? Why come armed to the teeth into a bakery?

His mates reminded her of the prisoners in the paper. Set, hard faces. The woman wore trousers and a man's shirt and jacket, her hair concealed under a scruffy bobble hat. Beside her, a wiry guy with cropped grey hair scanned the room. Sophie raised her hands and stood in front of Miss Kemble.

A man about Sophie's age stepped forward, moving like a soldier, precise and calculated. Clean-shaven, with brown hair and astute eyes, he held his pistol with easy familiarity. 'Who else is here?'

'Apart from us,' said Sophie, 'there are two women, a baby and a corpse. Mr Slater died yesterday.'

'I heard.'

So they were locals — or had good intelligence.

A sound from the back doorway. A young man hovered on the threshold, holding a dish covered by a cloth. 'I've bought a pie,' he said, then stopped in confusion, evidently not expecting armed assailants in a bereaved household. Before anyone else could react, the goon in charge casually aimed his pistol and shot the newcomer in the head. The young man crashed to the floor, his blood mingling with meat and potatoes from the smashed pie.

Miss Kemble cried out and clutched at Sophie.

Her mouth twisting in disgust, the woman in the bobble hat glared at the goon. 'That was unnecessary,' she said, in a strong Irish accent. She dragged the body into a corner, a thick red trail smearing the wooden floor.

Edmund didn't move, his face unreadable.

Sophie's heart hammered loud in her ears. She reached for Miss Kemble's hand and held it tight.

'Keep with the plan,' said the goon. 'Spread out. Clear the building.'

The Irish woman went into the parlour, the older guy and Edmund tramped upstairs, but the goon stayed in the kitchen.

He waved the pistol. 'I'm commandeering this building for the Communist party.' His clipped, educated accent jarred with his grubby jacket and trousers. 'More comrades will be along soon, and they'll need bed and board.' He turned to Sophie, his eyes narrowing with suspicion. 'And who might you be?' He took his time assessing, lingering on Sophie's mouth and chest.

Edmund had recognised her. Living at the Manor as a privileged guest could get her killed. If Edmund blabbed...

'Miss Green,' she said, giving the words a slight Derbyshire burr, a passable imitation of Maud. 'I'm a friend of Mrs Slater's.'

He pointed his pistol at her hat. 'That yours?'

'Yes, I saved up for the christening.' Her voice was hoarse, her throat dry.

He raised his eyebrows.

Stupid, bloody hat.

'*Miss* Green? A bit old to be single.'

She was eighteen, but people married earlier here.

'Nice dress and *very* nice watch.'

Sophie glanced at her wrist, dread turning into panic. A delicate gold strap and around the face tiny diamonds. A gift from Freddy Lacey.

Think.

She made her voice tremble. 'Actually, I'm a widow.' No need to act; she was shaking. 'I do plan to remarry…' No, widows kept on their wedding rings—

'A good-time girl … but classy.'

He thought she was a call-girl?

'You're not from the town.' He gave her a predatory smile.

She looked down, cowed, hoping to put him off guard. 'I've come from Derby.'

'You can cook, keep house?'

She nodded. He might not shoot a useful hostage.

The Irish woman returned. 'Ground floor clear.' She went upstairs.

'Who are you?' said Sophie, keeping the slight burr.

'Mr Barty Inkpin, at your service.' He did a sarcastic bow.

Was that really his name? She resisted an irrational urge to laugh, and a sudden volley of shots from the high street shocked the impulse away.

Maud and Lizzie rushed in from the parlour with Rose who was asleep, despite the noise outside.

Inkpin waved his pistol again. 'Slow down, ladies.'

Sophie had done kickboxing at school. Kicking wasn't an option now, literally hobbled by her narrow skirt, but they had to escape before his mates returned—

Inkpin clicked something on his pistol, pocketed it and smiled at Maud. The same smile he'd given Sophie: paper-thin charm, entitled lust. That moment of inattention was all Sophie needed. She launched herself forwards and punched him on the jaw as hard as she could.

He staggered in shock, his eyes wide. She grabbed the pistol from his pocket, aimed at his chest and pulled the trigger.

Nothing.

She tried again. Why didn't it fire? Actually, bad idea. Get away, not alert his friends. 'Out,' she yelled to the others.

Lizzie dashed through the back door with Rose, Miss Kemble close behind, but Inkpin tripped Maud as she ran by. She fell with a yelp.

Inkpin lunged for the pistol in Sophie's hand and she backed away, casting around for anything to use as a weapon.

Her hatpins. Razor sharp.

She yanked out a pin and drove it at his heart. After an instant's resistance of fabric and flesh against steel, it slid in. Smooth and silent. Just a trickle of blood.

Inkpin crumpled to the floor, twitched and stilled.

Sprawled beside him, Maud stared at Inkpin. And the pin.

Sophie hauled Maud to her feet, a drumbeat pounding in her brain. *Move.* She stepped towards the doorway, slipped on the murdered boy's blood, scrambled up, and walked out as fast as was possible in her tight skirt.

Outside, more gunfire sounded from the high street, and Rose woke up and wailed, the sound piercing and shrill.

In a garage by the alley, Miss Kemble scrambled into the front passenger seat of a van. Reverse-parked, it looked almost modern, with a regular roof and long chassis. Lizzie handed up a red-faced, bawling Rose to Miss Kemble.

'Maud, get in the passenger seat.' Lizzie's eyes were like Maud's in determined mode. Maud clambered in, clutching her right arm.

Lizzie opened the van's rear doors, frantically beckoning Sophie to climb in.

The vehicle's floor was level with Sophie's knees. She jumped sideways and forward, in a rubbish Fosbury flop, and landed inside.

Lizzie jumped into the driver's cab and put her foot down, but the van lurched. Sophie fell out and hit the ground with a hard thump.

By the time she raised her head, the van was disappearing down a side road through scrubland.

The garage wasn't visible from the bakery, but they'd search for her…

Hide.

She opened a side door to the alley. Empty. And the shooting had stopped. She could go along the passage, but out in the high street they'd see her from the bakery. Maybe she should go behind the shops, then onto the road? No, the militia might have spies or supportive locals who'd turn her in. A disguise, an old coat or overall from a washing line? In the shop yards, there were washing lines, but all empty — unsurprising given the weather.

But she couldn't stay here.

Between the first and second shop was a narrow space filled with rubbish: dumped beer barrels, dirty sheets, glass bottles and old newspapers. She eased around a broken wire fence and lay behind the barrels on her stomach, closing her mouth against the stench.

Inkpin's mates must have found him by now. Speared.

Should have taken the pin out, hidden it, kept them guessing. She was hiding too close—

A man's voice. 'They're long gone. His father will blame me. I'm not taking the rap.'

'We've got the building.' The Irish woman. Authoritative, calm.

More voices, low and angry.

The same woman. 'Get everybody in and secure it.'

More grumbling.

Silence.

Cold minutes passed. At least the rain had stopped. Sophie's knuckles throbbed from punching Inkpin, her spine ached from falling off the van, and regret and horror soured her throat, her mind full of the innocent boy. But all she felt about killing Inkpin was relief and defiance. He'd surely murdered other innocents.

A quote from one of her mother's faith books came into her head, serene and unwelcome: *when you see the light in each and every person, you should never extinguish it, for a greater good or self-defence…*

Sophie held her jaw to stop her teeth chattering and checked her watch: half one. If the militia hadn't blocked the road, Maud would be safe at the Manor.

It started to rain and she closed her eyes. Rose screaming … the inability of babies to sense danger and keep quiet was a *big* evolutionary flaw. How had humans survived?

She half dozed, shivering and wet. Was she a murderer? Desperate self-defence — most people would understand that. Wouldn't they?

Childhood memories had faded, but her parents' ideals had left a big imprint. She'd embraced their pacifism. Fighting in wars held no appeal and defending herself in the playground hadn't counted. And in history lessons, she'd parked the notion that but for millions of allied soldiers in World War Two, evil would have triumphed.

Not thinking about difficult stuff had worked pretty well. Just hadn't bargained for 1925 and a psychopath.

Her parents might still exist in some way, beyond the veil of death, but hopefully they couldn't see her here. They'd be distraught, believing she'd burn in their imagined hell…

CHAPTER 3

A rustling sound in the pile of rubbish. A smooth brown rat paused, right by Sophie's face, and stared at her.

Only a rat. At home, she'd campaigned to stop animal testing in labs — including rats, but she put her hands over her face. Didn't want to be bitten.

Her mind drifted to Hugo. They'd attended the same school but hadn't been friends. And so much had happened since they'd arrived here, stumbling out of the portal that had been disguised as a lift. She'd positively disliked him, but in Shorten that had changed fast. Curiosity, attraction, then she'd fallen madly—

'Quiet and slow.' Hugo's voice.

Was she hallucinating? Sophie cautiously raised her head. Hugo and a gardener from the Manor were creeping past her rubbish space towards the bakery. Sophie checked her watch. Nearly three. Maud must have raised the alarm.

At over six foot, Hugo was gangly thin beside the shorter, thick-set gardener, his dark hair ruffled as if he'd run his fingers through it. Both men were aiming a shotgun in front of them, looking like Wild West sheriffs, except Hugo was wearing a brown, boxy suit.

Sophie stood up and hissed, 'Here.'

Hugo saw her and his shoulders sagged in relief. He pointed behind him and whispered, 'Everyone's by the police station. *Go.*'

Hugo had played soldiers in the Combined Cadet Force at school, but he'd got this wrong. 'There's loads of them. You'll be a sitting duck.'

'We're seeing if there are guards.'

'You shouldn't risk tipping them off.' She pointed at her squalid hide out. 'You could put rubbish in that alley by the garage and set it on fire. The bakery will go up and they'll leave. No bystanders in there, apart from Mr Slater, and he's dead.'

'Change of plan,' said Hugo. 'We use the petrol cans in the cars.'

They hurried by the shop yards, Sophie managing to keep up. 'Where's the police?'

'Two dead, three wounded,' said Hugo. 'Shoot out at the station. Militia couldn't get in, so they went for the bakery.'

'But more police will come?'

'No.' Hugo was in brisk military mode, his square-jawed face tense. 'They cut all the phone wires.'

They'd reached the high street. Lizzie's van and the Laceys' cars, one green and one red, were in the middle of the road. Skewed, as if they'd just stopped rather than parked. Near the vehicles were gardeners and gamekeepers from the Manor, carrying shotguns, ammunition belts slung over their shoulders.

Sir Richard Lacey stood by the green car, talking to John Watkins, Hugo's valet and Maud's husband. Next to them was Freddy Lacey, heir to the Shorten estate. Tall and wiry, with short sandy hair, Freddy was habitually laid back. But today he looked as wired as Hugo.

Richard, Freddy and John wore their regular suits, but had shotguns too. Against the backdrop of a florist shop awning and a traditional English barbershop ... surreal.

Freddy sprinted to Sophie and pulled her painfully close, jamming her into the gun slung across his chest. 'Thank God.'

After a moment, he said to Hugo. 'How many?'

'Didn't get that far.'

They joined the main group and Sophie explained to Richard her arson idea. Everyone except Hugo stared at her as if she'd grown two heads.

'It's a good plan,' said Hugo. 'Minimum risk to us.'

'We could set the fire after dark,' said Freddy.

'No,' said Richard, 'harder to pick them off.'

'Once the fire catches, if there are buildings across from the bakery and we can get inside, when the militia run out, we'll see them,' said Sophie.

Richard nodded. 'Town houses.'

'Behind the bakery, there's wasteland. We could use the van for cover.' Sophie had watched a lot of action movies. 'The trouble is...' She bit her lip.

Richard frowned. 'Yes?'

'There might be more exits.'

'There aren't,' said Richard. 'Mrs Slater drew us a map.' He showed her a rough pencil sketch.

Gathered around Richard, the gardeners listened, guns slung over their coats like prohibition gangsters.

'They could be in the town houses already,' added Sophie, shivering in her wet clothes.

'They're all in the bakery,' said a smart, jowly man she hadn't noticed.

'Miss Arundel, this is Mr Morgan,' said Richard. 'He's been kind enough to allow us to assist.'

'I am the mayor of this fine town. Good afternoon.' Mr Morgan tipped his bowler to Sophie. Given the circumstances, a bizarre gesture. 'Madam, I'll find you a coat.'

'That would be kind.'

'So, we start the fire,' said Richard, just loud enough for everyone to hear. 'We go in the van and catch them as they leave out the back.' He pointed at some gardeners. 'Find a vantage point in the houses overlooking the bakery. Think … finishing off a fox den.'

Horrible analogy. 'They might surrender,' said Sophie.

Richard shook his head. 'They're linked to the group that attacked Manchester. They'll come out shooting.'

The mayor handed her an old man's coat, black and tatty. 'Apologies. Best I could do at short notice.'

'Thank you.' She slipped it on.

'I've got matches,' said a red-haired lad. 'I'll do the fire.'

'Good man.' Richard turned to Hugo.

'Won't take long.' Hugo gave a curt nod.

No was on the tip of Sophie's tongue. 'If they spot you, they'll shoot. With this coat, I'm shabby, invisible. Can I borrow your cap?' Without waiting for an answer, she grabbed it from a gardener and put it on. 'See?'

Hugo's mouth thinned into a stubborn line. 'No way.'

'You're being irrational,' said Sophie. '*I* have to go.'

'Absolutely not,' said Freddy, so loudly, there was a communal intake of breath.

'I'm going,' said Hugo. 'End of.'

'But,' said Sophie. 'I—'

'Enough,' said Richard.

She was beaten. Richard was in charge. Helpless and angry, she gave the gardener his cap and ignored Freddy.

Hugo was being stupidly noble, but Freddy was well out of order.

Hugo and the red-haired boy carried cans of petrol out of sight beyond the shops, and Freddy squeezed Sophie's hand. She didn't respond, anger simmering as her brain ran through scenarios: snap decision, bad timing, and Hugo could be clumsy, held his shotgun gingerly, as if it could misfire or jam…

Cold fear circled in her stomach. The place where Hugo had gone from sight was silent and empty.

,'He'll be fine,' said Freddy, with unconvincing confidence.

As they waited in the road, time crawled by, and Sophie felt sick. How long? Five, ten minutes? Longer?

'There,' said Freddy.

Hugo was running towards them, followed closely by the red-haired boy.

'It's done,' said Hugo. 'Went up fast.'

Richard addressed Freddy. 'You're with me.'

'We'll go to the town houses,' said Hugo.

'Sophie, stay close,' said Freddy.

'She'll be safer with me,' said Hugo, 'inside a building.'

'I can hear you.' Sophie glared at them. Why were they talking about her as if she wasn't there? Were they in shock?

Freddy whispered in her ear, 'Keep safe,' and ran to the van.

'You too,' Sophie called after him.

Richard, Freddy, and some gardeners piled into the van. The mayor led Sophie, Hugo, and the remaining men behind a row of houses.

Crackling. The fire must have caught.

Years ago, barefoot on a beach, she'd stepped on a lit cigarette end. The pain from that tiny flame had been unbearable, horrific. And at school, that remembered agony had given history lessons and accounts of 'witches' burnt at the stake a too-real resonance. Sophie resisted reaching for Hugo's hand, balling her fists in the pockets of the huge coat.

'Unsettling times.' The mayor knocked on a door.

A man with a bushy beard and tiny round glasses pulled the door ajar.

'May we come in?' asked Mr Morgan.

The man nodded. If he'd said no, Sophie sensed they'd still have barged in, but sheepishly. As they trooped up narrow dogleg stairs, the homeowner locked the door behind them.

'I tried to shoot a pistol in the bakery,' Sophie said to Hugo, 'but it wouldn't work.'

He pointed to a lever by the trigger on his shotgun. 'Safety catch.'

She hit her head with her hand. Idiot. But she'd never touched a gun in her life, and she'd had seconds…

'Sir?' Reynolds beckoned to Hugo from a small room. The floor was bare wooden boards, the only furniture a bed with an iron bedstead and purple quilt.

Hugo joined Reynolds and warily looked out a window, keeping his body by the wall. Waving flames obscured half the bakery, flickering up the external walls and leaping across the roof.

Hugo opened the window, and a bitter burning smell and crackling noise invaded the room. 'When they shoot, bullets will ricochet off the walls and that bedstead. One shooter per bedroom, backup shooter on the landing. You two set up in the house that way, you two the other side.' He gestured right and left, and the four gardeners thumped down the stairs. 'Reynolds, take cover with the mayor and Miss Arundel.'

Hugo knelt, rested his shotgun on the sill and settled the butt into his shoulder. But Sophie hesitated. With all her soul, she wanted to say, 'I love—'

Bang.

'Go to Reynolds,' ordered Hugo. 'Now.'

Something zapped by Sophie's left ear and she left quickly. Beside the doorway, Reynolds was sat with his back against the interior wall, his knees drawn up, holding his shotgun with the butt on the floor. She sat on the other side.

Hugo fired. *Bang* ... bang. *Bang.*

The mayor was pacing on the landing. An alarming metronome, humming to himself.

'Mr Morgan,' said Sophie, 'you need to—'

The mayor fell with a juddering thud onto the half landing on the stairs. His eyes turned glassy.

Bang. *Bang.*

Reynolds didn't move.

Neither did Sophie, though her corset was painfully digging into her hips. 'He's dead.'

'Yes, Miss.' Reynolds' voice was calm and quiet.

Sophie had given a name to how everything here — however dire — was understated: the Shorten Code. Underplaying bad stuff helped, but not always.

Bang, *bang* ... bang.

'The lads next door are gamekeepers,' said Reynolds. 'They won't miss.'

Finishing off a fox den. She'd never kill an innocent animal. But terror blocked the thought, her mind racing. They were trapped here. Hugo—

Bang.

She put her hands over her ears.

CHAPTER 4

*R*eynolds' brow was sweaty. So was Sophie's, despite a chilly breeze rolling through the landing from the open window, stronger than the heat from the bakery.

For now.

Even over the guns, the fire was loud, chaotic sizzling of brick and unknown things that nobody should hear burn.

Finally, the shooting stopped. Sophie was desperate to check on Hugo but she rested her head back on the wall. Be safe, be safe.

As if in answer to her thoughts, Hugo appeared in the doorway, pale but unhurt. 'Let's go.'

They went downstairs, stepping gingerly around Mr Morgan. 'I'm sorry about the mayor,' Hugo said to the bearded man.

The man's eyes widened but he only said, 'These things happen.'

As much as they could in the cramped hall, Hugo and Reynolds kept their shotguns up, ready to shoot. The homeowner opened the front door, Reynolds and Hugo stepped outside, and Sophie followed.

Billowing clouds of smoke had turned daylight into premature dusk, embers floated in the air, and acrid fumes invaded Sophie's nostrils and throat. She pulled up the borrowed coat to protect her face.,The bakery was an invisible core inside an inferno. In the distorting light of the flames, smooth pools on the tarmac road were red and shiny beside contorted bodies.

'We're done.' said Hugo, lowering his shotgun. Reynolds slung his across his chest.

Hugo linked arms with Sophie and strode off. She struggled to keep up, taking quicker but smaller steps like a determined puppet on strings. The gamekeepers from the adjacent houses were also rushing along the street, fleeing the living, roaring hell.

By the police station, there were only trails of smoke in the sky, and people hurrying from the fire packed the road: men, children, and women with babies.

Parked by the Laceys' cars was a bright red fire engine. Smaller than a modern one, it was open, with a ladder connected to a wheel at the rear. Three firemen wore navy uniforms with polished buttons. On their heads were pointed helmets.

Hugo let go of Sophie's arm and said loudly, 'I'm afraid the mayor is dead, but the baker's family is safe.'

The crowd started whispering.

'Are all the militia dead?' asked an elderly lady in a threadbare cloak.

'The ones who came out the front are,' said Sophie.

The woman's mouth tightened. Had her son or daughter been in the militia? They hadn't all been cold-blooded killers. When Inkpin shot that boy, that Irish woman had been revolted...

The van turned onto the road and stopped. In the gloom, Sophie could make out Freddy in the passenger seat, unhurt. She drew a deep, grateful breath.

Richard climbed out and addressed the fire fighters. 'The area's safe.'

The firemen promptly sped off to the blaze, and Sophie felt guilty, and sick. This had been her idea.

'Four escaped,' said Richard. 'We have one wounded and a fatality. We should go.'

Fatality. Please not Maud's John.

The van and two cars arrived at the Manor in convoy. Passing through open ornamental gates, they stopped in a line on the wide gravel drive.

Freddy jumped out and ran to help a skinny man struggling to get down from the van. The man's left arm was limp and bloody.

Three gardeners carried a boy towards the servants' hall, the first holding his shoulders, the second supporting the body and another his legs. They paused as a woman in loose black trousers and a dark shirt ran across the drive. She cradled the boy, shaking her head. 'No, no, no.'

Sophie scurried over to her. Lucy Hemmings, the head gardener, was her friend.

When Sophie saw who they were carrying, she faltered. The red-haired boy who'd volunteered with Hugo... She swayed and Richard caught her. 'Deep breath,' he said, 'and another one.'

Sophie stumbled along the thick studded ramp that bridged a dry moat to the house. In the hall, the butler, the housekeeper and Anne Lacey were standing like silent sentries. Anne's eyes were dewy bright.

'The militia's gone,' said Richard.

The butler and housekeeper exchanged a relieved glance, embodying more than professional understanding. This house nourished many layers of friendship.

'Chin up.' Richard gave Sophie a meaningful look and she nodded.

No need to tell Anne details. No need to tell anyone.

Sophie squeezed Anne's hand. Anne had come through the portal many years ago. She could never replace Sophie's real mother, but they'd forged a strong bond.

Hugo strode down the corridor that led to their rooms, and Sophie took rapid, short steps to catch him up. 'I'm glad you're okay.'

'And you.'

But he retreated to his bedroom so she retreated to hers. Whatever he'd done today, he wanted no comfort from her.

In her room, Maud was sat in the chair, clutching her arm.

Sophie petted the dogs who noisily greeted her. 'Mr Watkins is okay.'

Maud's drawn face crumpled in relief. 'Would you mind if I didn't help you dress for dinner, Miss?'

'Not at all.'

Maud hurried out.

Inside the grate, warm flames flickered safely, but Sophie's clothes were wet and sticking to her, and she was bone-achingly cold. She lay on top of the coverlet, unable to undress; the buttons on the gown were all on the back.

Maud had seen her kill Inkpin. Had Maud bailed because she couldn't stomach being near her? The dogs jumped onto the bed, sensing Sophie's turmoil, and snuggled close.

Maud was her friend, or had been…

Knocking. Excited barking.

Sophie blinked.

Hugo was by the door, dressed in old-fashioned black tie. His white shirt had a stiff, winged collar, his black wool jacket was scallop-shaped and was longer at the back, down to his knees.

Sophie checked her watch. 7.25 pm. Must have fallen asleep. 'What's happening?'

'Nothing.' To her surprise, Hugo sat on the bed and covered her right hand with his. 'How are you feeling?'

Still half asleep, her bruised knuckles and the tingle from his touch snapped her awake. She withdrew her hand. 'Fine.'

'Dinner's in thirty minutes.'

The last thing she needed was a formal meal. 'Maud's in no state to get me dressed.' She stood up. On top of a toiletries cupboard was a jug of water. She poured some into a bowl and rinsed her face.

Hugo grimaced. 'We're friends, right?'

'Yes.'

'You really stink.'

'Thanks for that.' She rang the bellpull. 'How's the man with the bad arm?'

'If the wound doesn't get infected, Freddy's valet should recover.' He hesitated. 'That young gardener died instantly, wouldn't have felt any pain.'

Sophie pushed away the memory of the boy on the drive but the boy in the bakery replaced it, and she gagged.

'Have a bath. You don't have to come to dinner.'

She was in bits. He must be too. Was he haunted by the faces of the people he'd shot? She wasn't up for asking him.

'The attack on the town is just the start,' said Hugo. 'When was the last time you thought about the lift puzzle?'

He was trying to distract her. A team of scientists had theorised and speculated, even camped out at the lift spot twenty miles away. They hadn't found the portal. Unlikely she and Hugo would. But she regularly re-read her notes. 'A few days ago.'

Hugo stroked Charlotte. 'Richard's going to say a few words about Andrew Cousins.'

'The red-haired boy?'

'Yes.' Hugo got to his feet.

If he could face eating in the dining room, she could. One more challenge. 'I'll call for you as normal.'

He paused at the door. 'Sure?'

She nodded. He was acting as if he'd spent the afternoon in the drawing room, not at the O.K. Corral. But he'd probably offloaded to John.

As Hugo left, a maid came in and wrinkled her nose. Miss Parry was only fifteen, probably hadn't finished Maid-Tact training…

Yes, Sophie Arundel needed a bath.

Twenty minutes later, Sophie was clean and dressed in her favourite red evening dress. Though it appeared formal, the gown was technically a 'tea dress.' No corset required.

Every day, Maud wound Sophie's hair around scrunched balls of paper called 'rats,' so when she put Sophie's hair up in an artful bun, her locks appeared wavier and fuller. Styled with Miss Parry's help, Sophie's reflection in a tall, free-standing mirror looked normal. Well, Shorten normal.

At dinner, the butler, Mr Crawford, was the same as usual: dignified, inscrutable. But the footmen, who usually whispered to each other, were silent. Richard had been given a detailed account of Andrew's character and aspirations, and as Richard paid tribute, though she hadn't known the boy, Sophie wanted to cry. But everyone else was holding it together.

Block this out, think about a happy time. Winning the kickboxing final at school and hugging Isha, her BFF…

The first course of mushroom soup was deep and nourishing, and Sophie relished its comfort and heat. The fire in the grand fireplace looked good but didn't affect the temperature in most of the room. After three months here, she'd become used to the splendid dining room with its dark-panelled walls, old portraits, and bare oak floor. The only rug was underneath the banqueting table: long and narrow and royal blue.

Sophie didn't take her elaborate place setting for granted: a sapphire mat edged with delicate gold leaf, silver cutlery laid for five or six courses, and the handwritten menu card in a silver holder. But she wasn't *quite* used to a footman placing a large cotton napkin on her knees whenever she sat down.

After the meal, she stood up to accompany Anne. Charlotte stood up too, resigned to leaving the men to their whisky and cigars.

Anne had told Sophie that she still thought the convention odd. Before stepping through the portal, Anne had been at university in the 1980s. Well before Sophie had been born, but relatively modern.

As they left, Anne suggested missing coffee and Sophie gratefully agreed, beyond tired.

'If I'd had *any* inkling about the militia…' Anne hugged her. 'I would never have let you go.'

Thanks to press censorship and upbeat stories, nobody had known. How many other towns, unprepared and undefended, were now run by militias?

When Sophie fell asleep, her final thoughts were of the bakery…

Fire chased her. Flames wrapped round her body, a sizzling, hissing snake. Pain and terror and despair—

She woke, her heart hammering, and mercifully slid back into sleep.

Safe at school in her dorm.

Making out with Hugo. He tugged down the straps of her top and kissed her shoulders, his lips warm but making her shiver. 'I know about Inkpin,' he whispered, 'and I've told Freddy.'

Hugo morphed into Freddy.

'You smell horrible.' Freddy pointed a pistol in her face and fired.

CHAPTER 5

The next morning at seven, Maud lit the fire in Sophie's bedroom, not once looking in Sophie's direction. Feigning sleep, Sophie told herself that Maud wasn't stepping back from their friendship, only following the Shorten Code…

Strange that Maud was so obsessed with dignity and behaving properly and yet was such a gossip. Yes, they'd been friends, but Sophie knew not to share *anything*.

But Freddy would hear about Inkpin. Might have already.

As Maud left, closing the door softly behind her, the diamond-paned windows rattled with a burst of rain, and Sophie pulled the bulky bedclothes up to her chin, wishing she could feign sleep forever.

Freddy didn't know her, so he'd set her on a pedestal. She might have kept her balance on the wretched thing if she'd shot Inkpin rather than skewered him. But Hugo would surely understand? Unease slid down her spine. No. The story would grow in the telling. Not one pin but two. Or three. Cackling with laughter as she did it. And even *exactly* what she'd done — that image — would stay forever in Hugo's brain.

She turned onto her side and her mind meandered back to the portal. In 2017, in the students' union, she'd assumed the lift had been painted gold for an art project, that the maths signs and childlike sketches on the doors were random. But those images had been symbols and the pictures destinations, like place names on a bus.

And the portal didn't show itself to just anyone.

Over three decades, only six people had stepped through it. Anne had been the first and Lucy Hemmings, the head gardener, the second. Lucy had arrived with another girl, Janet, who'd died a few years later from an infected scratch. Alan Parkes who ran the village pub had arrived next, and after him, Sophie and Hugo.

With so few 'visitors,' as the locals called them, Hugo had speculated that they shared a rare gene. Wacky, but all they'd got—

Maud came in holding a tray with tea and toast.

Usually a chatterbox, she stayed entirely silent as Sophie dressed, and Sophie was glad to call on Hugo. But on the way to the dining room, he was silent too.

Freddy and Anne weren't at breakfast and Richard hid behind the paper.

After the meal, Richard stood up and Hugo hastily got to his feet. Hugo worked in the estate office, was keen to prove himself; eventually might make estate manager.

As Richard left, Sophie waylaid him. 'Can we talk in private, please?' She couldn't face telling Hugo, but she needed to tell Richard, hopefully *before* he heard a garbled version.

Richard gestured for her to walk with him. 'Let's go to the large drawing room.'

After a moment's hesitation, Hugo carried on to the

office, and Sophie followed Richard to the oldest part of the house, the dogs in her wake. Jack was really Richard's dog, but Jack had formed a reciprocated attachment to Charlotte, and when Jack's eyesight deteriorated, Sophie had taken on minding him.

In a few minutes they were in the large drawing room. It *was* large, like a hall inside a castle. A double-height ceiling coffered into rectangles showcased the Lacey coat of arms in the centre, a royal blue 'L' outlined in gilt amidst brown, prancing stags. A grand piano graced one corner of the room and across from it on a walnut cabinet was a gramophone with a polished brass trumpet. Weak sunlight streamed through Jacobean stone-framed windows, flickering over a wide, medieval fireplace. The grate was empty and the air cold.

Sophie closed the door, the dogs mooched about and she perched on a dark pink sofa.

Richard settled himself in a dark leather armchair, his brown eyes concerned. 'The fire brigade telephoned last night. Two buildings by the bakery were destroyed, but they stopped it spreading. Heavy rain helped.'

She couldn't dress this up. 'I killed one of the militia.'

Richard gaped.

Sophie summarised, not glossing over the pin, but her description sounded too clinical. A soldier delivering a report. 'He'd just shot an innocent boy in the head.'

Very slowly, Richard exhaled. 'Do you know who you … dealt with?'

'It sounded like a stage name. Barty Inkpin.'

Richard gaped again. Becoming a habit. 'Are you sure?'

'Certain. He told me.'

'Bartholomew Inkpin is, *was*, the son of Albert Inkpin, the leader of the Communist Party. If *anyone* from that group identifies you, he'll hunt you down.'

'Mr Hunter was with the militia. He recognised me.'

'I thought he was in custody,' said Richard. 'The police are trying to identify the bodies. Mr Hunter might be dead.' He hesitated. 'Who else knows about this?'

'Only Mrs Watkins, but as she does, so will most of Shorten.'

'Mrs Watkins and her sister retired early, and Mr Crawford has told the servants that if they talk about who was involved, or *any* details, they'll be dismissed.' Richard shook his head. 'I was concerned about reprisals … but this is something else.'

Mr Crawford was a formidable butler, but nobody could stop gossip. 'If the militia do find out it was me, I'm nobody. Won't they be busy targeting other towns?'

Richard shook his head again, exasperated. 'Did you read in the paper about the Bellamy fire?'

'Yes, back in August.' A mob had torched a country house. The homeowner had been killed.

'It wasn't a random attack.'

Sophie frowned. What did this have to do with her?

'Two weeks before he was murdered, Mr Bellamy and his gamekeepers confronted a small militia group on his estate. Mr Bellamy shot one of them and the man subsequently died. The mob set the fire, but the militia planned it, riled people up.'

'That wasn't in the paper.'

'It's not common knowledge.'

'If you don't mind me asking,' said Sophie, 'how do you know this?'

'I have friends in London who keep me informed, particularly of anything that could affect the estate. Inkpin Senior isn't a small-town militia leader, Sophie. He started the militias. They all report to him. And he hasn't lost a foot soldier. He's lost his *son*.' Richard got to his feet, walked over to the empty fireplace and turned to face her. 'He won't bother stirring up a mob to avoid blame. He'll send his best.'

Cold spread through Sophie's guts. 'It's only a matter of time, isn't it?'

'I don't believe any of the servants are passing information to the militia but that could still happen by accident, through gossip.'

'Mr Crawford—'

'He's contained idle talk in the Manor.' Richard sat in the dark chair again. 'The problem is the bakery survivors. What *they* know.'

'When Mr Hunter found Barty Inkpin,' said Sophie, '... dead, he'd surely have told them my name?'

'Even if he didn't, the survivors know *how* Bartholomew Inkpin died, and his father will quickly establish the link between Mrs Slater, her sister, and the Manor, which can only lead to you. Once Inkpin Senior is certain, he'll act.'

'Actually,' said Sophie, 'he might not.'

Richard looked puzzled.

'He might think a girl couldn't have killed his son.'

'I beg your pardon?'

'It sounds crazy, but at home until really recently, the belief that women couldn't do certain things was so accepted, it led men to disregard what was obvious. So, in World War Two, women flew fighter planes between factories and airfields. There was more than one instance when a girl landed a plane and the men at the airfield refused to believe she was the pilot. They even searched the plane to find the "real" pilot.'

'Is flying an aeroplane incredibly difficult?' asked Richard.

'Don't think so. You just have to take lessons.'

'*Inkpin dying by a lady's hand is preposterous...* Yes, playing along with that assumption could give us some time and, with luck, throw them off the scent.' Richard nodded to himself. 'You need to bury your head in romance books, appear to have no interest in serious matters. I'm going to arrange regular security briefings, but it would be inappropriate for a well-bred young lady like yourself to attend. And we shouldn't meet again, not like this, closeted together. The servants will notice and talk. Of course, they might conclude that I'm an older man, enamoured...' Richard gave a self-deprecating shrug at the notion. 'But it would only take one person to get wind of the unusual circumstances of Inkpin's demise, and that would quickly reach the town—'

'I can act dumb,' said Sophie.

Richard gave her a respectful half nod. 'I'll keep you informed of security improvements using a hidden compartment in the library. No one knows of it outside the family. Look for a narrow window and below it, press a nick in the wood. Read the notes and burn them.'

'A bit cloak and dagger.'

'But efficient. It worked in the sixteenth century, so should work now.' He steepled his hands. 'We can refill the moat, not keep it too clean, and reinstate the drawbridge. Shorten Manor won't be an easy prize. They'll need heavy artillery to get in.'

It was Sophie's turn to gape.

'The wider estate, the cottages, they'll be more difficult to protect.'

'Why would the militia target cottages?'

'Why fight your way into a fortified Manor when you could take estate families hostage?'

'The police,' said Sophie, 'or the army—'

'The militia might surrender, but what if they don't? A pitched battle through people's homes ... I won't risk the lives of women and children.'

Sophie swallowed. He'd surrender the Manor — and her.

'But we have time to put measures in place.' Richard

stood up. 'And over the centuries, these walls have successfully shielded more than a few individuals who didn't want to be found.'

She wasn't reassured.

He came over to the sofa and sat beside her. By the grate, Charlotte opened one eye, but Jack didn't stir. 'If you hadn't all escaped when you did,' said Richard, 'it could have turned out very badly.'

'Human shields.'

'What do you mean?'

'Gunmen hiding behind civilians, so good guys won't shoot.'

'That's appalling,' said Richard. 'Now, for your own safety, you must learn how to handle a firearm. I'm going to ask the gamekeepers to share their expertise with the gardeners, so Miss Hemmings can show you, but discreetly. *No one* else should know. Not even Anne.'

'I promise.'

'We'll get through this.' Richard patted her arm and got to his feet.

She stood up and followed him out into the corridor.

As Richard headed towards the office, Sophie paused and petted the dogs. She and Richard had reached an understanding. She trusted him — just not with anything to do with the portal. Richard worried that if she could, Anne would go home, so he'd never let Reynolds drive them to the lift spot to test theories. But for now, that was academic. She'd run out of ideas.

She walked to her room, ruminating on Richard's advice. Keep busy. Keep a low profile.

CHAPTER 6

Once a week, Sophie worked in the office, updating tenants' records and cottage inventories. It was good to be useful. At weekends, she read in the small drawing room with the boys, or drank tea in the large drawing room with them, listening to scratchy music on the gramophone.

But this morning, it was routine weekday stuff. After she'd walked the dogs, Sophie changed into trousers and a top borrowed from Lucy, went to the other side of the house and unlocked a door — Sophie possessed the only key.

Against a wall were stacking chairs and a dusty, rolled up carpet. Beyond a cobwebbed window was a dense row of elm trees. A natural privacy barrier.

In the centre of the floor was a punch bag on a stand. Anne and Lucy had helped set up this space so Sophie could practise kickboxing. Hugo and Freddy also knew about it. But as the hobby would alarm suitors, Maud — and everyone else in Shorten — believed Sophie practised a more demure activity: mini-archery.

Following the workout, she had a bath with Maud in tow,

in case she slipped. The hip bath did have tall sides. The rest of the morning, she spent in the library. Like the large drawing room, the library held less appeal on colder days, but apart from Anne or Hugo returning a book, Sophie was rarely disturbed. And with so many classic novels, she was spoilt for choice.

In the early afternoon, Sophie walked the dogs again and at three precisely, changed into a tea dress and took tea with Anne, before changing back into the full Monty — corset obligatory. Yes, it was Groundhog Day, but after Inkpin, emotionally exhausted, she welcomed the familiar routine.

After tea, Sophie's thoughts returned to the red-haired boy who'd died, Andrew Cousins. Lucy had only recently hired him. She should go and comfort her.

Sophie set off with the dogs across the lawn towards Lucy's cottage. She adjusted her small, turquoise velvet hat as she walked and did up the cloak she'd borrowed from Anne. Sophie's hat and cape had burned with the bakery. Hopefully, so had her hat pins and any other evidence.

The borrowed duck-egg blue cape had a hood. More like a cloak from a fairy tale than a regular coat.

On the way, a bower caught her eye, the trees and bushes dressed in rich autumn finery, orange, purple and rust-red. Even within the moat, the Manor's gardens were big enough to get lost in, with groves, lawns and flowerbeds, and meandering gravel paths.

Sophie crossed the moat over an ornamental stone bridge, passed three imposing greenhouses and turned right along a narrow lane lined with elms. The trees' leaves were bright yellow, some fluttering on branches, others spread around the trunks like showy skirts. She tasted rain on the breeze, pictured it nourishing the earth beneath her feet and savoured the rural quiet. Soothing. A pause before winter.

Lucy's cottage was on the left, a few yards from the road.

She wasn't in, so Sophie sat on a battered chair on the porch while Jack stayed by her legs and Charlotte sniffed at the grass. 'It'll be dark soon, so she'll be here,' Sophie told the dogs. 'If you can't see, you can't garden.'

Sure enough, Lucy came striding along, her coat flapping. When Sophie had asked Anne how Lucy could openly wear trousers, Anne had said that over time, Lucy had become an honorary man. Proving her worth gradually, with small steps. Maybe Sophie Arundel could do that too?

'I would have texted,' said Sophie, as Lucy opened the door, 'but I've lost your number.'

Lucy winced at the weak joke. 'That takes me back.'

In the kitchen, a narrow iron stove was still warm, and Lucy added more coal. She ran water into a bowl from a tap on a stone basin and placed the bowl on the tiled floor.

As the dogs slurped, Sophie draped her cape over an upright chair by the window, sat at a wooden table, peeled off her gloves and removed her hat. Lucy wouldn't tell on her, and not even Maud could see inside Lucy's cottage.

'Andrew's funeral will be in the village church, not the estate chapel.' Lucy's slight cockney accent was more pronounced today. 'As it is, the church won't be big enough.' She sat down abruptly. 'He'd just turned sixteen, Sophie. I should never have let him go.'

Her words were an eerie echo of Anne's. 'Richard said Andrew approached everything with gusto.'

'He did.' Lucy stood up and took teacups from an oak dresser. 'Thanks for coming round. I have to set an example in public, but I don't with you.' Tears glistened on her cheeks.

Hoping to distract her, Sophie shared how she'd given relentless understatement here a name.

'The Shorten Code... You're right. It really is a thing.' Lucy filled the kettle and the dogs lay by the table. 'Hugo did really well at the bakery. The gamekeepers were singing his praises.'

'But he's too obsessed with the lift.' Sophie sighed. 'He *so* wants to go home.'

'And you don't? I'd have thought after the bakery—'

'Not anymore.'

Lucy raised her eyebrows.

'There are some things I'll never get used to, but Anne protected me when I struggled to fit in here, and at some point … she became a second mother.'

'But you must miss your real mother?'

Hugo knew about her parents but no one else did. 'My parents died in a traffic accident … years ago.'

Lucy swallowed. 'I'm sorry.'

The kitchen faded. Sophie was at school in a dark-panelled room with a too-loud clock, tick tock, tick tock. And the scent of wood polish… The moment she'd learned her parents were dead was always there, beneath her regular thoughts. She exhaled, hauling herself into the present.

Lucy took a jug of milk from a larder by the back door.

'For Hugo's sake, I can't give up on the lift puzzle.' Going home through the portal wouldn't change how he felt about her. Or didn't. And more than anything, she wanted him to be happy.

Lucy put the jug on the table. 'I know we're not supposed to talk about the bakery—'

'Last visit to fashionable market town.' Couldn't risk being ID'd as the girl with the pin.

'You'll have to go back for the funeral on Sunday.' Lucy wiped her eyes with her hand.

That was true. If she didn't attend, that would be noticed, seem odd. Sophie went over to the dresser, picked up a tin and put it on the table.

'Must have been horrible.'

'It wasn't that bad,' lied Sophie, opening the tin and taking a chocolate biscuit.

'Mrs Slater seems to be recovering herself.'

'If it's like at home,' said Sophie, 'people are pretty resilient.'

'While mum was in hospital, an IRA bomb went off a few blocks away. I don't miss that.' Her mother had passed away before Lucy came to Shorten.

The kettle was humming softly, would take a while to boil. Lucy sat down. 'I can join you for another workout next week.'

'Sounds good.' Sophie was teaching Lucy how to kickbox. 'I hear the gamekeepers are giving the gardeners shooting lessons.'

'We had the first session this afternoon.'

'I'd like to learn too, for self-defence.' Sophie's voice was casual. 'But it can't become general knowledge.'

Lucy nodded. 'Unladylike and would freak out the servants.'

'Could you teach me?'

'It's straightforward and you can practise aiming.' Lucy frowned. 'Let's hope you never have to do it for real.'

At eleven the next morning, Sophie joined Hugo and Freddy in the large drawing room. Richard had allowed the boys a rare break.

Hugo rang the bellpull for coffee and walked to the fireplace to light kindling already set. Freddy dropped *The Times* on a table and put on his favourite music. He'd shown Sophie how the gramophone worked. It wasn't complicated. He adjusted a lever so the 'brake' was on, turned a handle until he felt resistance, and carefully lowered a needle onto the record. After he released the brake, the disc turned and the melody started.

Sophie now loved *The Lark Ascending*. Almost as much as Freddy did.

Freddy sat beside her on the dark pink sofa opposite Hugo, and the dogs lay by the grate.

Hugo glanced at the paper. 'Anything about the bakery?'

'A couple of photographs.' Freddy shrugged. News took a day or more to reach the national papers. The local rag had reported the fire but played down the militia.

Freddy seemed cheerily unaffected by shooting who

knew how many people. But another thought surfaced. An unwelcome one. Freddy had killed birds since he was a child, hunted foxes and deer, didn't care about their suffering either. How could she marry someone like him?

'I guess the bakery's minor stuff,' said Hugo, 'compared to the cities.' Rioting had been going on for months, fuelled by unemployment and poverty.

Sophie leaned forward and unfolded *The Times*. Barty Inkpin's face stared out of the front page. *This newspaper understands that Mr Bartholomew Inkpin, the only son of the leader of the British Communist party, has died in Derbyshire.* Sophie's throat seemed to close and she fought to keep her face blank. Vague was good. Anyway, *Inkpin Killed with Pin* would have been in bad taste, or maybe that detail had been lost in the blaze?

Underneath Inkpin's picture was a tiny photo of the woman in the bobble hat. *Joan Small's whereabouts is still unknown.* There'd been news articles about Joan in the summer. She'd set up a militia in London, The People's Training Corps, showed women how to fire pistols.

Sophie sat stiffly in her chair, thinking about Edmund Hunter. One word from him and Inkpin would have shot her. And Edmund was likely dead. She drank her coffee, fancying it smelled of smoke.

Hugo took the paper and Miss Parry arrived with coffee and bourbon biscuits. A few minutes later, Hugo put aside *The Times* and asked Freddy how rain affected crop yields.

The boys knew nothing about Inkpin. If she hadn't been trussed up in a corset, Sophie would have sagged with relief.

After coffee, Freddy and Hugo stood up to leave.

'See you later,' said Sophie.

Freddy paused. 'What time?'

'It means goodbye,' said Hugo. 'Actually, I'm not sure what

it means. You can say that, never intending to see the person again.'

Freddy looked nonplussed. 'How strange.'

After they left, Inkpin seemed to watch her from *The Times,* his dead eyes boring into her skull. Sophie dropped the paper in the fire — pointless, but made her feel better — and headed to the library.

The large space was gloomy, despite the tall arched window and healthy fire flickering in the grate. Bookshelves covered the walls, right up to a high vaulted ceiling, largest books at the bottom, smallest at the top. Unknown servants regularly dusted but scents still lingered: fragile vellum, leather bindings and centuries-old ink.

As the hounds settled by the fire, Sophie scanned the room. Tucked in an alcove was a narrow window with a single column of glass. She'd never noticed it before. Wooden panelling flanked the bottom of the sill.

Feeling like a spy in a period movie, she pushed on a tiny, natural indentation and the panelling dropped down, revealing a note. *Moat filling slowly. Workshop says three weeks to replace the drawbridge mechanism. At least a day to install it. Vulnerable till then. Stay alert.*

For centuries, the medieval drawbridge had been used as a simple bridge between the drive and the house. In its place now was a temporary metal ramp.

Sophie closed the gap in the wainscot until it clicked, hurried to the fireplace and burned the note.

A week after the bakery fire, Sophie walked with Hugo and the Laceys through Little Shorten, past Alan Parkes's ramshackle, half-timbered pub, and neat cottages over-looking a village green.

As they continued on, up the steep lane towards the church, Sophie's mind was full of Andrew and how he'd died, but she was also aware of what couldn't be seen from the path. Above a stained-glass window on the chapel was a frieze, sticking out from the wall like a gargoyle: two youthful faces looking in opposite directions, the back of their heads touching. The symbol of Janus, Roman god of doorways — and portals.

A century in the future, there was no Little Shorten. Instead, there was a university campus and angular modern buildings. Only this church survived there, with the frieze.

Inside, individuals and families were wearing ordinary dark clothes, but the Laceys were in full mourning, and as a permanent house guest, Sophie was too: bombazine mourning dress, black veiled hat and a long black coat.

'You wouldn't normally, Miss,' Maud had said. 'People die all the time, but Mr Crawford said this was special.'

Andrew's sister gave a moving tribute as their parents were too upset. The chapel was packed but the service felt intimate and, yes, special. In her whole life, Sophie had only attended one funeral. Her aunt had tightly held her hand. Sophie remembered nothing else about it.

The following day, a second funeral was held in a larger church in the market town. Paid for by public donations, the vicar leading the service paid tribute to police officers, Mr Slater and the Mayor, and the young man murdered in the bakery, Robert Miles.

As Sophie walked behind Anne out of the church, mourners in the crowded pews watched them. If Inkpin Senior's goons were in the congregation, a veil wouldn't protect her.

Don't look round. Act. Normal.

~

Safely in her bedroom, Sophie thanked Miss Blackmore for minding the dogs and tried to relax. No need to visit Shorten town ever again.

After dinner, Sophie left as usual with Anne and Charlotte. According to Hugo, women 'withdrawing' at the end of dinner wouldn't change for years. He'd studied this period at school.

In the small drawing room, coffee was already made. The room wasn't 'small,' but it was cosy, with a heavy sideboard, floor lamps and sofas. Sophie sat opposite Anne on a green damask-covered couch, picked up a cup and saucer from a coffee table and took a sip.

'Mr Denning should have left a card by now,' said Anne.

A guest at the Manor ball in August, there'd been gossip that he was keen on Sophie.

'Rupert Denning's obviously a catch,' added Anne.

At home, Sophie had been looking forward to university, particularly meeting fit boys. But when the way back had disappeared with the portal, the freedom to date whoever she liked had gone with it. Forget gorgeous or intriguing, suitors had to be well off.

'Though he's a bit wild.'

Rupert had been expelled from Oxford University for setting fire to his room. 'Wild might be *interesting*.'

Anne didn't smile. 'Radden Hall is very grand but doesn't have a moat. If this trouble gets worse, you'd be safer here.'

'When was the moat last used, in an actual battle?'

'Seventeenth century, in the Civil War. It's in *A History of Shorten*.' Anne shook her head. 'I'd thought it would be nice to fill the moat, but to look pretty, not to be a security feature.'

1920s England in Sophie's history books had been largely peaceful, as the country recovered from the loss of life in the first World War. But here that war had never happened. That discovery, days after she'd arrived, had stunned her. Not her past at all. A parallel universe.

'Tell me *good* things about the London trip.' Anne topped up her cup from a silver pot.

They'd been guests of the Maine family. Hugo had spent most of the visit flirting with Clarissa Maine. Not a good thing. Torture. But Sophie finished her coffee and tried not to dwell. 'Clarissa wore mascara and lipstick. I meant to get some—'

'Scandalous,' said Anne.

'Even if Clarissa's using it?'

'Even if she is.'

'A *little* mascara?'

'No. Anyway, you don't need any. It's actually quite awful once you reach my age, not being able to conceal anything. Perhaps in a few years...' Anne looked directly at Sophie. 'I can't keep up with all the new families. Could you accompany me on the next visit?'

'What does it involve?'

'Welcoming them, making sure they're settling in all right. When you're happy with how it works, you can do visits by yourself.'

Sophie had never enjoyed meeting new people, but how hard could it be?

CHAPTER 8

The next morning, Sophie called on Hugo to go to breakfast.

He wasn't quite ready, so while he tied his shoelaces, she sat in a leather armchair by the fire, the dogs sprawled at her feet. She'd left his door ajar as she always did, mindful that to marry some gullible wealthy boy, Sophie Arundel's reputation had to be spotless.

She liked Hugo's room with its soft scents of tobacco and whisky. With an overcast sky outside, two mullioned windows made the most of the limited light. His mirror was plainer than hers and his bed simpler, the rosewood bedstead having no canopy or curtains. But the navy rug on the floor was plush enough to sink into. Good on cold mornings.

An opened envelope was on his bedside table, addressed in loopy, elegant handwriting: *Hugo Harrington, Esq. Shorten Manor, Derbyshire.*

A heavy feeling settled on Sophie's shoulders. 'From Clarissa?' She pointed.

He finished with his laces and looked up. 'Yes.'

'Pillow talk?'

He flushed. 'Some, but she's also telling me what's happening in London. I think she listens in on her father's phone calls.'

Lord Maine was a bigwig in the government.

'Militias now control eight boroughs. The Cabinet think this is a revolution, the same as happened in Russia.' Hugo stood up and placed the envelope in a small cardboard box on a writing desk. He unlocked a drawer and brought out a notebook with *Lift* written on the front. 'I'm out of ideas.' He peered at it, as if the title would inspire him.

'I'll read my notes tonight. You never know, my brain could find the crucial clue while I'm asleep. Obviously, I'll crack this first.'

'It's not a competition.' Hugo shot her a roguish half-smile.

She made herself roll her eyes, even as inside a misguided butterfly danced a jig. Hugo's eyelashes were amazing, dark and long and perfect... Okay, now she was torturing herself.

When they'd arrived at the Manor, baffled and terrified, she'd called for him before meals, but that had just carried on. Why not meet in the dining room like normal people?

From tomorrow, she wouldn't seek him out unless she had a concrete idea about the portal.

Hugo put back the notebook, relocked the drawer, pocketed the key and strolled towards the doorway.

Sophie followed. He wouldn't understand if she stopped calling by, would ask questions...

In the corridor, Hugo said, 'On the upside, no more scary notes.'

'Yes, not missing those.'

As soon as they'd come up with lift theories in the summer, they'd received anonymous letters. Scrawled in capitals had been a threat: if they ever opened the portal, they'd die.

They'd pretended to give up on the lift and, yes, the notes had stopped. But they'd never worked out who'd sent them.

As he walked, Hugo pushed his hand through his hair. 'It's surprising how quickly I've adapted to life here.'

'How do you mean?'

'Tapping out a quick text reply seems unreal, as if I never did it, and writing by hand is therapeutic. I've never done it before.'

Sophie had. Thanking mourners for their cards after her parents' funeral.

'And I really look forward to Clarissa's letters. Savour her handwriting, read them over and over.'

She nodded automatically. Despite knowing how he felt about Clarissa, his words hurt anew.

After breakfast, the boys went to the office and Sophie walked the dogs, keeping Charlotte's retractable lead attached to Jack's collar. She carried a regular lead but rarely used it. Charlotte was fine to run free.

As Sophie started across the lawn, a gardener stared at her. The retractable lead looked out of place, and so did Charlotte. Her brown curly fur was classic labradoodle — a breed yet to be invented.

The sky was clear and the late October breeze invigorating, pushing Hugo to the back of her mind. Warm in her velvet hat, woollen cape, and a cream scarf, Sophie ambled past the bower, over the half-full moat and into an orchard, the trees a glorious medley of red, yellow and amber. The leaves rustled, and the scent of damp earth and fallen apples was autumn-sweet.

Beyond the orchard, she followed an unfamiliar path between tilled fields and coppices, and the dogs ran and snuffled.

Up ahead were a young couple and a toddler. The woman was short and curvy, wearing a long, too-tight mac and a battered hat. As they drew nearer, Sophie attached Charlotte's lead. Didn't want her bouncing up. 'Miss Sophie Arundel.'

'Mrs Betty Hill. And this is my brother, Will Mason, and my son, Frank. How do you do?'

'How do you do?' said Sophie, though it was an entirely pointless question. No one ever said, 'Terrible. You?'

Betty smelled faintly of lavender, from perfume or soap. Her brother's face was gaunt and his suit was way too big for him.

Sophie looked down at the toddler. 'Hello, Frank.'

Frank turned his face into his mother's mac, as children do when meeting strangers.

'We're helping out at The Crooked Gate,' said Betty, 'in Little Shorten.'

Alan's pub. Surprising. Alan valued his own space, didn't employ staff.

'We're allowed to walk here?' asked Betty.

'I'm sure nobody would mind,' said Sophie. 'It's lovely countryside.' The Lacey estate stretched for miles, as far as the lane where the lift had opened, and beyond.

Will gazed around. He was far too thin, as if he'd been stretched up while on a fad diet. 'So peaceful here. Like all of Shorten.'

This family hadn't heard about the militia. Mr Crawford's dismissal threat must be working.

'We've come from Derby,' said Betty, 'got burned out.'

Sophie nodded. In the rioting and looting, many streets had been gutted.

'You came from the same place as Mr Parkes,' said Betty, 'through a lift?'

'I did.'

'Mr Parkes has told us incredible things,' said Will. 'That people can fly to Australia, that men have walked on the moon.'

'All true,' said Sophie.

'Mr Parkes said that after he arrived, scientists hoped to open a safe route to the future,' said Betty.

'Mr Harrington, who came through the portal with me, he still misses home.'

'Mr Parkes is happy here,' said Betty.

'I am too.' And Sophie was. Even with torture underwear and appearing demure to ensnare a suitable boy, Anne's maternal love trumped it all.

The family headed to the road to Little Shorten and Sophie unclipped Charlotte's lead. Hugo's lack of interest in anything other than friendship was wearing her out, but she found solace in the quiet and the dogs' delight in a new route and fresh scents.

Charlotte bounded off towards a drystone wall. Sitting on the wall was a girl in a pinafore dress and threadbare shawl, about ten or eleven, still wearing her hair down. The girl shrank backwards in alarm but when Charlotte nuzzled her legs, she stroked Charlotte's head. Jack stayed close to Sophie.

'Penny for the guy, Miss.' The girl was holding a cloth scarecrow. 'For bonfire night. *Canny to stay sober, 27th October, gunpowder, treason and plot.*'

Bonfire night at home was 5th November. *Remember, remember, 5th November* rhymed better—

The girl thrust out the scarecrow that represented Guy Fawkes, who centuries ago tried to blow up parliament. 'Penny for the guy, Miss.'

'I'm sorry, I haven't any money.' Awkward.

The girl shrugged.

'You must be cold.' Sophie took off her scarf and offered it.

'No, Miss, Mam will think I stole it.'

'She won't. I'll tell Lady Lacey I gave it to you.'

The girl jumped off the wall and sprinted away.

In the Manor, Maud folded up Sophie's nightdress and put it in a drawer. She seemed more her usual self.

Sophie shut the bedroom door. 'Can I ask you a delicate question?'

'Miss?'

'Are you happy to be my lady's maid?'

Maud frowned. 'Of course, Miss.'

'After the bake—'

'We can't speak of it.'

'Without saying what happened, could you see yourself staying with me?'

Maud frowned again. 'If it wasn't for you, Miss, I'd be dead or worse. And for Mrs Slater, it's been a comfort.'

'Sorry?'

'She didn't realise who they'd murdered until after,' Maud whispered. 'Before she married Mr Slater, she was sweet on Mr Miles.' Maud stuck out her chin. 'I'm proud to be your lady's maid.' She glanced at the closed door. 'Though I can't say why.'

Intense relief.

'The memorial fund has raised plenty to rebuild the bakery and, in the meantime, Mrs Slater's going to rent a place nearby.'

'Wouldn't she feel anxious, living there?'

'The town's raising its own militia,' said Maud, 'and a

gamekeeper's teaching us how to fire a pistol. They won't catch us on the hop again.'

After Maud left, Sophie said to the dogs, 'This is how it starts. One group gets tooled up, so everyone does. This England might never get back to normal.'

Jack ignored her but Charlotte tilted her head, meaning, 'I know.'

CHAPTER 9

'Today is All Hallows Eve. Appropriate, given the sad circumstances.' Richard was addressing the servants as well as everyone at the dinner table.

'All Hallows Eve at home is the last day of October,' said Sophie. Every year there'd been a church service to remember family and friends who'd passed away.

Anne nodded.

'Is it Halloween today too?' Sophie's parents had disapproved of all things 'magical,' so at boarding school she'd adored dressing up.

The Laceys looked baffled but Hugo smiled, remembering 'Hadley Halloween.' Students and teachers had dressed up at Hadley school, and Sophie had partied with her friends, like Hugo had with his.

'Our modern Halloween came over from the States,' said Hugo. 'Children and some adults dress up as ghosts, witches or vampires, anything wacky. Children knock on neighbours' houses and say, "trick or treat," and receive sweets.'

'My speciality was witches,' said Sophie. 'Glam make up, pointy hat and wand.'

'I don't remember that at all,' said Anne.

Richard coughed. A deep, raspy cough, and he couldn't stop. He drank water and finally it abated.

'When's the manager starting?' Anne asked, her eyes concerned.

'In a fortnight, and I'll step back.' Richard covered his mouth with a handkerchief and coughed again. He drained his water glass. 'Now, where were we? Halloween.'

'Carving pumpkins and eating spooky cupcakes.' The fair-haired footman served Sophie a helping of piping hot mushroom soup. 'Dressing up was only some of it.'

'Did you dress up?' Freddy asked Hugo.

Hugo seemed to pull his attention from something else. 'I did.'

'I loved being a witch,' said Sophie.

Freddy pulled a face.

'A pretty witch,' said Hugo.

'Witches have grey hair,' said Freddy, 'and big noses.'

'They're just women, of all ages,' said Sophie, 'who know about plants and healing.'

'*Bewitched*.' Anne giggled and explained a 1970s TV show to her bemused husband.

Sophie blew on her spoon and enjoyed the soup, wishing she could cast a love spell on Hugo. No. That never worked in stories.

'Bonfire night tomorrow,' said Freddy. 'Wizard fun.'

'It's held in a field,' said Richard, 'outside Little Shorten.'

Sophie's stomach muscles tightened. Standing around outside, she'd be an easy target.

As if he'd read her mind, Richard added, 'We'll be taking extra precautions this year.' He tasted his red wine. 'The Manor has organised bonfire night in the village since the seventeenth century, initially to quash rumours that we'd been part of the Gunpowder Plot to assassinate King James.'

He gestured at a portrait on the wall. '*That* Richard Lacey was a committed Catholic.'

The man in the oil painting had neat brown hair, a goatee beard, wore a ruby doublet, a white shirt, and a square lace ruff that stuck up like a sail behind his neck. Richard, in black tie, could have been the same man ... except for a ruthlessness about the eyes and lips that the long-ago artist had caught. Otherwise, the two Richards were as alike as her and Granny Collins.

In Sophie's aunt's house was a faded photo of Sophie's grandmother as a teenager, staring out from bleak post-Blitz London. At least one family friend had remarked on the resemblance. If World War Two still happened — it would be called *the* World War here — she'd likely live through it herself.

'We think time passes more slowly here,' Hugo said to Sophie. 'Imagine if it passed a *lot* more slowly. We might have found ourselves in Shorten in 1605, witnessed the Gunpowder Plot first-hand.'

The difference in the rate that time passed was so tiny that Hugo's manual watch from home kept the time. But the difference between universes had cumulatively grown over millennia. That explained why this parallel world was a century behind home.

'I'm glad I didn't come here then,' Anne said to Richard. 'They'd probably have thought me a witch.'

'But what an experience.' Hugo set down his wine glass. 'Would have been incredible.' He didn't seem to be joking.

'Maybe for a short while,' said Sophie.

'No anaesthetic,' said Anne.

'Or dentists,' said Sophie. To avoid impersonating a rabbit, she'd worn a brace until she was sixteen. Freddy was smiling at her. He had good teeth. She acknowledged the footman as he spooned cabbage onto her plate. The main course was lamb with new potatoes — and quiche. Once Anne had discovered Sophie was vegetarian, every meal had included quiche, without bacon.

'We've got priest holes,' said Freddy, 'in the small drawing room and the servants' hall.'

Catholics in Tudor times had risked their lives to protect clerics, even building concealed rooms. Sophie had seen them, visiting grand houses on public tours with Aunty Wendy.

'There's supposed to be a ghostly priest who walks through walls,' said Anne, 'but I've never seen him.' She seemed disappointed.

'My father swore he glimpsed him once, on New Year's Eve,' said Richard, 'but he'd drunk a fair amount.'

After dinner, Sophie went with the boys to the drawing room.

'Can you find the priest hole?' Freddy sat on the green sofa and steepled his hands, reminding Sophie of Richard.

The dogs settled by the fire, uninterested in hidden rooms, and Sophie and Hugo tapped for hollow sounds on walls, but within a few minutes had to admit defeat.

Freddy pointed to a cupboard. 'In plain sight.'

The cupboard door curved out and down from the top. Sophie opened it. Inside were shelves and piles of linen.

'Hold these.' Freddy handed her the sheets and blankets and removed the shelves. He adjusted loose floorboards with his foot and easily took up the boards.

Steep stone steps disappeared into darkness.

Charlotte left Jack by the grate and growled at the entrance, tense and alert. Hugo peered over Charlotte's shoulder at the stairs, his blue eyes curious. 'What's down there?'

'A couple of chairs,' said Freddy. 'No natural light.'

'That's really cool,' said Hugo.

'Cool?' said Freddy.

While Hugo explained what cool meant, Sophie imagined being in there, not knowing if she'd ever get out. Better to know the facts. 'Freddy, is there stuff about the priest hole in *A History of Shorten?*'

'Might be. It's very long.'

They replaced the floorboards and returned the linen, but Charlotte only stopped growling when Freddy closed the door.

'Would you mind if we have coffee in here?' Freddy rang the bellpull.

This was a surprise. 'Don't you want to drink manly whisky?' said Sophie. 'Shoot the breeze?'

'My father's not feeling well,' said Freddy. 'My parents have retired early.'

Miss Parry came in.

'Coffee for three, please,' said Freddy, 'and could we have a tin of chocolates?'

Miss Parry left and Freddy said, 'My father's been working too hard.'

Hugo nodded. 'And the paperwork keeps piling up.'

'Rest helps the brain,' said Sophie. 'Work smarter, not harder.'

Hugo raised his eyebrows. 'Easy for you to say.'

Freddy frowned at Hugo, who looked sheepish.

Miss Parry soon returned, laid the table with crockery and poured coffee. Freddy opened a round cream tin with green leaves pictured on the lid. He offered the tin to Sophie and she chose a round chocolate. She'd enjoyed chocolate biscuits here and chocolate cake, but not straight chocolate.

The confection was smooth and sweet. 'Yummy.' She sipped her coffee.

Freddy gave the tin to Hugo and turned to Sophie. 'I'm sorry about the bakery. You must still be so upset.'

Sophie spluttered, hot coffee going down the wrong way. After she'd recovered herself, she said, 'I'm okay, thank you.' He was being polite. If Freddy knew about Inkpin, he wouldn't be watching her like that. Concerned and fond.

'No more visits to the town,' said Freddy.

'We shouldn't let it change the way we live,' said Hugo, channelling what politicians said.

'Nothing's more important than keeping Sophie safe — I mean, us,' said Freddy.

'Hugo's right,' said Sophie. Or he would be if she wasn't the girl with the pin.

Freddy placed the tin in front of her and she selected a different chocolate, shaped like a leaf, popped it in her mouth but stopped mid-chew. With an effort, she chewed more and swallowed it. 'That tasted odd ... woody.'

'Cook's made them for Hugo,' said Freddy, 'but we can eat them too.'

Sophie wrinkled her nose. 'There's a bitter aftertaste.'

'It's the marijuana,' said Hugo, as casually as if he'd said cherries, or butter.

She took another leaf-shaped chocolate and examined it. 'Seriously?'

'Hugo's a serious person,' said Freddy, chuckling.

'My head aches sometimes, and it helps.' In the summer, Hugo had been injured in a riot in London.

Sophie ventured a small bite. 'You did harder stuff at home.'

Hugo glanced at her. 'What?'

'In the lift, you said that if it was a drugs trip, it would wear off.'

He laughed. 'I was speaking from general knowledge, Sophie, not experience.'

Back then, she'd thought the worst of him. She finished the chocolate, feeling foolish.

'Marijuana won't be criminalised for decades,' said Hugo, 'or might never be.'

'In your future, this is illegal?' Freddy pushed his sandy fringe from his eyes. 'Why?'

Sophie considered. 'If you smoke a strong sort, you risk mental problems, and it can make you passive or tempt you into serious drugs.'

Freddy took a chocolate. 'Dr Griffiths says it's harmless.'

The Laceys' doctor had given Sophie an arsenic remedy when she'd first arrived at the Manor, but she held her tongue. Change the subject. 'I was walking the dogs and met a nice family. Betty … Hill, her toddler and her brother.'

Freddy slowly put down his cup.

'They're staying at The Crooked Gate,' said Sophie. 'Mr Parkes has been telling them all about the portal, how scientists here tried to find a safe route to the future. Think how many benefits it would have brought … scientists, politicians, ordinary people free to come and go, learning from each other's cultures.' Sophie warmed to her theme. 'Better painkillers—'

'Actually,' said Hugo, 'it would be catastrophic. In a few years, you'd have airports, shopping malls and who knows what diseases going both ways. With the unemployment here, there'd be so many refugees, our government would install border controls, secure units for illegal immigration, and all the rest.'

'The Prime Directive,' said Sophie, gloomily.

'Prime what?' Freddy picked up his cup.

Hugo summarised the rule that tied the hands of captains

in *Star Trek*, stopping them from interfering in less advanced societies.

'But by the end of the episode, they usually get around it,' added Sophie.

Freddy finished his coffee. 'We're just fine as we are.'

CHAPTER 10

'We should put a sign to the Manor near the lift spot, to help future visitors,' said Hugo, as they walked towards their rooms after coffee. 'Just a sign wouldn't make the portal appear, so wouldn't worry Richard.'

'Or rile up the creepy note writer,' said Sophie. 'What about an arrow, pointing to the right?' In the other direction, the lane led to a small hamlet.

'A large stone on the verge opposite the portal site,' said Hugo, 'so a new visitor couldn't miss it. It could also have the Janus symbol, matching the frieze on the church.'

'The last thing a traumatised traveller needs is a mysterious symbol.' Bonkers clues were annoying and overrated.

'Janus is pretty well known, probably why the sculptor chose it.'

Only if you'd done Classical Studies in the top set at Hadley. Sophie hadn't. After her parents' death, her grades had taken a nosedive. 'Too obscure.'

'It needs to be a picture in case a visitor doesn't speak English.' Hugo had on his earnest face.

'All the visitors speak English.'

'In the future, they might not. The portal on this side moved around when it got blocked, so could the one at home.'

Years ago, the portal here had been in Little Shorten.

'The portal only moved down the lane from the village,' said Hugo, 'but it could have gone to any place where there's another weak spot in the universe or a tear.' Hugo's grasp of theoretical physics, like hers, owed more to *Star Trek* than an in-depth knowledge of science. 'Outer Mongolia, the Amazon jungle... And if the portal at home did move, it's quite likely visitors in the new location wouldn't understand English.'

'Or recognise the Janus symbol.' Sophie folded her arms.

'Possibly.'

'Let's cover all the bases. Add a smiley face.'

'An emoji?'

'Yes, but not showing teeth,' said Sophie. 'That could look aggressive.'

'I'll ask Freddy if there's a local stonemason who could make it.'

Sophie rubbed her eyes.

'Tired?'

'Not sleeping well.'

'Nightmares?'

She nodded.

'You should take it easy, not overexert yourself.'

'That's what Freddy would say.'

A flicker of emotion passed over his face. Annoyance? Regret? No, she'd imagined it. 'I'll be fine tomorrow. Planning to *overexert* myself with Lucy in a workout.'

But as Sophie went into her bedroom, a hollow feeling surged and deepened. She wasn't fine, and never would be.

~

The following morning, Sophie determined to keep going and stay busy.

She changed into her trousers and top, picked up the embroidered bag with her initials on, and set off to the 'gym.' Maud came too. Sophie's outfit was not 'respectable,' so Maud chaperoned her there and back.

Lucy was waiting. Maud sat on a wooden chair up the corridor with the dogs and began darning Sophie's petticoat.

Once Lucy and Sophie were inside the room, Sophie hastily relocked the door.

'I really look forward to these sessions.' Lucy grinned. 'No responsibilities … just fun.' She placed her palms flat on a wall and stretched. 'I can meet you at half two tomorrow at the armoury, take you through the basics, shotgun and pistol.'

Sophie put down the bag and started her stretching routine. The thought of handling firearms made her nerves jangle, but she nodded.

'According to *The Derbyshire Times*, four people died in the latest riot, but Miss Parry's sister says it was hundreds.'

'The national papers also under-report stuff. Do you get *The Times* delivered?' Sophie yawned as she stretched.

'No, but it's always in the servants' hall and occasionally I sneak a copy.' Lucy stopped stretching. 'The old Poor Laws can't cope.'

'Sorry, Poor Laws?'

'Literally, laws for poor people. Nobody wants to end up in the workhouse, but they're turning families away. No wonder there are riots.'

'I think you've cracked punches. Now for kicks.' Aiming carefully at the punch bag, Sophie demonstrated a slow motion-kick. 'Now you.'

Lucy kicked, *not* in slow motion.

'Impressive.' Sophie whistled.

'I've been practising in the cottage.'

'Can you do it with your left leg?'

Lucy did a less impressive kick.

'How are the shooting sessions going, with the gardeners?'

'Finished. Done. But knowing *how* to shoot isn't the same as being confident. There'll be refresher sessions twice a week.' Lucy kicked again with her left leg.

'It's a shame we have to do this in secret.' Sophie did a flurry of punches. 'At home, girly kick-ass moves are given proper respect.' In her last term, the whole school had turned out for the county kickboxing final, gone berserk when she'd won.

'Feeling homesick is natural,' said Lucy. 'Mr Parkes is really interested in your ideas about the lift. The new gardener said he was talking about them in the pub.'

'But Alan doesn't want to go back.'

'I don't either, but I'd love to know how it works. I'm sorry the visitor dates didn't work out.'

They'd analysed the visitors' arrival dates for a pattern, hoping to predict the next portal opening. But there was no pattern and, anyway, Alan Parkes didn't fit.

'The idea that we share a rare gene is fascinating.' Lucy steadied the swinging punch bag.

'But we've no way of proving it, and even if we could … by itself, it doesn't help find the lift.'

Lucy let go a clean, explosive punch.

'Do more left leg kicks.'

Lucy managed a wobbly kick.

Sophie steadied the punch bag again. 'I'm getting better at pretending to be a docile decoration.'

Lucy leaned against the wall, watching Sophie kick and punch. 'I knew a little about horticulture and wasn't afraid of hard work … so eventually I was accepted. After that, it was dead man's shoes. In my case, literally.'

Whatever obstacles Lucy had faced, she'd never given up. Like Anne, a daunting role model.

'And you're not on your own.' Lucy tried another leftie kick. 'Hugo must be in the same boat.'

'He's posh, so for him Shorten Manor isn't that different to what he's used to. And male clothes here aren't so different. Sometimes, I feel as if I'm a man in pantomime drag. Except it's a performance that never ends.' Sophie shrugged. 'But at least in the Manor, I'm able to do this, and wear a tea dress for a few hours in the afternoon, and for dinner.'

'Don't envy you all that,' said Lucy.

'If I do marry and move away, this will stop.'

'Unless you marry Freddy.' Lucy shot her a mischievous grin.

'No signs of him proposing.' Sophie rummaged in her bag on the floor, took out two water flasks and handed one to Lucy. 'I'm in no hurry.'

'But you like him?'

'Very much.' Sophie unscrewed a flask and gulped a big swig. 'And I fancy him. Win, win.'

Lucy drained her flask. 'Sometimes … compromise is good.'

Half an hour later, after a bath, Sophie was in the library, unfolding a note from the cubbyhole. *Gamekeepers and gardeners armed tonight. Keep close.* She clicked the hiding place shut and burned the paper in the grate.

While the dogs dozed by the fire, she climbed a ladder attached to a bookcase. There were four ladders, all tall enough to reach the highest shelves. She scanned some titles and carefully leaned, to send the ladder sideways. Lean too far and the ladder slid alarmingly fast.

Sophie pulled *Middlemarch* off the shelf. She'd enjoyed extracts at school. Would the novel be the same here?

She climbed down and switched on a heavy brass lamp. In this 1925, grand houses had electric lighting, not gas. She dragged a wingback red chair closer to the fireplace and, careful not to disturb the dogs, settled down to read. Within seconds, the library door opened.

It was Freddy, looking like he'd lost something.

Charlotte bounced towards him, Freddy ruffled her head but his brown eyes were on Sophie. 'Do you mind if I join you?'

His formality was endearing. 'Shall I ring for coffee?'

'No, I can't stay long.'

She checked her watch. Half eleven. He rarely took time out from the office. She put the book aside and got to her feet. 'What's up?'

'Needed a break.' He gave her a nervy smile and patted Charlotte who was burying her muzzle between his legs. 'I thought you'd be in here.'

'I love reading, experiencing other worlds … pretend ones.' But she was glad of his company.

'Fiction can be diverting, but I often skip to the end.' Freddy left the door ajar and moved a black leather chair nearer the fireplace.

'That does defeat the purpose,' said Sophie. 'And the best bit. Getting lost in the story.'

'When I was in Cambridge, working on a problem, I'd lose all sense of time.' He sat down. 'Even forget where I was.' Freddy had a maths degree, was maths-obsessed.

'Is there always an answer?'

'Usually. And when you find it and prove the formula, it's

wonderful.' He glanced at her and grinned. 'All is right on earth and in heaven.'

'Heaven is supposed to be perfect, though nobody ever gives details, just clouds and harps.'

'I wonder how it will really be? How it will feel?'

Sophie frowned. 'It's made up.'

'You aren't a Christian?'

When her parents died, her faith had died too. 'I'm an atheist.'

Freddy's eyes widened. 'There was an atheist at Cambridge.' He made it sound like a freak medical condition. 'So, if you have a dilemma, or find yourself in trouble, you can't pray?'

'If I was reduced to praying, Freddy, the situation would be pretty hopeless.'

'But you could do a wicked deed, and if you thought God didn't know, it wouldn't trouble you. And you'd do more.'

A mantra from one of her father's sermons echoed through Sophie's mind: *follow God's teaching or suffer eternal damnation.* 'There's no need to imagine an all-powerful being, or heaven and hell, to do the right thing, Freddy. That's down to character … and circumstances.'

'You don't believe in hell?' Freddy's expression was intent, serious.

Sophie frowned again, bemused why laid-back Freddy Lacey was worrying about this. 'I wouldn't waste a second of your life thinking about hell. It's an invention, meant to frighten and control.' He hadn't seemed traumatised by the bakery, but she added, 'If we hadn't defeated the militia, they'd have hurt a lot of people.'

Freddy nodded and looked down, apparently studying his shoes.

CHAPTER 11

How we think and feel, what we cling to, our shared beliefs, our hopes and fears, these bind us together. But every one of us is also an enigma, to others, and sometimes to ourselves.

On her first ever date at home, Sophie's boyfriend had explained how a racing car worked, described in loving detail how the engine had been improved, how parts of the body work had been reshaped. He'd been baffled that Sophie didn't find cars fascinating, and she'd been baffled that he did.

Freddy's belief in hell was just as baffling to Sophie, but whatever he was worried about was presumably real. She leaned forward in her chair. 'What's this about?'

'Nothing in particular. Do you believe in evil?'

Okay, this was strange, but she went with the flow. 'Actually, I do.' Inkpin shooting Robert Miles... 'When I learned about World War Two, I wondered whether evil could be akin to a virus, spreading and infecting people.'

'There are evil people in the second war?'

Sophie told him about the horrors of the Holocaust.

After a few moments, he said, 'I hope that didn't really occur.'

'Maybe it won't here.' Time to lighten up. 'A lifestyle or belief thought to be so dreadful that a person's executed or locked up in one country, might be fine somewhere else. It's subjective, depending on culture and religion.'

'What sort of thing?'

'If someone is gay.'

'Being happy can be a crime?' Freddy shook his head.

'Sorry, no, gay also means homosexual. Back home it isn't illegal in many countries. And other stuff has changed. How we treat animals, though there's still a way to go.'

'I have no idea what you're talking about.'

'I campaigned against using animals to test cosmetics and medicines.'

Freddy made a face. 'You'd rather experiment on *human beings*?'

'Actually, yes. They can give their consent. And we don't have to eat animals either.'

'You're a vegetarian.' Freddy pronounced 'vegetarian' like a difficult foreign word.

'Charlotte used to be too. She ate veggie dog food.' Charlotte wasn't keen on salad and vegetables so, in Shorten, Sophie had to feed her meat.

Freddy's brow creased, resembling a puzzled bear.

'Tins, from a factory.'

'Most peculiar.' Freddy glanced over at Charlotte, sleeping by the fire. 'You'll be telling me next you celebrate her birthday.'

March 26th. Of course she did.

'I still don't understand why you're so concerned about animals?'

'The skeletons of dogs, horses, or even bats, they're all based on the same template as humans, and eventually, as we learn more, nobody will want to kill animals for food, or any other reason.'

Freddy looked blank.

'Okay, for example, monkeys in zoos who break up rocks at night to throw at visitors during the day. Planning for the future. They feel pain and fear like us. *We're* animals.'

'That's not right.' Freddy sat back and crossed his legs. 'Ascribing our feelings to animals is anthrop…'

'Anthropomorphism,' said Sophie. 'Attributing human attributes to animals, gods or objects.'

Freddy nodded. 'We've evolved to eat meat.'

'But we can change. Evolution hasn't stopped, Darwin knew that.'

'Darwin?'

'*The Origin of Species*,' said Sophie. 'Theory of evolution.'

'Wasn't that Mr Wallace?'

Poor Darwin.

'Is Mr Darwin important,' said Freddy, 'in your universe?'

'Just a bit.'

'Hugo's grandmother keeps chickens,' said Freddy. 'He says they have different personalities. He ate the eggs but never the chickens.'

'My aunt kept chickens. Tracy, the mother hen, was fierce — and quite mean.'

'I teased Hugo, I admit,' said Freddy, 'pointed out he loved beef.'

'What did he say?'

'That he was glad he didn't know any cows—'

A light knock on the open door.

'Sorry to interrupt,' said Hugo. 'Your father needs you to finish the latest crop yields graph.'

Freddy jumped as if he'd been caught doing something dubious and hurried out.

Sophie bit her lip. What was up with him?

Hugo sat in Freddy's chair and stretched out his long legs by the grate. 'Interesting chat?'

'We talked about religion and evil and animals.'

'I thought...' He drove his hand through his hair.

'It was odd, as if he was sounding me out.' Sophie hesitated. 'He was shocked that I'm an atheist. Could be the end of a beautiful friendship.'

Hugo took off his suit jacket and laid it across his lap. His sleeveless jumper — diamond-patterned, grey and navy — made him seem particularly old-fashioned. 'Your friendship is safe. If you embraced Satan and performed rituals on the lawn, Freddy would excuse you.'

Not sure that was true. 'He is ... kind of naïve.'

'He is.' Hugo checked his bow tie was straight. He randomly wore bow ties, as well as regular ties.

'Freddy was asking me about evil, seemed stressed. I said you don't need a faith to make good choices.' She picked up *Middlemarch*.

Hugo was watching her, his face enigmatic.

She turned to the final paragraph. Yes, the ending was the same. She read aloud. '... *for the growing good of the world is partly dependent on unhistoric acts; and that things are not so ill with you and me as they might have been, is half owing to the number who lived faithfully a hidden life, and rest in unvisited tombs.*'

'I think that's an optimistic view. With every generation, life doesn't always improve.'

'There's bound to be ups and downs. I'm not putting this out as a grand theory.' She shut the book more abruptly than she meant to. 'You're contributing here, and I'd like to. Somehow.' Her parents were gone but a childish part of her wanted them to be proud of her.

'I'm helping with the security plan,' said Hugo, 'but it's mostly common sense.'

'Filling the moat's taking ages.'

Hugo yawned. 'It is huge.'

Sophie yawned in sympathy. She'd sleep better once the moat was full and the drawbridge up.

Hugo hurried off to work and Sophie tried to focus on *Middlemarch,* but couldn't settle. The boys were planning, scheming. Not a surprise party. No one here knew her nineteenth birthday was this week. Or was it her twentieth? Her birthday in October would have been a month after she got in the lift, but in Shorten it had been July. Had she travelled backwards two months or forward ten?

Rationally, a birthday was simply another day, not an unwelcome, husband-hunting milestone. But as each year passed, finding someone decent — anyone decent — would only become more difficult.

<h1 style="text-align:center">CHAPTER 12</h1>

That evening, nobody dressed up for dinner.

'Perhaps we're having street food?' said Hugo, as he walked with Sophie and the dogs towards the dining room where 'snacks' were set out. He was still wearing his baggy office suit.

'Shorten street food. Right.' She giggled and couldn't stop, her ribs pressing against her corset.

Hugo stopped walking. '*Sophie.*'

'Give me a minute.' It was years since she'd battled an out-of-control giggles fit. She finally stopped but got hiccups.

'Freddy's found a stonemason to carve the Janus stone.'

Between hiccups, she said, 'That's good.'

'By the way, I explained to Freddy that homosexuality isn't compulsory at home. He was confused.'

'I didn't tell him that ... but thanks.'

The meal was hardly a snack but could have been street food, if served in a street: quiche, jacket potatoes, meat pies, grilled chicken and sausages.

'We don't eat at the bonfire,' said Anne, 'so do tuck in.'

Sophie half-stopped a hiccup. 'Where's Freddy?'

'He has a migraine,' said Anne. 'Needs to rest until it goes away.'

He'd been fine earlier, but migraines could come on fast. Sophie felt for him. She'd suffered from occasional migraines, been grateful for modern meds. 'I can't go either. Every year, Charlotte has to be distracted with cuddles and loud music. I guess Jack is the same. I thought I'd sit with them and put a record on.'

Sophie hadn't enquired about dog-sitting. Miss Blackmore and Maud enjoyed only half a day off a week, so Bonfire Night was precious extra downtime.

Richard leaned under the table and gave Jack and Charlotte a sausage. 'Dogs know to keep away from fire.'

'The bonfire's not the problem.' Sophie swallowed a mouthful of quiche. 'It's the fireworks.'

'There aren't any,' said Anne. 'Frightens the horses. Literally.'

An hour later, when they drew up outside Little Shorten, the bonfire was already alight and the field crowded.

Sophie climbed out of the car, keeping the dogs' leads short. The primeval excitement she usually felt on Bonfire Night was absent, replaced by worry. It took all her willpower not to put up her hood, though hiding her face wouldn't have helped. Other women wore thin macs or shapeless brown coats; her expensive cloak was akin to a fluorescent vest. Richard and Hugo carried shotguns under their coats, but not being gun-savvy, Sophie hadn't requested one.

Manor kitchen staff were cooking on braziers, giving out pies, and Alan Parkes was at his pub stall, serving beer and drinks.

'Would you mind getting hot chocolates?' Richard gave Hugo coins.

Hugo gave Sophie a resigned look. 'Coming?'

'What are friends for?' Alan wasn't exactly fun to talk to.

They joined the drinks queue, closely followed by two gamekeepers. Betty was helping Alan serve.

'Four hot chocolates, please,' said Sophie.

Alan gave her a curt nod. He was around fifty, bald, and heavily built, and exuded the air of a man with a grudge against everyone and anyone. But in August, he'd risked his life to get Edmund arrested. Must be as nervous as Sophie Arundel.

'How's business?' asked Hugo.

'Going fine,' said Alan, with a half-smile. 'Better with company.'

Betty looked embarrassed.

That was why Alan had taken them in. But Sophie wasn't judging. Life was hard outside the Manor. In Betty's position, she'd have done the same. Just not with Alan. Icky thought.

Sophie took two steaming cups and hurried over to Richard, who accepted his with enthusiasm. 'Nothing like hot chocolate on a cold evening.'

'Absolutely.' Sophie stamped her numb feet and accepted her drink from Hugo. The chocolaty goodness was creamy and sweet.

Anne, Richard, Sophie and Hugo stayed in a huddle, surrounded by gamekeepers. The security detail made this weird for the Laceys, but the villagers and servants were in high spirits, chatting and laughing. More families arrived, milled about, and swelled the pie queues. Maud was arm in arm with John, her round face happy and animated in the light of the bonfire.

'This is great,' said Sophie, trying to relax. 'Who needs fireworks?'

'At home, fireworks get more spectacular every year,' Hugo said to Richard. 'They're done through computers.'

'The machines you've talked about before. But someone physically lights them?'

'I think they press a button,' said Hugo. 'I'm not sure how it works.'

'The fireworks were incredible at the Sandhurst ball.' Sophie's friend, in the year above her at school, had enlisted in the Army. 'Lily won the sword of honour. Amazing day.'

'Lily,' said Richard. 'I'm sorry, Sandhurst?'

'The army officers' academy,' said Sophie.

'I know about Sandhurst,' said Richard, 'but I must have misheard. Who was graduating?'

'Lily,' Sophie repeated.

'How could she graduate?'

Sophie shrugged. 'Like everybody.'

'Female and male officers are trained the same,' said Hugo.

'If my phone hadn't died in the lift,' said Sophie, 'I could have shown you photos.'

Richard shook his head in disbelief.

A group of young women laughed, pointing at a lad dancing in a circle to an imaginary tune, waving his cap in the air. Men nearby clapped and grinned.

'Time to go,' said Anne.

The party was just starting, but the sturdy walls of the Manor held more appeal.

In her room, Sophie lay on the bed fully dressed, waiting for Maud to return, and her mind wandered. Lily. She'd never see her again. Or Aunty Wendy, or Isha.

Why hadn't she paused before getting into that lift in the

students' union? Upset by losing Charlotte when she'd bolted, the rush of relief once she'd caught up with her. Understandably distracted...

Charlotte had screeched to a halt by Hugo who was in front of the lift, then moved closer, almost touching his trainers. Engrossed in his phone, Hugo hadn't noticed Charlotte or the paint job on the lift.

Sophie sighed. She shouldn't beat herself up. Only an insane person would have worried a lift might be a portal into a parallel universe.

She fell asleep, dreaming of gold doors.

CHAPTER 13

Sophie lingered by the moat the following morning, keeping Jack close. In a household preparing for war, nature's murmuring beautiful quiet seemed perverse. The air tasted clean and fresh, and a soft autumn breeze caressed the water, sending lazy ripples to the edge. Charlotte stroked the surface with a paw, contemplating a dip, and Sophie hastily ushered her away. Sophie was meeting Richard in the office. *Not* the place for Happy Wet Dog.

Near the alley that led to the gardens was a neat pile of wood, remnants of a rickety bridge to the front drive. Sophie headed in the opposite direction, towards a square redbrick building.

The bookkeeper wasn't in, and the boys were out walking the estate. Richard removed a roll of paper from a safe and put it on Sophie's desk. Back at his own desk, he steepled his hands. 'Until the stone bridge is dismantled and the drawbridge installed, the militia can simply walk in, so our knowledge of the house, the interior layout, will be crucial.'

The document unrolled like a scroll. 'So detailed,' said Sophie. 'This is the only copy?'

'There's a duplicate in the safe.'

'I'll study this in here, then explore on foot.' She was familiar with only part of the Manor. 'That'll help me remember.'

Richard explained the plan for protecting her and Sophie swallowed. 'What about the dogs?'

'We'll stash them downstairs, behind the kitchen.'

'What if the militia torch the house?'

Richard gave her a cynical smile. 'They won't. They want a headquarters. A defendable one.'

Given the choice, she'd rather be shot than burned alive.

'We're clearing the hedges and trees outside the moat. With a clear line of sight, we should be able to neutralise a small group.'

Yes, common sense. A superstitious shiver ran through her, as if her parents could hear her thoughts.

It took three hours to check out the Manor, excluding male servants' rooms in the basement and female servants' accommodation in the attic. From the ground floor, a wide oak staircase wound past leaded windows up to rooms with furniture covered in dustsheets, last used when guests had stayed over for the summer ball.

On the second storey was a nursery, an old-fashioned swing cot distinct under a white sheet. The mantlepiece was bare except for a sepia photo in an oval silver frame. Sophie blew the dust from the glass and smiled. Even at four, wearing what seemed to be a girl's sailor dress, Freddy was instantly recognisable, staring into the camera, his eyes mischievous.

After lunch, Sophie searched the library for *A History of*

Shorten. It could have stuff about the priest hole, secret passages…

A History was on a bottom shelf, resplendent in mottled green leather. Lugging the book onto a side table, she sat down and rested it on her lap to read the dedication. *Sir Frederick Lacey dedicates this work to all the souls who have lived in this blessed place. Shorten Manor, 1847.* She turned the page. *There has been a dwelling here since the Roman occupation in 43 AD…*

Sophie skipped forward. *The De Lacey family were gifted the estate in 1066 by William the Conqueror… In 1606, Thomas Garnet hid in a priest hole, narrowly avoiding torture and execution… Besieged by the roundhead army in 1644, the Laceys held out for three weeks before surrendering, thereby saving the Manor from bombardment and ruin…*

'Shorten's a microcosm of this world's history,' Sophie told the dogs. 'I'll read a little every day, maybe find a guide to hidden passages.' From a pocket, she fished out a mechanical pencil and a notebook with a plain cardboard cover. Her skirts were narrow but had cleverly concealed pockets.

The notebook contained portal ideas, so overnight was kept on top of the wardrobe. If Maud the Gossip Queen found it, everyone would be fully informed. Sophie had drawn maths symbols from the lift: infinity and Pi. Other symbols had been unfamiliar — so forgotten. Underneath were pictures she'd sketched from memory, clear but clumsy. She was no artist.

There'd been four, including a big house symbolising the Manor. Anne and Lucy had only seen the Manor picture. Alan had seen other images: a mansion in flames and a forked road or river, signifying his break from the Laceys and taking a different path — running a pub.

Alan could have come through another lift from the students' union, or the images might change, like refreshing a web page. And a while ago it had occurred to Sophie that the images could be tailored to each visitor. Hugo had been impressed when she'd mentioned this, speculated about 'super advanced algorithms.'

Sophie checked her watch. 'Nearly half two. Let's meet Lucy.' The dogs wagged their tails, keen for an outing.

Outside, she cut down the alley and hurried past the office towards the servants' hall. Once a medieval keep, the entry door was set inside a much larger one — two storeys high with iron studs. The fair-haired footman stood by the entrance, smoking a cigarette. He gave Sophie a respectful nod, and she acknowledged him before continuing to the armoury, the last structure within the moat.

A twelve-foot wall enclosed the armoury courtyard, save for a walk-in gap. Lucy was waiting beside a squat, unassuming building. While Charlotte and Jack patrolled the courtyard, pretending to be guard dogs, Lucy unlocked a metal gate and Sophie followed her in.

Guns were stacked to the ceiling. 'More rifles were delivered this morning.' Lucy opened an interior door. The smaller room had cardboard boxes on steel shelves and grab-size drawstring bags hung from wall hooks. Lucy delved into a box, put a handful of bullets into a bag and filled a second bag with cylindrical objects. She stepped back into the main space and locked the side door. 'One spark would send this up, take the stables and servants' hall with it.'

Sophie gulped, picturing the footman smoking his cigarette.

'You're coming to Richard's briefing? Anne will be there.'

The girl with the pin would *not* be going. 'You could give me the essentials in the gym?'

'Okay.' Lucy put a shotgun on a table. 'Do you know how to use this?'

'No clue.'

Lucy touched the same lever Hugo had shown her. 'If you don't release this, you can't fire.'

In the bakery, pulling the pistol trigger, over and over…

'And if you forget it's open, you'll shoot your foot off.'

Sophie winced. 'Got it.'

'Next time, I'll show you how to take it apart, clean it and keep it in good nick.' Lucy extracted a cylinder from the bag. The tube was wrapped in paper, a brass disc sealing the bottom.

Sophie had attended a shooting party here but been excluded from the shooting part. 'What's that?'

'Shotgun cartridge.' Lucy demonstrated how to load, and the firing action.

Sophie examined the gun, familiarised herself with the moving parts, and Lucy adjusted a sling, so the gun rested on Sophie's chest. Sophie slid off the sling, put the gun aside, and Lucy picked up another firearm.

'Rifle.' Using a bullet from the other bag, Lucy loaded the rifle and explained how it worked. 'Much more accurate over a distance.'

'What sort of distance?'

'Say, if you're firing across the moat.'

'I can't imagine doing that.'

'You won't be able to properly practise,' said Lucy. 'Need to conserve ammo.'

The shelves had looked well stocked, but what did she know?

'I'll store the shotgun and rifle for you at the cottage.' Lucy selected a pistol. 'Same principle, slightly different.'

Sophie got the hang of it in five minutes.

CHAPTER 14

Half an hour later, Sophie heeded Anne's advice about small cottages and large dogs, and left Charlotte and Jack with Maud.

'The cottage isn't far.' Anne marched down the lawn, balancing a basket against her hip, a soft grey hat matching her kid gloves, a pale coat skirting her ankles. When she'd learned that Sophie's scarf was with Guy Fawkes Girl, Anne had grumbled but replaced it. The new one matched the blue cape.

In Sophie's basket were housewarming presents: bread, butter and jam. Anne had a tin of black tea, a steamed pudding and cake. Wedged upright in both baskets was a bottle of milk.

Anne led the way across the bridge and by the greenhouses, but Sophie couldn't keep up. Anne did this every day. Corset pressed against ribcage, walking, talking, all the while holding a precarious weight. No wonder she'd looked puzzled when Sophie had asked for a gym.

Sophie set the basket down to catch her breath, wanting to swear but too concerned with breathing.

Anne paused. 'Not much further.'

Sophie picked up the basket, and they walked together towards a row of cottages.

The door of the middle cottage opened a second after Anne's quiet knock. A teenage girl stared at them, a toddler clutching at her thin brown skirt.

'May we come in?' said Anne.

The girl gestured them inside. She had a pinched, pale face and wary eyes.

Compared to the Manor, the sitting room was tiny. A baby in a cot took up one corner. The only other furniture was an old stove, a scarred table and four upright chairs. There was no fire in the grate and no carpet on the boarded floor. This was a side of the estate Sophie had never seen, tucked away like something ugly hidden in a pocket.

Anne put her provisions on the table, removed her coat and hung it on a hook by the door. Feeling awkward, Sophie did the same.

'Mrs Evans, how do you do?' Anne's tone was matter of fact, and she continued chatting, addressing the girl, though Mrs Evans said nothing. And as Sophie laid out her supplies, Mrs Evans stayed silent, avoiding eye contact.

'Can I boil some water?' said Anne. The girl gave an almost imperceptible shrug.

Anne handed Sophie a saucepan. 'There's a tap beside the road.'

Sophie gladly went outside. If she'd been that girl, she wouldn't have welcomed two overdressed, patronising visitors.

While Sophie twisted a large iron tap and filled the pan, a horse and cart clattered up and stopped. A thick-set man hauled a bulging sack from the wagon and stomped off behind the houses.

Inside the cottage, Anne was still talking to the tongue-tied girl. 'Oh, good, the coalman's here.' Anne opened a back door and a tremendous hammering noise made Sophie jump. The man had emptied his sack into a cellar in Mrs Evans' yard.

The baby began wailing and the toddler cradled him with practised ease, making shushing noises.

'Morning,' said the man, directing his greeting vaguely in their direction.

'Morning,' said Anne. 'Getting colder.'

The man put his hand to his cap in a salute and walked from the yard. Mrs Evans seemed bemused.

'Maybe we should go?' Sophie ventured quietly to Anne.

Anne shook her head. 'We need to get the fire lit. Should be enough coal to last the week.' She passed Sophie a black metal bucket. It had jug lips on two sides and a carrying handle. 'Fill this up.'

This seemed to galvanise Mrs Evans. 'This way,' she said, and walked out the back. Sophie followed with the pail.

Mrs Evans transferred coal into the bucket with a shovel, and Sophie carried it inside. Anne had wedged old news-paper and sticks into the narrow fireplace and found matches. With perseverance and coaching with bellows, the fire caught.

'We'll make tea,' said Anne, smiling at Mrs Evans.

Sophie was tasked with boiling the pan of water on the stove, found a teapot, and what appeared to be a ragged doll's hat — a tea cosy. It fitted snuggly, holes accommodating the handle and spout.

They sat around the table while the baby sprawled on the floor, playing a hand-gripping game with the toddler. Mrs Evans poured tea, picked up her cup and saucer, and said, 'This is very kind of you.' She smiled, a hint of healthy pink dimpling her cheeks.

The merry fire and hot tea had transformed the room — and Mrs Evans.

'We welcome every new family.' Anne addressed Sophie. 'Mr Evans is working in the greenhouses, helping to ensure we have vegetables through the winter.'

For the first time, Mrs Evans made eye contact with Anne. 'He didn't believe a woman could be head gardener.'

'I presume he does now,' said Anne.

'I wasn't sure about coming here,' Mrs Evans blurted. 'I've lived in Derby all my life.'

'I understand your husband worked in a car factory,' Anne prompted.

'When it burned down there were so many men out of work, I knew we had to move, find a different trade, take anything.'

'Was anyone hurt?' asked Sophie.

'Oh, Miss, it was horrible. Started at night, arson they reckoned. Nobody died in the fire, but people were killed in the riot after.' Mrs Evans shuddered. 'We locked ourselves in, our windows got smashed, took the army three days to clear the streets.'

Anne nodded in sympathy.

'Miss Hemmings' letter came just in time.' Mrs Evans finished her tea. 'But I worry for my mother. She's nearly fifty, has problems with her heart. She hasn't written…'

Twenty minutes later, walking to the Manor, Sophie reflected on the visit, swinging her empty basket. The instant they'd entered Mrs Evans' home, Anne's actions and words had been a masterclass in benevolence, disguised as routine.

'Mrs Evans will be okay,' said Sophie, going with Anne into the small drawing room.

'I think so.' Anne sat on the green couch. 'Her husband was fortunate to be taken on. The office receives more requests by the day.'

Sophie warmed her hands by the fire, feeling guilty. As 'visitors,' she and Hugo had been unknowingly privileged. Turned up and moved in.

'Can you see yourself helping on a regular basis?'

'Absolutely,' said Sophie, 'but there's a lot to learn.'

'I dreaded visiting families with Richard's mother. She came across as awkward and condescending. Once I treated it as an induction course for wives, part of their employment package, it worked better.'

~

In her bedroom, Sophie stretched luxuriously. Mid-afternoon, wearing loose underwear and a 'casual' tea dress. Heaven.

She checked her pistol was safe in her beside drawer, picked up *Middlemarch* but then dropped it with a thud, startling Jack. 'Anne helps people here and she's good at it. Yes, the visitors have a rare gene, but we have another thing in common.'

A skill.

CHAPTER 15

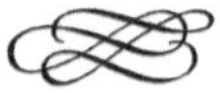

Sophie retrieved the notebook and pencil from the wardrobe and sat at her dressing table to write. She'd allocated each visitor a page: *Anne, Lucy, Lucy's friend Janet (deceased), Alan, Hugo, Me.*

She scribbled under each name.

Anne brought expertise, changed how families are treated.

Lucy had studied the history of domestic horticulture, directly relevant to the Manor gardens.

Alan previously worked in a pub.

Hugo's helping with the estate, using his family's farming background.

Janet's degree was in computer science, not much use here.

My skill — unknown.

Yes, these skills were commonplace, but only a very few people also had the visitor gene. Shame she and Janet didn't fit.

'Time to check the mail.' The dogs, who'd been snoozing by the fire, jumped up and followed her out.

Sophie read Richard's latest note, and when Hugo

finished work, she waylaid him near the anteroom to explain her idea.

'My family have farmed for generations, but I had no hands-on knowledge,' said Hugo. 'And aren't useful skills built on many smaller ones, each requiring aptitude and practise? Whatever combines with the gene may be more specific and immediate. Perhaps the visitor's state of mind?'

'A state of mind … that could be anything.'

Hugo looked glum. 'Richard's learned through his contacts that the militia's regrouping in Derby.'

Sophie knew this. 'Apparently, he has friends down in London who "keep him informed." No idea how they'd know what's going on in Derby.'

'Richard didn't expect to inherit the Manor,' said Hugo. 'Before his older brother died, he worked in London, in the War Office. They have men all over, including Derby.' He lowered his voice. 'Shooting militia members is one thing, but if a mob attacked the house … shooting civilians?'

'You wouldn't want to, but if they were bent on killing us—'

'Even if children were in the mob, like in London?' Hugo swallowed. 'Freddy saw the bodies.'

The fair-haired footman approached them and held out a silver tray with a card on it. 'Miss?'

'Thank you.' After Sophie picked up the card, the footman turned on his heel and left.

Thick white paper, the size and shape of a playing card. Engraved in gilt in the middle was *Rupert R. B. Denning-Lytton* and below, *Radden Hall*. 'The top corner's turned down. Rupert left this in person.'

Hugo peered over her shoulder. 'So, he's serious.'

'Two months since the ball. Why now?'

'Etiquette? Considered vulgar to call too soon?'

An incredibly boring boy had called on Sophie in the

summer. She'd learnt the correct way to reply. 'I'll post him a "Sophie" card.'

Later, when she saw Hugo before dinner, he seemed stressed, gestured for her to go into his room.

'Richard's been pushing himself too hard,' said Hugo. 'He has pneumonia.'

Sophie heart missed a beat, lost for words. With no antibiotics, pneumonia could be a death sentence.

'It's just us for dinner. Anne and Freddy are staying with Richard.'

The following day, Sophie felt guilty about agreeing Rupert could call, given Richard was so ill, but told herself Anne dearly wanted her safely married.

This was a strange birthday.

In the small drawing room, she took a fountain pen and a card from a sideboard. Larger than Rupert's card, hers had *Miss Sophie Arundel* printed in a floral font and near the bottom, *Shorten Manor*. After a disastrous first attempt, she was getting the hang of fountain pens and could write a few words without splodges. She carefully inscribed *Morning* on the card. When Rupert received it, despite her writing *Morning*, he'd deliver another of his cards with a date, and a time in the early afternoon. A confusing convention, its origin long forgotten.

All that day and the next, Richard's wife and son didn't leave his bedside. Hugo went to work, Sophie walked the dogs or read in the library, but found herself reaching for non-existent briefing notes. She and Hugo continued eating in the dining room, though it felt awkward, outnumbered by Mr Crawford and two footmen, and seated at a banquet-sized table.

First thing on Saturday, Maud had news. 'He's passed the crisis point, Miss.' She put the tea and toast tray across Sophie's lap. 'But it could be a false dawn. My mother rallied before the end.'

'All we can do is hope,' said Sophie, alarmed at Maud's uncharacteristic pessimism.

'Everyone's praying, Miss.' Maud prodded wood in the grate with a poker.

Supernatural beings here were likely as unresponsive as at home.

'Praying didn't help my mother,' added Maud, picking up on Sophie's scepticism, 'but there was only me and my sisters.'

Did she really believe prayers were like petitions, every signature increasing the power to persuade or demand?

The next day, when Sophie and Hugo arrived at the dining room for lunch, Anne and Freddy were there. So was Richard.

Sophie impulsively kissed him on the cheek. 'How are you?'

'On the mend.' He looked tired and thin, but this surely meant he wasn't dying? 'Not going to the office yet. Doctor's orders.'

Anne's body language was *very* clear. Returning to work wouldn't happen for eons.

'We've got the essentials covered,' said Hugo, nodding at Richard.

After lunch, Sophie told Maud about Richard, but, predictably, she already knew.

Ten minutes later in the small drawing room, Sophie settled down with *Middlemarch*, and Hugo came in. As it was a Sunday and the weekend, he wore male Shorten Casual: same baggy trousers, long-sleeved shirt, sleeveless jumper — but no jacket.

He sat on a cream sofa opposite her. 'There's been … a development.'

Secret squirrel stuff. Without Richard's notes, she was behind the curve.

Hugo drew a deep breath. 'Lord Maine knows I have no money, but Clarissa's provided for.' He smiled. 'He'll give his consent if I propose.'

CHAPTER 16

In pivotal moments, when something or *someone* is irrevocably lost, time distorts. Seconds become minutes, minutes become seconds. Whatever time is really doing, it leaves only a few breaths to grapple, to agonise, before granting too much time to deny and — sometimes — to accept.

Marry. Clarissa.

Sophie stared at Hugo with her mouth open. The crackle of flames in the grate and her own breathing grew louder and louder, and the weft and weave of the silk in her skirt shimmered and blurred.

Cold reality roared through her like a fire hose.

Breathe.

But her heart was crushed by an invisible vice.

'Out of the blue.'

It wasn't. Exchanging love letters...

She'd thought she'd accepted how he felt, but she hadn't.

Block it out.

Charlotte left Jack by the fireplace to lean into Sophie's

legs, knew she was upset. No tears. A blotchy face would only mean humiliation, even more distress.

Out of her body, seeing the scene in the room from above, herself and the dogs and Hugo, a paused video … floating far above the Manor, suspended, nothing, nothing.

'This made me refocus on the lift puzzle, Sophie. *Really* focus.'

He said something else. Complicated, abstract, unimportant.

She put her hand to her temple. 'Sorry, splitting headache.' Numb and empty, she rushed out and down the corridor as fast as she could. She wasn't up for a lift talk. If he'd discovered the Theory of Everything, she didn't care. Just across the threshold into her room, she threw up.

Maud leapt from the armchair and a novel fell to the floor with a thwack.

'Sorry … migraine.' Sophie wiped her lips with a handkerchief and swigged water from a glass on the bedside table. 'I'll clean up the mess.'

'Aspirin, Miss.' Maud rummaged in the toiletries cupboard.

Sophie swallowed two pills with the remaining water.

'Don't worry, Miss, I'll clear it up.'

Sophie felt guilty but climbed on the bed and lay down. A migraine was a convincing lie.

She let sleep take her and, slipping into oblivion, the abject misery faded.

For the rest of the day and the day after, Sophie lay in bed with the curtains closed, and a numbness slipped into her and spread. Like a sci-fi robot, she seemed to be the real Sophie, but she wasn't. She couldn't Feel.

Anything. And she welcomed in the numbness as a long-lost friend.

That night, she dreamed she flew around the university tower block, students in identical silos…

Sophie sat up, disturbing Charlotte who'd been lying across her arm. '*Misery*. We were all miserable at the university. That's a state of mind.' Jumping out of bed, she opened the curtains and let in early morning light. She grabbed her notebook from the wardrobe and found the relevant notes.

Lucy. Mother died. No other family. Never settled at Uni. Depressed.

Alan. Hated working at the Uni bar.

Charlotte opened her eyes and yawned. 'And I wasn't having fun.' Sophie drank a half-full glass of water. 'Hugo was only there because he'd lost his place at Oxford, couldn't face retaking his A levels.' Charlotte closed her eyes, uninterested. 'But I wasn't *miserable*, just stressed. I don't fit.'

She returned the notebook to the wardrobe and glanced at the dogs dozing on the bed. 'Come on.' The numbness was embedded, allowing her to return to the fray, to act and to talk, and Robot Sophie's armour was polished. Battle-ready. 'Time to face the day.'

'Has the migraine gone?' asked Hugo, as they walked to breakfast.

'Under control.'

The fair-haired footman was by the dining room's double doors, holding a tray with another card. On it was scrawled *2 pm*. Rupert had delayed leaving the first card but the second was outrageously fast. 'No date. He's calling today.'

Hugo raised his eyebrows.

Freddy wasn't at breakfast. Neither was Anne.

Towards the end of the meal, Sophie said to Hugo, 'Have you time for a quick walk?'

Richard gave them a slight nod. He hadn't made much of a dent in his bacon and eggs and his cheekbones were too prominent.

Hugo turned to Sophie. 'A short one. Ten minutes.'

She fetched her cape, a fur hat and kid gloves from the bedroom. She hated the fur hat, but Maud had insisted. 'Bobble hats aren't right for a lady.'

Hugo was waiting on the terrace. He also wore a fur hat with a formal dark-grey coat that made him look familiar and yet unreal. An unfeasibly fit suitor in a period Netflix show.

Embrace the numbness.

They strolled over a frosty lawn and the dogs raced around, their paws leaving patterns on the grass. The air smelled sharp and pure.

'These gardens are so beautiful,' said Hugo, 'even with the washed-out colours.'

Only a few trees still had leaves, brown and fawn and yellow. Autumn surrendering to winter.

They reached the bower, the bushes as skeletal as the trees. In the middle was a stone seat and beside it an old sundial. Sophie sat down and tapped her feet against the cold. Good that she was Robot Girl. Entirely detached, she was acting in a play without the faff of remembering lines. The dogs stretched and yawned, and Hugo took off his hat.

'Are you more used to hats?' Robot Sophie sounded the same as the real one.

Hugo shrugged. 'Not really, you?'

'A hat diva.'

He laughed and her robot armour wavered. Search for the numbness.

'Has the migraine come back?'

'Not yet.' Robot Sophie did banter and believable lies. Interesting.

'I've been thinking about Janus but getting nowhere.'

She outlined her misery theory.

'Richard told me Anne had a serious riding accident before university, that she blamed herself for the horse's death, so Anne fits.'

'But I don't.'

'I don't either,' said Hugo. 'The pressure was off. I knew I could get a first there without working *too* hard. See my friends at weekends.'

She'd planned to visit Isha. The gene plus misery idea was pants.

Hugo left for the office and Sophie headed to the library. She dropped more wood on the fire, kept on her coat and sat in the red chair to read *Middlemarch*. But Robot Sophie wasn't reading, just turning pages.

An hour later, Freddy joined her, and Sophie shut the book.

'Work is getting impossible. Thank goodness the manager starts next week.' Freddy rang a bellpull. 'Hugo'll be along in a minute. We can have elevenses in here.' He stirred the embers with a poker and settled himself in the black chair.

'With a new manager, will things change, going forward?'

'Forward?'

'Will the estate be run differently?' Why had she said, 'going forward'? Who had time-turners to stop time, or go back?

'Everything's changing, regardless of who's manager,' said Freddy. 'We need to make the Manor more secure.'

Sophie nodded vaguely, as if she didn't know. Talking to Hugo had worn her out and she didn't need another intense talk with Freddy. But actually, she *did*. Rupert might not work out and she had to marry … someone, before her hair went grey. 'Freddy, you know last week we talked about animals?'

'Hmm?'

'You hunt them.'

Freddy shrugged. 'Yes.'

'Could you stop? Hunting, I mean?'

'If we didn't cull deer, the woodland would suffer.'

Sophie looked sceptical.

'Deer strip bark off older trees and kill them, and they eat the shrub layer. That's food for nightingales and willow warblers. And they damage cereal crops too. We have to keep a balance.'

'Couldn't you fence off the forest bits and the fields?'

Freddy shook his head. '15,000 acres? It's not practical.'

'How big is 15,000 acres?'

'Twenty-four square miles, give or take,' said Freddy. 'They don't suffer. One clean shot.'

This was hopeless. She avoided his eyes, imagining how much it hurt to be shot.

'You're still feeling rotten.'

'It's getting better.'

'I know what will help. When I was small, Mummy said it could cure most things.'

A wonder cure would be good, but not if it sent away the numbness. Anyway, wouldn't work on a robot.

Freddy got to his feet, walked to where Sophie was sitting, and kissed her on the cheek. 'There. That should do it.'

She could love Freddy. Maybe nag him about hunting over months — or years? She stood up and kissed him near his sensual mouth.

Someone dropped a book near the door.

Hugo.

Lucky it wasn't Anne who'd seen. She would have been

scandalised... How curious. This numbness filtered out important thoughts and focused on trivial ones. Freddy held her hand and a longed-for comfort seeped past her armour. But as Hugo picked up the book and strolled in, despair overwhelmed her. Pleading another headache, she fled to her room.

Everything, good and bad, passed in the end. This would too.

CHAPTER 17

*D*espite feeling numb or maybe *because* she felt numb, Sophie was up for Rupert Tea Date.

According to convention, after drinking tea together, she'd have an inkling whether she'd like to marry him, sleep with him for the rest of her life, and bear his children.

No worries.

Ten minutes before two, Rupert Denning was shown into the small drawing room. He was early. Anne had said suitors were never early.

Charlotte bounced up and tried to kiss him on the mouth, but he just smiled and ruffled her head until she calmed down.

Good start.

Rupert looked the same as he had at the ball, except now he wore a baggy suit. As tall as Freddy, Rupert had unfashionably long blond hair down to his jawline, a pointed, clean-shaven chin, and startlingly blue eyes.

Sophie got to her feet, nerves swirling. Her robot armour wasn't working. Was it Hugo specific? Rupert smiled again, this time at her, and Sophie's nerves swirled faster. He really was ridiculously handsome.

She gestured at the green couch. 'Please, sit down.' Under Anne's tutelage, she'd rote-learned the etiquette for these dates. After ringing the bellpull for tea, she sat on the cream sofa, her posture corset-straight.

'Thank you for letting me call.' Rupert watched her, his eyes playful. 'As with Lady Lacey, your story of a magic portal … rather improbable.'

Straight to the point. If he thought she was a charlatan, why was he here? But she kept the thought to herself, remembering Anne's instructions: *stay calm, on no account let him touch you, hold your hand...* Sophie smoothed out a wrinkle in her skirt. 'The portal isn't magic. We think it's a machine.'

'And where you say you're from, that's the future?'

'Not *your* future. History's unfolding differently there.'

'In what way?' He was either genuinely curious or trying to catch her out.

'We had a terrible war, a world war. For some reason, you didn't. And we had no riots in the cities, or militias.'

Her seriousness seemed to impress him. 'The scientists found nothing.'

'There's a theory about multiple universes, based on complicated maths. It explains *this* England and doesn't rely on physical evidence.' She shrugged. 'But it's just a theory. Can't help me find the portal.'

Miss Parry came in with a tea tray. She laid out crockery, poured tea, and put down a plate of biscuits. But as she left, she couldn't help herself. She glanced at Rupert, then at Sophie, and grinned. Rupert, with his back to the door, didn't see.

Yes, he was off-the-wall fit. Somehow, Sophie kept a straight face. 'Did you really set fire to your room in Oxford?'

The question was probably 'unladylike,' but this was impor-tant info. He might be insane.

'I did,' said Rupert, 'for a bet.' He shot her a wicked smile. 'And before you ask, I was stone cold sober.'

'Was it worth it?'

'No. Winning a bottle of claret … *not* worth being sent down for. A chair was lost and a rug ruined. But the rug was frightful. Purple flowers.' Now his face was deadpan. 'It was only a little fire.'

Sophie giggled. 'What did you study?'

'Dreamy poetry and thoughtful novels.'

'What's your favourite?'

'*The Prisoner of Zenda*,' he said, promptly. 'Not high litera-ture. Adventure with a happy ending.'

'I must read it.'

'The best books are a solace,' added Rupert, 'an escape from mortality.'

Clever as well as fit.

'Assuming I believe you hail from … a different future, tell me about it.'

Where to start? 'Women have the same rights and respon-sibilities as men. Mostly.'

'Mostly?'

'Childcare still largely falls to women,' said Sophie, 'but to give you an idea how different it is, we've had two female prime ministers.'

'Do they make more emotional decisions? Kinder ones?'

Sophie considered. 'No.' She reached for a biscuit but remembered Anne had told her not to eat on the date because it was 'undignified.'

'Do you have similar laws, conventions?'

'I believe so, but in England we've abolished capital punishment.'

He hesitated. 'What about social rules, between the sexes?'

Sophie hesitated too, uncertain whether he was sincere, or flirting, or both. 'We have marriage, but if it doesn't work out, divorce isn't frowned on. We have effective contraception, which is free, so women can decide when or if to have babies.' She hadn't said, 'sex,' but that's what he'd asked about. Had she been too forward?

Rupert laughed, a clear, joyous laugh. 'You must have been dismayed to end up here.'

'At times it has been difficult.' Understatement.

'Notwithstanding convention, if two like-minded people form an alliance, they can have a splendid life.' The invitation in his eyes was clear. She should have looked down, played demure, but she grinned.

Anne came in and Rupert stood up.

'Lady Lacey, I find Miss Arundel perfectly delightful.'

If Anne was surprised by his declaration, she didn't show it. 'I'm glad.'

'I will take my leave.' He looked at Sophie and, ensuring Anne couldn't see, he winked. He turned to Anne. 'May I call again?'

'Of course.'

Anne accompanied Rupert as he sauntered out and Sophie, as was proper, stayed in the drawing room. She hadn't drunk any tea. Neither had Rupert.

A few minutes later, Anne returned, closed the door, and leaned back against it. 'You like him.' It was a statement, not a question.

'He's clever and witty, so, yes.'

'If you married Rupert, you'd definitely be—'

'Financially secure.' Those were Anne's favourite words in relation to Sophie Arundel's husband-hunt.

'But I'd worry about you living in Radden Hall,' said Anne, 'with all this trouble going on.'

Radden Hall was thirty miles from the Manor. Not seeing Hugo every day would make this easier.

'The *eldest son*,' said Anne. 'In a few years, you'd become a duchess.'

That was crazy, yet a duke's son had made her laugh and sent the numbness away. An impressive feat in itself.

When Sophie called for Hugo to go to dinner, he ushered her into his room, leaving the door slightly open. He perched on the edge of his bed. 'How was Rupert?'

'Why are you whispering?'

'Why do you think? I don't want your love life to be common knowledge downstairs.' Maids were always in the corridor and had incredible hearing, almost as good as Charlotte's.

Sophie sat in his leather armchair and considered fobbing him off. Her interaction with Rupert had been unexpectedly intimate, private. No, she and Hugo were in this together. He'd reminded her of that in the summer.

She told him everything, from the moment Rupert arrived. When Hugo didn't respond, she added, 'He's got a brain and he's fun.'

'Freddy says Rupert had a risqué reputation at Oxford.'

'How does Freddy know? He went to Cambridge.'

'Every year at the boat race. Word got around.'

The boat race was held in London, raucous students from both universities lining the Thames. 'Is this opinion about Rupert yours, or Freddy's?' Freddy was Mr Proper.

'Mine *and* Freddy's.'

'Anne wouldn't have let Rupert call if he wasn't respectable.'

'Rupert's reputation is for stuff that doesn't travel to Anne's ears, or Richard's for that matter. He has mistresses.'

'So? Isn't that the equivalent here of *girlfriends*?' Sex before marriage wasn't allowed, so posh boys slept with regular girls, actresses or opera singers, but married posh ones. Sophie smiled to herself. She couldn't imagine Freddy chatting up a glamorous actress—

'Rupert's in another league. Prostitutes, rent boys ... he's worked through half of London.'

She sighed. 'I thought you'd be glad I'd found someone who doesn't bore for England.' The empty feeling was back, with a new layer of regret.

'I'm not judging him, Sophie. You just need to be careful.'

Sophie stood up. 'It's not like he's going to propose next week. That would be way too fast.'

'By your own account, Rupert's unconventional,' said Hugo. 'If you accept him, you can't ever change your mind. He might sue.'

'What?'

'I'm not certain that was still done in the 1920s at home, but it may happen here. Breaking an engagement, reputational damage. A big deal.'

'Rupert wouldn't do that.'

'Are you sure?'

'I've talked to him for twenty minutes.' Sophie stepped into the corridor, feeling a bit light-headed. 'Okay, I'll put him off ... until I am sure.'

CHAPTER 18

After breakfast the next day, as Lucy was too busy for a workout, Sophie called by her cottage. Lucy put the kettle on, and hardly pausing for breath, Sophie talked about Rupert.

'Fit, clever and rich,' said Lucy. 'What's not to like?'

Between drinking tea and munching on chocolate biscuits, Lucy summarised the latest security measures. Richard's notes had resumed, so Sophie merely nodded at appropriate points.

'There was trouble at The Crooked Gate last night,' said Lucy, 'over bread of all things.'

'Really?' Servants from Little Shorten sent food parcels to their relatives in the market town and Derby. 'So, people in the village are going hungry now?'

'Mr Hunter's family are. He was the only one in work. His brother stole the bread.'

Edmund's body hadn't been identified by the bakery. He must have died in the fire. But Joan Small had somehow escaped, been spotted near Shorten station. Joan's disgust when Inkpin had shot Robert Miles in the head … good she'd got away.

'Any more lift puzzle ideas?'

Sophie summarised her skill and misery theories and why they were rubbish.

'Back in two ticks.' Lucy went upstairs and returned with a painting the size of a paperback. 'It doesn't rescue the skill idea, but Janet painted this. It's my favourite.'

Sophie examined it, moving closer to the window. A dreamy summer watercolour: the moat's sandy interior in shadow, lawns a soft green, and sunlight playing on the orchard's plump, pink blossom. Muted colours, separate but in harmony. 'Beautiful.'

Later that morning, Freddy joined Sophie in the library.

Today was Wednesday. Another rare elevenses break for the boys? 'Where's Hugo?'

Freddy picked out a book from a shelf. 'Out of sorts. Gone for a walk.' He sat in the black chair and opened *The Foundations of Geometry*.

A blast of wind rattled the window and rain lashed against the glass. Had Hugo made himself scarce so Freddy could propose?

Stop Freddy popping the question, buy time to suss out Rupert. Not mad, but wonderfully bad and dangerous to know. Talk about safe stuff. She shut *Middlemarch*, her mind wandering to the cute picture of Freddy in the nursery, then to the summer, and another photo. Freddy had a print of it. 'I guess the framed picture of us and Hugo at the ball has been lost in the post.'

'No need for a frame,' said Freddy. 'I have it here.' He patted his chest.

'Oh, okay.' He'd said he'd get it framed. She must have misunderstood. 'Show me it again?'

He pulled out a notebook from an inside jacket pocket and removed a picture wedged within the pages. The outer edges were frayed thin, but the sepia image was clear. Sophie was wonderfully grand in her ball dress, posing between Freddy and Hugo in posh white tie, and had held her smile, despite the five seconds or so she'd had to stay still.

But the boys looked stern, old-fashioned. Almost as if the picture was taken in another century. Young men long dead. Sophie took a slow breath. Get a grip. Old pictures were as misleading as airbrushed selfies.

'Are you still missing home?' Freddy slid the photo carefully inside the notebook and returned it to his pocket.

'A bit. I think I always will.' She leaned nearer the fire. 'I was only at Uni for a few hours.' She'd explained what 'Uni' meant. It was called 'college' here. She warmed her hands. 'Freshers' Week would have been fun.'

'What week?'

'New students joining societies, getting drunk,' said Sophie. 'Did you have parties at Cambridge?'

'We did.'

'All those clever girls.' She gave him a cheeky grin.

'None at my college.'

'Oh, so the parties were just with boys?'

'Local girls, from the town.' He shut his book. 'Were there many ladies allowed in your college?'

'It's not a case of *allowing* them, Freddy. In my subject, English, there were far more women than men, but in the maths department it was the other way around.'

'Undergraduates must marry while reading for their degree.'

'I'm not sure many do that,' said Sophie. 'My parents met as students. Married a few years later.'

'Why did they wait?'

'Until they'd sorted a career and a house. Most couples tie the knot in their late twenties or thirties. Or never marry.'

'That's sad,' said Freddy. 'Who would want to live on their own?'

'No, I mean, they move in together *before* marrying, make sure they're suited.'

'Live in sin? What happens to the children?'

'Nothing,' said Sophie. 'They adopt their father's surname or mother's. Sometimes it's confusing, but there's no stigma.'

'Have you lived with someone?'

'I haven't.' First Rupert asking personal questions, now Freddy. Distract him, keep talking. 'I got into the lift the day I arrived at Uni. Had no time to meet anyone.'

'Except Hugo.'

'But I knew him from before.'

'He says your school had girls and boys mixed up.'

'Yes.' This was turning into a job interview. 'They take the same classes but live in separate houses until the sixth form. I was in Ada.'

'Interesting name.'

'After Lord Bryon's daughter. She realised machines could do a lot more than add and subtract.' They'd told Freddy about modern computers.

'The only lady at my school was Matron,' said Freddy, 'and she didn't count. Did that make it nicer? Mine was all right, but older boys picked on the younger ones.'

'I can't judge. I only went to mixed schools. There was an effective system for reporting bullying, but girls are under pressure to look sex— Um pretty, from when they're really young. And it can be a distraction from studying. I suppose that's true for undergraduates as well.'

'Unimaginable … my college having girls.'

'Makes parties more enjoyable,' said Sophie. 'Obviously, people drink too much, get carried away.'

'Did you get carried away?' Freddy flushed.

Sophie laughed. 'No, I told you, I didn't get the chance.'

Now he seemed taken aback.

'Girls have to be careful. Actually, so do boys. If a girl tells the police a boy did something without her consent, the girl has the option to be anonymous, but the boy's name is dragged through the mud, even if he's done nothing wrong. And the mud sticks forever.'

'Only the chap's reputation is damaged,' said Freddy. 'How odd.'

'There's a huge database. You type a name into your phone and in seconds find everything about them. People are trying to change the law, so silly things children do are deleted.'

'You mean impropriety.'

'Relations between the sexes are relaxed,' said Sophie, 'but there are rules. Girls should consent to everything. There was a lecture about it in the first week at Uni.'

'A lecture?'

'I couldn't go. I was *here*.' She shrugged. 'I might not have learned much. It's just decent to respect other people's wishes, isn't it? Obvious.'

Freddy abruptly stood up and, with equal suddenness, sat down again. 'I don't think it's obvious. I think it's difficult.' He hesitated. 'I need to tell you something. What you've been talking about, um, happened to me.'

'Someone tried to … a man?'

Freddy vigorously shook his head, as if fending off a wasp. 'Of course, not a man. A girl.'

That serious discussion about evil… 'You'd never do that, Freddy. You haven't an aggressive bone in your body.'

'You don't understand.'

'Then tell me.'

'You mustn't repeat this to a living soul. Not my parents, not Hugo.'

Keep calm. Whatever Freddy wished to confide, it was serious. But rape? 'I promise.'

He drew a deep breath. 'It was hard to smuggle girls into the College, so we'd go to inns, hotels. We had drinks and music and it was jolly, but the girls were pushy.'

'Pushy?'

'Kiss you out of the blue, while you were speaking to them. This particular girl, her brother had moved to Derby, and I chatted to her about the estate. Other chaps disappeared upstairs with girls, so I did too. We were in this room and she started kissing me so I kissed her back. It felt wrong but she was so keen, it seemed rude not to let her. She undid my trousers and lifted her skirt—'

'You were uncomfortable, wanted to stop, leave.' Sophie was in automatic reassurance mode, though her brain raced.

'Exactly. She smelt of, I don't know what, and she made me pull on this horrible thing.' He exhaled, very slowly. 'Afterwards, she kissed me on the forehead and left. At the College, nobody mentioned what they'd done.'

'A difficult situation but it wasn't your fault. You were unprepared. Was the girl upset?'

'No.' He frowned. 'But I felt dirty, guilty.'

'Did you meet up again?'

'Absolutely not.'

'So, put it down to experience.'

Freddy briefly closed his eyes. 'She's staying at The Crooked Gate. Betty's son ... he's mine.'

The library was unnaturally silent, as if all the books were listening, holding their breath.

Betty. She said they'd come from Derby. Her brother had lived in Derby while Freddy was in Cambridge. Betty must have travelled to Shorten *via* Derby from Cambridge.

Sophie met Freddy's eyes. 'When did you first meet?'

'Four years ago, in a pub near my college.' Freddy fidgeted on the edge of his chair.

'Since she got here, she hasn't tried to contact you?'

Freddy shook his head. 'Perhaps she's waiting until he's older, to see if he resembles me?'

Betty's child was about three. Sophie couldn't remember his face. Bonfire night … Freddy had stayed at the Manor to avoid Betty — and Frank.

'I'll ensure he's provided for.'

Freddy was jumping the gun. By his account, Betty had been careful to avoid getting pregnant. It was excruciating but she made herself say, 'The thing you pulled on, it didn't break or split?'

Freddy cringed. 'No.'

'He's not yours.'

Freddy looked unconvinced.

'We learn about it in school.'

'Schoolmasters talk to children about *this*?'

'I know it sounds bizarre,' said Sophie, 'but children study relationships and the practicalities, so when they grow up, they have babies when they want to.'

'Your world's very different from here.' He stared at the floor. 'You're *sure* he's not mine?'

'Yes.' As Betty was a party girl, most of the College cricket team were likely in the frame. But why had she moved here? Cambridge was a hundred miles from Derby and Shorten. 'She could still claim he's yours.'

Freddy swallowed.

Sophie's instinct to side with the underdog battled with an unexpected urge to protect Freddy. His family had taken her in and now he'd shared this, trusted her. Yes, he was a landed gentleman, but he was … *too* gentle. 'Look at me.'

He reluctantly met her gaze.

'It's her word against yours, and you're Freddy Lacey. She's a barmaid.'

His mouth compressed.

'If she does write to you or start a rumour, we'll sort it.'

'Pay her off.'

'Give her claim credibility and she'll come back for more.'

He paled.

'We spread a counter-rumour that Betty's a prostitute.' In a very short time, Sophie had learned a lot from Freddy's mother, including the terrible power of gossip. 'Make it so uncomfortable for her she'll leave, take her son and brother with her.'

Freddy gaped. 'I can't do that.'

'If she falsely claims Frank is yours, for money or influence, it's a declaration of war.'

'But saying she's a … too dishonourable.'

'She'd have weighed up the risks.'

His jaw tightened.

'Blackmail? The gloves come off.'

He frowned. 'All right.'

'But…'

'But what?'

'That would be the nuclear option.'

'Nuclear?'

'A last resort,' said Sophie. 'I only talked with her for a few minutes, but she wasn't destitute and desperate. And she didn't seem like a girl set on blackmail.'

Freddy frowned again.

'Shall I make you feel better? In my England, she could have posted an embarrassing photo so all your friends and family could see it.'

'Why would anyone do that?'

'If couples fall out, for revenge. Mostly done against women.'

'Horrible.'

Sophie leaned towards him, her hands clasped in her lap. 'You were what, seventeen, when this happened?' Freddy had passed the Cambridge entrance exam a year early.

He nodded.

'If that's the worst thing you've done, you can rest easy.'

'I used to cheat at poker. I saw all the cards in my head.'

'That's not cheating,' said Sophie. 'It's using your natural talents. Did you win much money?'

'At the start, but everyone caught on and refused to play.' He jumped out of his chair, stepped over the dogs asleep by the grate, and threw a log from a basket onto the fire. 'It means a great deal being able to tell you about this. You're a brick.'

'You may be worrying about nothing. If she was going to

spread rumours or confront you, I think she'd have done it by now. Her move to Shorten could be coincidence.'

Freddy sat down again. 'Making a connection between two, three or even four events, and on that basis alone reaching a conclusion … is foolish, in maths anyway.' He put his head back and exhaled. 'Yes, coincidence.' He was trying to reassure himself.

'I'll never tell anyone and from now on, we won't mention this, and you stop worrying. Agreed?'

'Agreed.' They shook hands.

Freddy stood up, kissed her on the cheek and hesitated, as if he wanted to say something. But he left, taking his geometry book with him.

After a moment, Sophie got to her feet and stood by the window, hoping the cooler air away from the fire would clear her head. Why had Freddy shared his most shameful secret with *her*? The secret itself was pretty tame, but his confiding, that was huge. Couldn't be unlearned, or forgotten.

Keeping confidences had never come naturally. She'd had to learn … to pretend to forget. But this changed their friendship, bound them with invisible threads of trust. And those kinds of ties were rarely cut — only when people really fell out.

Too wired to read, Sophie walked the dogs during a lull in the rain, then skipped lunch in favour of a midday nap. But sleep proved elusive.

Why hadn't Freddy confided in Hugo? And why had she imagined Freddy would propose? Wasn't as if they were having an intense affair. But boys here lived by a different set of rules and she was playing catchup.

Her one, short-lived boyfriend, Pete, had been consent-savvy, drilled into him by school. Yet she'd never thought about *his* consent. If he hadn't been keen, he'd have said so, untroubled by gallantry or politeness.

That night at dinner, Freddy looked relaxed, his secret re-sealed and safe, deep in his brain.

The next day, after work, Hugo called on Sophie while she slobbed in her tea dress in her room. He never did that.

'The Janus stone has been delivered to the stables.' He lingered in the doorway. 'Let's go see.'

Sophie put on her cape and hat, put Jack on the lead, and followed Hugo outside with Charlotte.

At the end of the alley, they took a path that led beyond the servants' hall. The stables mostly accommodated horses, but the nearest block was for cars. The place was deserted, wooden doors propped open, sunlight reflecting off the polished bonnets. The dogs darted inside, sniffed at oil cans, toolboxes — and the Janus stone.

The stone was hefty, two foot high and the same wide. On one smooth side, two youthful faces stared in opposite direc-tions, the back of their heads touching. Sophie moved closer. 'Identical to the one on the church, but not as fine.'

'Freddy told the sculptor to copy it.'

Sophie traced her finger over the carving. 'Janet was an artist. Lucy showed me one of her pictures, a watercolour of the Manor gardens. Impressionist faded colours, really imag-inative.'

Hugo stilled. 'Oh.'

'What's the matter?'

He swallowed. '*Not* imaginative. She painted what she saw. Muted impressionist shades. Exactly how Shorten is for me.' He gestured. 'Everything. The house, the estate. This garage.'

'It's the same as home.' But he'd always thought the colours here were 'wrong.' *These gardens are so beautiful, even with the washed-out colours.* She'd assumed he meant the onset of winter, the fallen leaves. She pointed at a car. 'Shiny red.'

'Not red, and faded, almost sepia.' He pushed his fringe away from his face. 'In the summer, Alan didn't say that Shorten looked different, and if Shorten was like that for Anne, she'd have mentioned it. So would Lucy.'

'I don't understand. Why would you and Janet see everything faded?'

He gave a low whistle. 'Janet didn't have the gene. And I don't either.'

'The lift, Hugo...' Sophie drew a slow breath. 'I'd presumed you were too busy with your phone to notice, but if you don't have the gene, *that's* why you couldn't see the gold doors, or the pictures.'

'Lucy mentioned something about Janet and the doors when we arrived...'

'She said Janet was tipsy, didn't notice the lift had been painted.' Sophie thought back to the busy students' union. 'And everyone else in the hall saw it as grey metal.'

'Janet just happened to be with Lucy, like I was with you.' He whistled again. 'Your misery theory.'

'What about it?'

'Every visitor with the gene was miserable at the university. Anne, Lucy. Alan and you.'

'I was on edge, having Charlotte along without permission,' said Sophie. 'Maybe with the gene, being stressed is enough?'

'No, there has to be an additional trigger. Lucy was depressed for months and used the lift countless times before she stepped through the portal.'

'Still, you not having the gene ... a big piece of the puzzle.' Sophie patted the stone. 'This is a lucky carving.'

He bit his lip.

'I'm joking.'

'It's a good copy. They could be male or female.'

Underneath the heads was an arrow and by the tip, a simple, smiley face. Not a round emoji-shape. Oval.

'I found Cicero's book on gods in the library,' said Hugo, 'thankfully translated into English.'

'And?'

'Not much on Janus. Major deity, associated with beginnings and ends, first dibs on sacrifices.'

'Yuk.'

'Not helpful,' said Hugo. 'I focused on the frieze instead.'

'Why is the symbol of a pagan god on an English Christian church?'

'Exactly,' said Hugo. 'And with young faces, unlike any of the images of Janus I saw at school, online, or in books.'

'Easier to carve? Maybe beards are tricky?'

'Given the quality of the church frieze, I've discounted that. *When you've eliminated the impossible, whatever remains, however improbable, must be the truth.*'

'Sherlock Holmes… I loved the TV series.' In particular, she loved Benedict Cumberbatch—

'I kept coming back to the same conclusion. The frieze on the chapel at home and the one here are identical. Either one sculptor travelled through the portal both ways, carved it on both churches—'

'Or there was a sculptor here and another version of them at home, who only travelled one way.' Parallel worlds were supposed to have some of the same people in them. 'And the two versions carved their friezes independently.'

'Either way,' said Hugo, 'they chose the pagan symbol because they encountered something or some*one* we didn't.'

'You've lost me.'

'The image is specific and deliberate, designed to deter

people from travelling between worlds. A *literal* warning about Janus, as in the actual god.'

'That's quite a leap.'

'Only if it's *impossible* Janus exists,' said Hugo. 'That's improbable, not impossible.'

Many myths had started as real events. Arthur and his knights, the stones of Stonehenge transported from Wales… but gods?

'If the lift is a machine, constructed eons ago,' said Hugo, 'Janus could have been one of the builders? A creature so technologically advanced, the ancient Romans thought him a god.'

'Who went walkabout but hasn't been seen since.'

'A guy with two heads would be memorable anywhere, in any period of history. That's where the logic breaks down.'

'I don't believe in gods.' But her assertion was defensive.

'Since we got in the lift, I'm open to anything.'

Sophie hugged herself, glad of her warm cape. His talk of machines and gods had given her goosebumps.

Hugo looked at the stone. 'We should take it down the lane. What's left of the militia are still in Derby.'

Sophie nodded. She was just paranoid.

'Mr Lear's organised patrols on the road and the estate.'

She hadn't met Mr Lear, but on Lucy's account the head gamekeeper was highly respected.

'And Reynolds is doing driving lessons. If a patrol gets ambushed, any man might have to drive.'

Women didn't patrol, not even Miss Blackmore or Lucy. Out of devilment, Sophie said, 'Strange… I didn't get the memo.'

Hugo gave her a wry glance. 'I'll make notes.'

Starting old-fashioned cars required a complex sequence of actions, tweaking buttons on the dashboard, more on the front of the car, and flicking over a crank.

'I'll copy your notes,' said Sophie, 'and if we solve the lift puzzle, we can steal an incredibly expensive car, you can get home via the portal, and I can return the car safely to the Manor.'

'I guess.' Hugo avoided her eyes. 'But who gets to drive is academic unless we can nail down when and why the gene triggers the portal.'

Sophie believed in genes, like she believed in molecules and atoms. An act of faith, not unlike her parents' belief in an invisible, silent god.

~

Over lunch, Anne said, 'It's only a stone. You should go when things settle down.'

'Reynolds isn't available, and the other driver's not well,' said Richard. 'They won't return to work until next week.'

Sophie acknowledged the familiar excuse with a nod. Beyond unlikely that placing a sign by the lift spot would make the portal open, but Richard's reaction was based on a new worry. Richard had heard squat about Inkpin Senior, but Sophie Arundel was safer not leaving the Manor.

After his parents left the dining room, Freddy said, 'I'll ask Reynolds to take us on Saturday.'

CHAPTER 20

*A*fter breakfast on Saturday, the dogs ran across the makeshift ramp towards the green car, and Sophie and Hugo followed. The engine was already running, but there was no sign of Reynolds. Someone else was behind the wheel, their face obscured with goggles and a cloth cap. The person gestured for them to get in. In the front passenger seat was the Janus stone.

'All set.' It was Freddy.

Sophie hesitated. Freddy knew how to drive, but only from a casual, five-minute chat with Reynolds. He'd attended none of the lessons.

'We shouldn't let it change the way we live.' Freddy was quoting Hugo's words after the bakery. 'We need to show an example.'

Was Freddy showing he was brave and decisive for her benefit? He kept glancing at her. Sophie sighed. Saying bad people wouldn't stop you going about your normal business was easy, doing it quite another. Freddy seemed to be testing them — why was unclear. She gave Hugo a pretend punch on the arm. 'Freddy's right.'

In the car were shotguns, but only two. Freddy hadn't brought a gun for her.

'I have driving coats.' Freddy handed them over.

Hugo slipped on the bigger, brown coat and Sophie put on the smaller one: emerald leather. If they had a spectacular crash, wearing leather like motorcyclists might shield them. Airbags and seatbelts wouldn't be invented for decades.

Hugo collected the guns and sat in the rear with Sophie and Jack. Charlotte jumped in, and they moved off … incredibly slowly.

'No need to break any speed records,' said Hugo, with mock cheerfulness.

They sped up, and the wind whistled around the half-height doors. 'Her limit is supposed to be forty-five.' Freddy had to shout above the wind. 'But I've done a scorching fifty.'

The speedometer was barely at twenty-five. Not exactly a boy racer.

'You can't drive *and* shoot,' said Hugo, giving a shotgun to Sophie.

Freddy muttered something and slowed for a bend.

Sophie didn't close her coat, draping some of it over the dogs. If they met any militia, she doubted she could aim while keeping Charlotte and Jack down in the seat well, but she checked the safety catch was on, practised positioning the butt into her shoulder, then rested it across her knees.

For twenty miles the road twisted and turned, looking the same after each bend. On both sides of a tarmac lane were high evergreen hedges, fronted by occasional silver birch and oak trees. They didn't see a soul.

Hugo spotted Charlotte's plastic bag, hanging forlornly from a branch. Sophie had tied it there to mark the lift spot.

Freddy positioned the car towards Shorten and parked. Hugo and Sophie climbed out with their guns, walked past an oak tree to the hedge, and scanned the air for a tell-tale square outline.

'Nothing.' Sophie bit her lip. '*Again.*' Days after moving into the Manor, they'd returned here, searched every inch beyond the tree.

Freddy stood by the car, staring at her.

'You're not going to turn off the engine?' Sophie asked him. It sounded loud in the rural quiet.

'No.'

Right. Reynolds must have got the engine running at the house. Freddy didn't know how to start it.

'Let's sort the stone.' Hugo placed his shotgun on the rear seat.

Sophie did the same.

It took three of them to pick up the stone. While they laboured to set it on the verge opposite where the lift had opened, the dogs ignored them. Jack mooched about and Charlotte snoozed in the car.

Once the stone was in the right place, Sophie untied the plastic bag from the branch of the oak. The tree was old, with an oval opening like a door near its base. She smiled to herself. When she was little, she would have imagined fairies.

The dogs started barking and the hairs on the back of Sophie's neck stood up. 'Someone's here.'

'Get in the car.' Hugo grabbed Jack's collar and they all scrambled in.

Freddy drove off at speed, narrowly avoiding the Janus stone and hardly slowing as they approached the first bend.

Two men were in the road.

CHAPTER 21

Sophie pushed the dogs further into the seat well. She clicked the safety catch and held the butt into her shoulder, her heart thumping and her mouth dry.

But the men were lounging on the verge chatting, their cycles flat on the grass. As the car passed them, they turned around. It was Alan and Betty's brother, Will. Alan waved, and Hugo waved back.

'It must have been them the dogs sensed.' Hugo's voice was shaky with relief.

'Heard them talking.' Sophie clicked her safety catch to on.

Freddy drove at thirty miles an hour on the straight bits of the lane, and Sophie's respect for him moved up a notch. No need to risk dying in a ditch. And like before, the road stayed deserted.

At the Manor, they left the guns with Freddy and he returned the car to the garage.

His parents were waiting in the hall with the house-keeper. Mrs Rawlings looked relieved, and Anne gave Sophie a hug, but Richard's mouth was compressed into a resolute line.

'No militia,' said Hugo, 'but we shouldn't have gone. I'm sorry.'

'From today,' said Richard, 'the garage stays locked.'

Sophie briefly met Hugo's eyes. If they ever solved the lift puzzle and needed the car, they'd have to break in.

Walking towards their rooms, Hugo handed her a folded sheet of paper. 'Driving instructions.'

'Thanks.' She'd study them later. 'You knew Freddy couldn't restart the engine.'

'Even knowing the sequence, without hands-on practice, it's hit and miss.'

That evening, when Sophie called for Hugo, he was still putting on his shoes, so she flopped into the chair by the fire.

'Richard quizzed me yesterday about the Combined Cadet Force at school. It wasn't idle curiosity.' He sat on his bed to tie his shoelaces. 'Parliament's amended the law on trespass. Landowners can defend themselves any way they choose.' He finished with his laces. 'The gamekeepers are hiding booby traps outside the moat.'

Sophie grimaced. The note from Richard she'd read a few hours ago had been unusually detailed. *The traps wound, not kill. Injured men slow down their comrades. Dead ones don't.*

'And now the government's requisitioned the Vickers factory, we might get a machine gun.'

She made herself look surprised.

'Richard doesn't share gritty details with Anne, doesn't want to worry her. Please don't say anything.'

'You're telling me.'

Hugo hesitated. 'It didn't occur to him I'd discuss it with you. You *must* keep this to yourself.'

'I will.' She'd never tell Hugo about Inkpin, or Richard's notes.

She stood up, flattered Hugo had confided, but not surprised. A fairy tale prince with modern updates… Just not *her* prince.

On the way to dinner, the fair-haired footman approached Sophie with a card on his tray.

Rupert.

Scrawled on it was, *Tomorrow*.

In the anteroom, Sophie showed it to Anne and she frowned. 'He should have waited for you to send him your card in reply.'

The following afternoon, Rupert strolled into the small drawing room. 'I've had a dreadful telling off from Lady Lacey, for *presuming* you'd wish to see me.'

Sophie grinned, but only said, 'Please sit down.'

He took a seat and petted Charlotte who nuzzled into his knees. 'Impressive guard on the drive.' The front door was now manned 24/7 as the drawbridge still wasn't ready.

'My reputation is precious,' said Sophie, mischievously, pretending to misunderstand.

Miss Parry brought in the crockery, poured the tea, and Sophie avoided looking at her, couldn't risk a fit of giggles.

'Seriously, you have it well in hand. Our security measures are proving more problematic.'

He talked to her like Hugo did. 'Most boys here assume my head's full of pretty dresses and sewing, wouldn't think of discussing this.'

'That's down to my mother. She's in prison at the moment.'

Sophie stared at him, open-mouthed.

'She insists on using false names to avoid special treatment.'

'Oh.' Rupert's mother must be a suffragette.

'She's in Walton jail in Liverpool. We've sent our barrister to get her out.' Rupert spoke flippantly but was clearly troubled.

'What's her real name?'

'Lady Georgina Denning-Lytton.'

'I hope she's released soon. I'll check the paper every day.'

'You won't find anything,' said Rupert. 'The government makes sure of that. A respectable lady prepared to go to prison? Far too embarrassing.'

'Has she been force-fed—'

'More than once, but she'll never be cowed.'

'She sounds formidable.'

'She is, and I'm proud of her, but I haven't inherited her courage.'

With every word he uttered, Sophie liked him more.

'But in the meantime, there are limits to how we can protect her. And ourselves. Radden Hall is four times the size of Shorten Manor. It's taken a week to track down all the access points into the main house, not counting windows. The formal hedges in the gardens provide cover for anyone coming in, so we're clearing all that.'

Sophie took a ladylike sip of tea. 'The most important thing is to ensure everyone in the household is loyal. Or the servants will unlock the doors, or worse, help torch the house.'

'You're thinking of the Bellamy fire.'

She nodded. Some of the arsonists who'd murdered Mr Bellamy had been his servants.

'The trials were brought forward. Four were hanged last week.' Rupert picked up his cup and saucer. 'My family has land in Virginia. Depending on how bad it gets, we'll go there.' He frowned. 'But I may be worrying too much.'

'*There is less danger in fearing too much than too little,*' quoted Sophie. Those endless Tudor lessons had been of some use.

When Rupert raised his eyebrows, she added, 'Francis Walsingham, spymaster for Queen Elizabeth the first.'

'First?'

Oops. Elizabeth the second hadn't been born yet. 'Good Queen Bess.'

'My brother is convinced we may lose our heads.'

'According to *The Times*, Mr Baldwin nearly lost his.' A suffragette — not Rupert's mother — had thrown a hatchet, missed the prime minister by inches. 'What does your brother do?'

'He's in the Derbyshire Yeomanry. Loves it.'

'You didn't consider joining up?'

'No,' said Rupert. 'All that standing about in the cold. Needlessly unpleasant.'

She smiled at him.

'What's that for?'

'You.'

'You like me.'

'I do.'

Rupert drank his tea. 'You should be clear what the arrangement would be if you became my wife.'

Hugo had been right. Rupert was proposing. Excitement, instantly followed by apprehension. She stared into her cup. 'I'm clear what marriage would involve. We don't need to discuss *arrangements*.'

'We do.' He put down his cup and saucer. 'You'll have money, status, respectability.'

'And you.'

'And me. But we would pursue our own interests, with no rancour.'

'Okay.' Best not to mention kickboxing, might put him off. Use the cover story. 'I do mini-archery.'

Rupert looked her in the eye. 'I'm talking about other … relationships.' He paused, letting that sink in.

She drew a startled breath. 'An open marriage. What is it called here?'

'If either of us starts to resent it, *adultery*.'

Sophie's brain stalled, then fired up. 'What about children? You couldn't be sure they were yours?'

'We'd have a son and heir first, and another one. Move on when you're ready.'

'You've thought this through.'

'You're shocked.' He seemed disappointed.

She was, though twenty-first century Sophie shouldn't have been. Lie. 'Surprised.'

'You need time to consider.'

'Yes.'

'I've learned to be cautious, and honest, *before* formally proposing,' said Rupert. 'Being turned down is … unpleasant.'

'You checked me out before deciding to call.'

'I heard about Mr Clutterbuck and concluded you're *remarkably* unconventional.'

At the summer ball, assaulted by the inebriated cleric, Sophie had punched him. Somehow, Anne had managed to spin it so people thought she'd 'fainted' against him, knocking him over. 'How did you find out what really happened?'

'Edward Armstrong told me he was tipsy, imagined you'd put Clutterbuck on the floor with a punch. Mr Garner said something similar. Unlikely they'd both imagined it. He stood up. 'Write to me when you've decided.'

'Of course.' She got to her feet and accompanied him towards the door.

'I may end up like the curate, but I can't resist.' Rupert lightly took hold of her shoulders and kissed her on the mouth. A gentle kiss but holding the promise of more. It was over before she could protest.

'That wasn't proper.'

'I'm not proper.' He shot her a conspiratorial grin. 'And neither are you.'

He left the room and Sophie didn't move, her lips tingling.

By the time Anne came in, Sophie had recovered herself. *She* needed to take this decision. If she told Anne about the 'arrangement,' Anne would take the decision for her — and in a heartbeat Rupert would be banished.

'He'll propose next time,' said Sophie, 'but it's too fast.'

'Engagements can last up to two years.'

Sophie rolled her eyes. 'I want to be sure *before* he proposes. I asked for more time and he's fine with that.'

'Don't keep him waiting too long,' said Anne, 'or he'll lose interest.'

Back in her room, Sophie sat on the bed. 'If Hugo felt differently, this "arrangement" would have been brilliant. Love with Hugo and security with Rupert.' Jack and Charlotte watched her quizzically. 'I know, it wouldn't have worked. Once Hugo marries Clarissa, he won't cheat.' He'd joked in the summer about 'turning to the dark side,' seducing maids. In some ways, he was as conventional as Freddy.

But Hugo had studied this period. Even though this England was different, he'd surely have some inkling whether Rupert's Bohemian offer was even practical?

With a heavy heart, when Hugo returned from work, she called on him.

'What's happened?' He stood up from a chair at the writing desk.

'I need your advice.'

'Sounds serious.'

'It is.' She shut the door.

'No, it needs to be ajar—'

'*Nobody* can overhear.' Privacy trumped a brief faux pas. She settled in his chair and told him what Rupert had said and done, including the kiss. 'I have no idea what to do.'

'More money and security than if you married Freddy.' Hugo turned the desk chair to face her and sat down. 'The Laceys have land but there's not a lot in the bank. They employ too many people.'

'And you know this, how?'

'I've gone through the books. The ledgers aren't locked up.'

'Enough cash to emigrate?'

'Yes,' said Hugo, 'but it would mean starting from scratch.'

'If I married Rupert, you could come with us to America.'

'With Rupert?'

'Help everyone start again. Freddy, Anne, Richard, Maud. Anyone who wanted to come.'

'But if we emigrated, I'd never get home.'

'That may be a pipe dream, Hugo. We've got bits and pieces of the puzzle, but we might never figure it out.'

He folded his arms. 'With Rupert's track record, you'd almost certainly catch a nasty disease. Maybe more than one. No antibiotics … syphilis causes horrible disfigurement. Not a nice way to die.'

Sophie winced. She hadn't thought of that. Since she'd arrived here, she'd hoped to meet a boy who wasn't any trouble. Rupert was devilish and gorgeous — the right sort of trouble — but the downside could be a deal breaker?

She got to her feet and walked to the fireplace. 'It's a real shame. He makes me laugh.' She took a log from beside the grate and dropped it on the fire. 'I'll turn him down, won't tell Anne the real reason.' She watched the flames embrace the wood. 'If he can't be a lover, he can still be a friend.'

Hugo stood up, turned his back, and moved the chair under the desk.

'I'll say I've gone off Rupert because he's too pushy.'

'And I won't share with Freddy *any* details of your date,' said Hugo. 'He'd be beyond shocked.'

That evening, in the anteroom, Anne was disappointed about Rupert, but also relieved. 'You'll be safer here.'

And after dinner, with a pang of regret, Sophie wrote to him, finalising a draft in pencil before copying it in ink onto watermarked cream paper, headed with the Laceys' coat of arms.

Sunday, 8th November 1925

Dear Mr Denning,

I very much enjoyed your company, but after careful consideration I don't believe I can make you happy. However, I really value your friendship, and if you ever need anything else that Shorten Manor could provide, do not hesitate to call.

Yours sincerely,
Miss Sophie Arundel

CHAPTER 22

In the Manor's entrance hall, tucked away in a corner, was a red post box, a miniature version of a regular one, with collection times printed behind a glass window. Signed above the rectangular gap to post letters was POST OFFICE and above that, flanking a raised outline of a crown, were the letters V and R: Victoria Regina. Queen Victoria's reign might be over, but this was still the property of the Royal Mail.

Sophie posted Rupert's letter and her mind wandered. If this trouble got worse, would the British royal family flee the country? They'd stayed during the blitz at home—

Mrs Rawlings marched out of her study. 'Good morning, Miss.'

'Morning.'

The housekeeper's hair was pulled into a severe bun, and with no make-up on her lined face, she appeared elderly and frail. But her brain was sharp, and she moved like a head-mistress on a mission. She unlocked the post box and slid a sheet of paper over the old one. 'Mail collection's been reduced to every other day.'

'Why?' Sophie peered at it.

'Whenever the postman calls, we're vulnerable, the same as with food deliveries.'

'Of course.' Tradesmen were delivering less frequently, at pre-arranged, irregular times. *Everything's changing, regardless of who's manager.* Freddy's words reverberated in Sophie's head.

Mrs Rawlings opened the front door. Women and children were walking in a ragged line towards the house. Armed gamekeepers and gardeners were also on the drive, including Lucy, her shotgun strapped over her coat.

This was a planned drill. The estate families had come from their cottages by the longer route, via the road. The aim was to have everyone in the servants' hall in less than an hour. Once the pretty stone bridge was gone, there would just be one way into the house, and to anywhere within the moat. The drawbridge would serve as a bridge *and* front door, secure inside a daunting ring of water.

In normal circumstances, Sophie would have been casually excluded, would have had to ask to take part. But she and Richard had already agreed her role — act conspicuously, decorously useless. Gossip flowed between Shorten Manor and the village, and *nothing* could connect Sophie to the girl with the pin. Richard had dubbed her contribution 'Operation Scarlet Pimpernel,' after a fictional French revolutionary spy. Appearing ineffectual and foppish, the Pimpernel secretly saved aristocrats from the guillotine.

Miss Parry stood to attention by the doorway, waiting to lead families through the house to the servants' hall. Sophie attached the dogs' leads. Jack would be confused and Charlotte's enthusiastic welcome could knock over a child.

Mrs Evans came in carrying her baby, her toddler by her side. She had an air of resigned weariness, and the other adults' faces were set, keen to get the drill over with.

Sophie moved back, near a grandfather clock, its sonorous ticking lost amidst children's excited chatter. For them, this was just a fun day out.

Richard, Freddy, and Hugo tramped down the stairs with shotguns, wearing gardener's brown trousers and shirts. Hugo had a greasy ammunition belt.

Smoothing a crease on her silk skirt, Sophie walked over to Richard. His cheekbones were sharp-angled, his eyes hooded. 'Lady Lacey's in the large drawing room,' he said, as if they were rehearsing for a dinner party. Anne was discreetly revising the Manor defence plan.

'You should join her,' said Freddy.

'Yes,' said Hugo, 'we've got this.'

Sophie turned around, channelled the Scarlet Pimpernel, and joined the families' line. She stayed with them down the corridor until she could slip into the library. Couldn't face Anne, needed to think.

Closing the door, she unclipped the leads and sat grumpily in the red chair. Freddy didn't know she had to act useless, so was seriously out of order, *again*. But neither did Hugo.

She took the notebook out of her pocket. Hugo's car instructions were between the pages. His writing was terrible. but she managed to copy them. After that, as she'd finally finished *Middlemarch*, she read *A History of Shorten*.

An hour or so later, she heard the families passing the library, returning to their homes. She reattached the dogs' leads and stepped into the corridor.

'How long did it take for everyone to reach the servants' hall?' Sophie asked an elderly woman with a pronounced stoop.

The lady paused, one wrinkled hand still on her walking stick. 'Miss Hemmings timed it. Fifty-six minutes.'

∼

When Sophie called on Hugo to go to lunch, he'd changed into his suit.

'What was that about during the drill?' She put his car notes on the writing desk.

'What in particular?'

She gestured inverted commas. *'We've got this.'*

He straightened his already straight tie, a sign he was worried about something. 'Wasn't worth making a scene. Under the surface, everybody's stressed.'

Hugo would make a skilful politician: diplomatic, with a dollop of cunning. And he had other talents. He'd done drama at Hadley, acted in loads of productions. Been quite good.

'I won't have Freddy giving me orders,' said Sophie. *'You should join her.* I'm going to put him straight.'

'For someone born in 1904, Freddy's pretty open-minded. Obviously, Anne's a massive influence, but he's a man of his time. And Shorten. You shouldn't hold that against him.'

Out in the corridor, tears pricked Sophie's eyes. Hugo was looking out for her, but his platonic kindness hurt so much, she felt utterly defeated.

∼

After lunch, Sophie waylaid Freddy before he left for work. Act smart. Rupert hadn't panned out, so Freddy was the last man standing. He'd kissed her on the cheek. Maybe he did want to propose but was waiting for the right moment? And if Richard could adapt and treat Anne as an equal, so could his son.

She checked the corridor was empty and said, gently, 'I can fire a shotgun and defend myself, the same way you can.'

Freddy seemed taken aback. 'But why would you?'

'I should pull my weight securing the Manor. If you have to protect me, you're not focused on keeping yourself safe.'

He frowned to himself. 'We're late.' He strode away, his strides resolute and awkward.

Charlotte nuzzled into Sophie's skirts. 'That went well.'

Hugo came out of the dining room, and she accompanied him to the office. He paused as they approached the alley. 'Guessing Freddy bailed?'

'He didn't understand or was embarrassed.'

'He'll come round. You guys need to meet halfway.'

The hollow sensation intensified into an ache. Focus on the portal. Help Hugo get home. 'We should include Freddy in brainstorming lift ideas.' Freddy relished puzzles. 'We'll swear him to secrecy. He won't tell his father, or anyone. The note writer won't find out.'

'I'd trust Freddy not to blab, but he doesn't want me to leave. He won't help.' Hugo stared down the alley. 'Freddy really likes you. Do you feel the same?'

Okay, not at school anymore. Far too old to be quizzed by a boy's best mate. She lowered her voice. 'I'd marry Freddy.'

Hugo looked relieved. After a moment, he said, 'We might figure out the lift, so you have to be absolutely sure you're staying ... before you commit.'

'I *am* sure, but even if I wasn't, I wouldn't get married, then abandon him.' Hugo didn't know her at all.

'He's financially secure,' said Hugo, deliberately imitating Anne. He smiled and adjusted his watch, so the face was square in the middle of his wrist.

Not actually laughing, but obviously found this *so* amusing. And now he'd labelled her a gold digger. 'I'd never marry for money. Aunty Wendy says women who do that, earn it, and not in a nice way.'

'That was sound advice, Sophie, but not for here. Think about your long-term health and any children.'

She turned and hurried down the alley, but Hugo caught her up. 'We've no money and limited opportunity to earn any. Living "happily ever after" is a nice-to-have. Marriage here is about survival.'

She stopped and faced him. 'Do you honestly believe that?'

'What's the proverb? When poverty comes in the door, love flies out the window.'

Why was she in love with him? Biology was a cruel mystery. She chewed her lip. 'What's happening about Clarissa?'

'Richard's helped with the etiquette. As a respectable suitor, I've written to Lord Maine, said I required a couple of months to arrange my affairs, even though I don't have any.'

'Are you nervous?'

'About the proposing or the marriage?'

'Both.'

'Not the proposal,' said Hugo. 'She'll say yes. The marriage part will be an adventure, but perhaps all marriages are?'

'You're in a philosophical mood.'

He shrugged.

Society weddings took months to plan, in any world. And day by day, every moment with him hurt a little more.

CHAPTER 23

Sophie shortened the dogs' leads to prevent craziness in the office.

Richard had allocated her the families' files because she was female and, yes, she could have objected, but open rebellion would have been a pointless indulgence. Mrs Evans would never have opened up to Hugo or Freddy, however tactful and understanding they'd have been. Anyway, it was academic. Anne wouldn't allow Mrs Evans — or any other Shorten tenant — to be a guinea pig for interesting social experiments. Women here were multi-taskers. Prisoners of the system *and* the guards.

Freddy was at his desk, and Richard was behind his though it was entirely empty. In neat piles on the boys' tables were previously out-of-control papers, and a shelf housed box files that used to be stacked on the floor.

An overweight, balding man was standing by Richard. He had a moustache that was oddly long across the top of his mouth, as if it was trying to wriggle off his face. He nodded towards Hugo.

'This is Mr Adams,' said Richard. 'He'll be overseeing security as well as the estate.'

The new manager shook hands with Hugo and, after initial confusion, with Sophie.

Mr Adams could see her now, but for a few moments she'd been mysteriously wrapped in an invisibility cloak. Maybe Mr Adams couldn't hear her either? She'd come up with ideas, but Freddy or Hugo would repeat them and receive the credit. Sophie knew how this worked.

'From today,' said Richard, 'if you have any problems, please liaise with Mr Adams.' Richard still asked perceptive questions but there were no gentle jokes over meals. He looked bone-weary, might never really recover.

After Richard left, Mr Adams took a graph from a drawer and showed it to the boys. Mr Adams was how Sophie had imagined an estate manager: sturdy, dependable, slightly deferential. Hard to imagine Hugo doing that job, even in a decade. Wrong somehow.

The dogs crawled under Sophie's desk, keeping close. Despite Jack's cataracts … enjoying their Happy Ever After. She sat down and thumbed through a ledger. Beside each cottage inventory was A, R, V or N: Active, Retired, Vacant, Needs Renovating. Something else had been written in Mr and Mrs Evans' column: F and a question mark.

'Family member,' Mr Adams said, when she mentioned it. 'A formal request to let a relative live with them. The relatives are usually elderly or sick and can't work. And when someone does move in, if other applications have been rejected, it causes ill-feeling.'

'What if there were set criteria?' said Sophie. 'Rules everyone accepts?'

'I fear guidelines would be difficult to draft.' Mr Adams smiled unexpectedly. 'Are you volunteering?'

'Of course.'

But five minutes later, she wished she hadn't.

'Specify an age limit,' said Freddy.

Sophie shook her head. 'Too arbitrary. A healthy fifty-year-old verses someone younger who's ill.'

'And how do you know how sick they are?' said Hugo. 'Doctor's notes are expensive.'

'People are bound to exaggerate and lie,' said Sophie, half to herself. 'I would.'

'We wouldn't realise until they got here and sending them back would be, um, tricky,' said Freddy.

Hugo addressed Mr Adams. 'Would it be worth me and Sophie going out to see them? Do an assessment?'

'How would you assess them?' Sophie asked Hugo.

'I don't know.'

They exchanged glum faces.

'I've drawn up benchmarks,' Sophie said to Mr Adams. 'Terminal illness, no money, but in the end, you'll still have to decide on a case-by-case basis.'

'Always good to check the logic.' Mr Adams rubbed his temple. 'I'll put up a list in the servants' hall. Accepted relatives, how they're contributing to the estate, plus up-to-date information on building more cottages.'

She should have thought of that.' 'Stop fake news before it goes viral.'

'Pardon?' said Mr Adams.

'If people can verify the facts,' said Hugo, 'they'll be more sceptical of inaccurate gossip.'

'I'll keep it up to date,' added Mr Adams, 'try to anticipate misunderstandings and grumbles.'

That evening, Sophie considered *not* calling for Hugo before dinner. But he'd wait around in his room for her. No, call early, tell him straight that she needed to step back from their friendship and why. Awkward, but he'd understand.

His door was open, so she knocked and went in. He was seated in the armchair reading a letter. Charlotte jumped up at him and he put the letter aside to make a fuss of her. After she calmed down, the dogs sprawled by the fire, their heads touching.

'Charlotte's a lucky dog,' said Hugo. 'Jack is too.'

He was joking. 'You don't believe animals fall in love—'

'You're getting me mixed up with Freddy.'

Was she?

'Most animals are promiscuous, like us,' said Hugo, 'but others mate for life. Also like us.'

Her cheeks felt hot. She couldn't tell him. She squirmed inside.

His eyes were on her face, puzzled.

'Forgotten something. See you at dinner.' She scuttled to her room.

The next morning, Sophie and Anne visited Mrs Evans. Half an hour later, walking away from the cottage, Sophie said, 'Her mother's not bad enough to come here.' If it had been down to Sophie Arundel, she'd have overstated the heart condition.

'She may qualify because she's *not* very sick,' said Anne. 'She can help in the house or if she minded her grandchildren, Mrs Evans could join the laundry team.'

Before lunch, Sophie met Hugo in the corridor and told him in a whisper about Mrs Evans' mother. The assessment was confidential and gossip gold dust.

'If this gets worse, it'll be more than the odd relative, Sophie. There'll be refugees the same as home, except they won't be fleeing wars in far off places.' He patted Jack and sighed.

'Are you okay?'

'Just tired. Slept badly.' He ruffled Charlotte's ears as she determinedly wagged her tail. 'I dreamt of home and when I woke up, for a second I forgot I was here.'

'Dogs live in the moment. We should too.'

'Carpe diem.'

'Sorry?'

'Seize the day.' He checked the passage was empty. 'Freddy's afraid that when he proposes, you'll turn him down.' Hugo said the words in a rush, as if he'd memorised them.

'*When* he proposes.'

'Definitely "when." My tips on *where*, a romantic Caribbean beach or a fancy hotel … weren't very helpful.'

'Not funny, Hugo.' She should spell out now she'd rather marry *him*. But he wouldn't believe her. Or worse, laugh.

Hugo checked the corridor again. 'Freddy's on the level, or to use a more Shorten expression, his intentions are honourable.'

A lifetime as a pitied spinster receded, but sheepish relief was instantly replaced by panic. Actually. Marry. Freddy. 'It's too soon.'

'The only way he's not proposing is if he knows you'll reject him,' said Hugo. 'He hasn't talked to his father, but he will soon, and given the family history, Richard won't block it.'

Resigned to marrying Freddy. No, *resolved*—

'Are you in love with him?'

She winced. 'That's a very personal question.'

'But a relevant one.'

'No, it's not. You think marriage is a meal-ticket.'

'Marrying *for* money isn't the same as marrying *into* it.'

A clever debating point but didn't help. 'I told you, I'll happily marry Freddy ... down the line.'

Hugo frowned.

'Okay, sometime soon.'

'How soon is soon?'

Marriage here was so ... final. Divorce was vanishingly rare. Social suicide. 'In a year?'

'Twelve months is respectable.'

The Manor was huge. If they fell out, she and Freddy could have separate wings? 'I fancy Freddy, so I'd say yes.'

'*So* glad you've stopped dithering.' Hugo turned away as he spoke, removed a speck of dust from his jacket. 'Freddy adores you.'

CHAPTER 24

After lunch, Sophie sat in the small drawing room by the fire. Another storm was brewing, splattering rain against the window.

Three weeks since the bakery, and thanks to Mr Crawford's dismissal threat, still no chit chat. But getting fired here didn't involve humiliation, hardship, and welfare — it meant starvation.

She scanned *The Times*. Good, nothing more about Inkpin.

The paper's editorial was a diatribe on the moral dangers of women showing off their ankles. All Sophie's skirts had been shortened, with no exciting consequences.

Across two pages near the front was an article headlined *Cambridge to be Rebuilt*. As usual, the story was upbeat, with black and white photos of residents temporarily housed in barracks, but a photo of a burnt-out street told the real story. Back in September, a bread shortage had sparked a riot and hundreds had been killed, many more made homeless. The town had taken the brunt. Most students hadn't been there, the academic year yet to start.

Betty, and that disturbing conversation with Freddy. With Cambridge in flames, entirely logical that Betty should flee to her brother in Derby. But Derby was also in chaos. Betty must have remembered Freddy talking about the Manor … travelled here on spec, hoping to find work on the estate, happened on Alan and the pub.

As if she'd conjured him up, Freddy strolled in.

'You're not needed in the office?'

'Hugo and Mr Adams have everything in hand.' He sat on the cream sofa. 'No point staying there out of habit.'

'I want to tell you something,' Sophie whispered.

He leaned forward.

'You don't have to worry about Betty.'

He looked horrified but Sophie ploughed on, told him about the Cambridge riot.

'I read about it. My college wasn't affected.'

'Freddy, most of the town was destroyed.'

'I didn't realise that.'

'How could you *not* realise?'

Freddy shrugged. 'Once I saw the College was safe, I didn't read the rest.'

His lack of interest and empathy for the people in Cambridge was concerning, but he'd lived a sheltered life. She summarised why Betty had ended up in Little Shorten. 'She lost her home. That's what brought her here.'

'Would explain why she hasn't done anything.'

'Exactly.'

Freddy let out a long, slow breath and sat up straighter. 'Tell me about your favourite stories again. The TV star one.' Freddy pronounced TV like a strange password. 'Man conquering the stars. I'd love to watch it.'

'Science fiction books are wonderful too. All those classics in your library. And fantasy novels. What about *Dracula*?'

'I've read it.'

'I loved a show called *Buffy the Vampire Slayer*,' said Sophie, 'about this girl with superpowers who fights vampires.'

'Sounds odd.'

'It's not really about vampires. More about growing up, how hard it is to be a leader, a warrior.'

'I love your tales from the future.'

'And I love telling you them,' said Sophie. 'But there are things I don't miss.'

'What things?'

'Finding it difficult to relax, take time out. Wasting time on social media.'

'Hugo's talked about this,' said Freddy.

'It's worse for children. If they're bullied at school, that carries on in the holidays via their laptop or phone.'

'They're machines. Why not disconnect them? The telephone stopped working last year, took weeks to repair. Nobody noticed.'

'They're addictive,' said Sophie. 'I turned my phone off before I went to bed, but if I forgot, a bleep would wake me up. And in the evenings, I'd finish prep with half an eye on messages—'

'May I kiss you?' Freddy's eyes were on her mouth.

Surprised, Sophie hesitated. This was happening way too fast. 'We might be seen.' The door was open, as was proper.

'We could go for a walk.'

Rain was bombarding the windows now, making them rattle.

'The storm will have blown itself out by tomorrow,' said Freddy. 'We should set off early, before breakfast.'

'Okay.' Freddy was not an early riser. He had an agenda. Likely a proposal agenda. *No changing your mind.* Hugo's warning about Rupert echoed in her brain.

~

First thing next morning, Sophie mentioned the Freddy-Sophie walk to Maud. 'Can you mind Jack? It won't be for long.' Jack required careful supervising and she might be distracted...

Maud nodded. 'Be careful, Miss.' Part of Maud's job spec was protecting Sophie Arundel's reputation. 'Plenty of gardeners about, clearing up.'

Acceptable chaperones.

The storm had raged all night, kept Sophie awake, but she felt better about today. When Freddy proposed, of course she'd accept.

'You could wear your new dress, Miss.'

The pale blue gown didn't have a hobble skirt. The fashion had arrived from Paris last month, allowed the wearer to move normally.

At eight, Sophie opened the door to Freddy. 'It's dry today,' he said, 'and not as cold.'

Sophie slipped on her cloak but didn't fasten it. She put on her velvet hat and kid gloves, followed Freddy through the house and across the terrace. Charlotte hurtled onto the battered lawn and raced around, deftly avoiding bits of bushes, torn branches, and a fallen tree.

'Morning.' Freddy nodded to some gardeners.

Despite nature's devastation, Sophie drank in a fresh 'after-rain' scent, and smiled. 'Walks are excellent for clearing your head.'

'Yes,' said Freddy, 'I find that as well.'

Most people probably never had an original thought in their lives. Depressing, though, that she was one of them. She paused by the moat. To fill it from the river, the gardeners had reopened a centuries-old channel. In the summer, she'd swum in that river, splashed in its clear, pure water. Sophie wrinkled her nose. The moat water was dank and dark and covered in mulchy leaves.

Freddy strode off to the bridge and she followed. The decorative stonework had been removed but the main structure was still intact.

'Dismantling this will take a few hours,' said Freddy, as they crossed the moat. 'Let's go further out, towards the river.' He glanced at the lowering sky. 'You can see the entire county when the weather's right.'

With no curious audience of gardeners. This *was* proposal day.

Beyond the bridge, Freddy kept up a brisk pace, but wearing the wider skirt she stayed with him through the orchard and along a steep path.

At the top, he gestured. 'Perfect view.'

'It is.' Even on a dull day, the panorama of the turbulent river rolling by neat fields was stunning. 'Where does Shorten land stop?'

'On this side. The river's the boundary.'

'What's that?' She pointed at a scruffy shed.

'Old shepherd's hut.' Freddy squared his shoulders, his soft eyes resolute. 'Sophie, may I kiss you?'

Anne's dating advice... 'I don't think we're allowed.'

'No one will know.'

She was being ridiculous. She was nineteen ... actually, could be twenty. Stepping forward, she put her arms around his neck. 'You're a rebel, Freddy Lacey.'

He kissed her, deliciously slowly, and a familiar tingling swirled, not as intense as when she'd kissed Hugo, back when they'd thought Shorten a dream, but mighty fine. Ignoring Charlotte jumping up to join in the cuddle, Sophie returned his kisses, gently, then urgently.

After a while, Freddy stopped kissing. 'May I ask you a question?'

Now the moment had come, panic set in. More time. A harmless lie. 'There's someone at home.'

'Are you engaged?'

'No, but I think about him—'

Charlotte barked. Her warning bark.

'*You. You.*' A man was shouting at them. Tall and gangly, in filthy, ragged clothes, he was by the shepherd's hut, gesturing with a tree branch. Freddy touched his chest and paled. This was Proposal Walk, so he'd forgotten his shotgun.

The man stumbled towards them, holding the branch as an enormous walking stick. Reason might sort this situation. Or not.

'Look here, old chap…' Freddy stepped in front of her.

Charlotte wagged her tail, but Sophie attached her lead. This man could have a knife or pistol.

Sophie had on stout walking boots and could kick. She'd need to get close, though, and he had the makeshift staff. 'Freddy, hold Charlotte.' She thrust the lead into Freddy's hand.

The place was strewn with branches. She found a reasonably straight one with a sharp tip and held it like a javelin. If push came to shove, this would stop Stick Man.

It did stop him. He stared and stood still. She stepped nearer, balanced the branch, and prepared to throw.

Freddy shot her an alarmed glance. 'Sir, you're on private land. You should return to the road. Over there.' He pointed past the hut.

The man shook his head.

'Lose the pole,' said Sophie.

The man frowned, seemed confused.

Sophie took another step. 'Put the stick down.'

He dropped it, swayed, and fell into a foetal position.

The man might be on drugs, irrationally violent. But something didn't add up. Sophie stood beside him, balancing the branch. Charlotte strained against her lead, trying to sniff him.

Stick Man didn't move.

Freddy kept Charlotte back. 'Is he dead?'

Sophie pressed two fingers to his neck. 'No, he has a pulse, but I've never seen anyone so thin.' Underneath the man's shirt, his shoulder bones loomed, angular and prominent, and his face was sunken and grey. 'I think he's fainted. Where has he come from?'

'No idea,' said Freddy, 'but we should go. Call the groundsmen out.'

As they ran down the hill, it started to rain. It was ten minutes before they saw anyone to alert, and half an hour before the man was carried to the servants' hall.

'He was leaning on that pole, Freddy, desperate for help,' said Sophie. 'I didn't need the branch.'

'Better safe than sorry. I'd never have thought of using a stick as a weapon. Goodness.'

Hugo came onto the terrace. He had new shadows under his eyes. 'What's happened?'

'A man on the estate,' said Sophie. 'He's in a bad way.'

'Sophie frightened him into a faint,' said Freddy.

'I did not,' said Sophie. 'I picked up a branch. As a precaution.'

'Like a spear,' Freddy announced.

'A spear,' said Hugo, slowly, finding this hard to process. 'Ah, channelling your javelin throwing.'

She'd channelled her inner *Buffy* but kept this to herself.

'Sophie threw javelin at school,' Hugo reminded Freddy.

'I'm double-jointed.' When Freddy looked puzzled, she added, 'Helps with the throwing.'

Two hours later, sat at the dressing table, Sophie recounted the entire adventure to Maud, minus the kissing and possible proposal, embarrassed that she'd almost literally got the wrong end of the stick. 'What's happening to him?'

'He's nearly dead from starvation, Miss, staying here until the parish decide what to do. He's not from Shorten, so not their business.' Maud fixed a stray lock of hair in Sophie's bun. 'But he'll be enjoying a nice roast meal.'

A half-remembered history lesson set off a klaxon in Sophie's brain. She stood up abruptly and knocked over the chair. 'I'm going to the servants' hall.'

Maud pursed her lips. 'No, Miss. The family don't go there, except in emergencies—'

'This is an emergency.'

'Whatever it is, Miss, I'll deal with it at lunchtime.'

'That will be too late.'

CHAPTER 25

*A*fter shutting the dogs in the bedroom, Maud reluctantly accompanied Sophie outside and down the alley. Sophie was hatless but didn't care. And Maud was so stressed, she hadn't noticed.

Freddy came out of the office and Sophie called his name. This produced a full-on frown from Maud.

'What's the matter?' said Freddy, glancing at Maud's worried expression.

Freddy had been sceptical about the Holocaust. She could only hope he'd trust her now. 'That man we found, he mustn't have a huge meal.'

'Why? It's what he needs.'

'Come with me. I'll explain in the servants' hall.'

'Very well.'

When Maud knocked on the regular-sized door within the enormous, castle-like gate, a maid opened it and gawped. The girl backed away, her eyes wide.

Sophie walked into a dining room bigger than the one in the Manor. This was socially very dangerous. Violating their private space.

Mr Crawford stood up from the far end of a central table, his expression unreadable. The room was crowded but if there'd been chatter before, it had stopped. Everyone stared.

Stick Man was munching on a sandwich. She might be too late.

Sophie swallowed. 'Mr Crawford, I appreciate this is unconventional, but I need to stop this man eating a rich meal.' Descriptions of liberated camps had given her nightmares. Keep it vague. 'Where I come from, there were people as malnourished as him, or worse. They were found, given army rations, bread, tea, but they'd eaten so little for so long, the richness and quantity of the food killed them.'

Mr Crawford's face was still expressionless.

'A soft, liquid diet is safest. Soup, milk, oatmeal, no sugar in his tea. Meat stew after a few days but small amounts, and no alcohol.'

Freddy cleared his throat. 'Lady Lacey supports Miss Arundel's account.'

Sophie shot him a relieved glance.

'No.' Stick Man struggled to stand up. 'I want some proper grub. *Please.*'

After a moment's hesitation, Mr Crawford nodded at Sophie and Freddy. Deference. Before Shorten she'd hated everything about it, but it might yet save Stick Man.

As they left, Sophie said to Maud, 'Thank you.'

Maud nodded.

'You were wonderful,' said Freddy to Sophie.

'You were pretty good yourself.'

'He'll recover?' said Maud.

'I don't know,' said Sophie, 'but he stands a better chance.'

'I didn't believe what you told me about those camps,' said Freddy, 'so I asked Mummy.'

'It was so horrific, people didn't want to believe it,' said

Sophie. 'Fear of the unknown is supposed to be more frightening than reality, but I'm not sure that's true.'

'You're not frightened of anything,' said Freddy, 'even Mr Crawford.'

'Confined spaces freak me out, and snakes give me the creeps.'

He shrugged. 'They're mostly harmless.'

'Are you really afraid of Mr Crawford?' Sophie's question was light-hearted.

'I was when I was younger.' Freddy caught Maud's eye. 'He's a good man.'

Maud did a bob curtsey. 'If you'll excuse me.' She hurried off.

Freddy turned to Sophie. 'See you at luncheon.' His eyes lingered on her mouth before he strode away.

In her room, Sophie was nearly bowled over by an excited Charlotte. After she calmed, Sophie sat on the bed and cuddled her and Jack. 'Freddy was brilliant. I've been living in this house for months, but I hardly know him.' The revelation about Betty had revealed surprising layers beneath the easy charm, and today he'd calmly and quickly assessed the situation, and her. 'Once Hugo goes to London, Freddy will have to take up the slack at work. He'll hate that.'

She picked up a glass of water by the bed. 'I should do Hugo's job.' She drained the glass. 'Knowledge of a possible future might help Stick Man, and benefit the estate in other ways?' Charlotte did her serious gaze. It meant, we're all right, but could also signal, this is a mistake.

'If crossing universes is a quest, that might be what success looks like?' At home, she'd been planning to study medieval English literature — knights and heroic deeds. And as with her pre-course reading, *Sir Gawain and the Green Knight*, the goal of this real-life quest — getting back through the portal — had initially seemed clear, but wasn't.

'The Manor's basically a farm, relying on cows and sheep to feed the local community. Maybe I can improve animal welfare?' She hadn't converted Freddy into going veggie, but instinct told her that Hugo's take on Freddy was sound. Freddy would do almost anything if she pushed … okay, worrying, not comforting.

That afternoon, the idea simmered as Maud helped her change into a cream tea dress with a wider skirt. In front of the standalone mirror, Sophie straightened the gown's high collar.

'He was so angry he couldn't have his dinner, Miss. Mr Crawford threatened to call a constable.' Maud hesitated. 'You were the same as ever, but I was surprised at Master Freddy.'

'Why?'

'I've never seen him so solemn and certain.'

'He hasn't always been like that?'

'No, Miss. When I first started, he'd never sit still. Once, he came into the kitchen, knocked over a whole pan of carrot soup.' Maud had been twelve when she began work here. Freddy would have been a young teenager. 'Two days to make. Cook was beside herself.'

'I guess solemnness comes with responsibility.' Sophie winked at her. 'You can be quite solemn.'

Maud smiled in recognition.

At that moment, Sophie wanted to quiz Freddy about his childhood scrapes. Yes, she hardly knew him, but that could be remedied fast. His proposal, thwarted by Stick Man, would have happened seconds after their first proper kiss, which was crazy, but a lot of Shorten stuff was crazy. He'd just been following the rules. And she needed to follow them too — before quietly breaking them.

She pondered her reflection. Shorten Sophie: hair up, the ankle-length dress overlaid with lace. Familiar, yet outlandish.

Freddy had looked gutted when she'd invented the fake boyfriend. The Clarissa bombshell hadn't changed how she felt about Hugo, but her feelings for Freddy had evolved.

They'd be happy.

CHAPTER 26

The following morning, Maud's psychic powers, honed by years in the Lacey household, were audibly humming like a broken live wire. 'You look chirpy, Miss,' she said, as she brought Sophie tea and toast.

'It's a nice day.' Sophie gestured at the French windows and a dull sky outside.

Maud smiled and added wood to the fire, which she'd lit an hour before.

She knew about Freddy. How could Maud possibly know? Impending proposals were delicate matters. Richard and Anne wouldn't have breathed a word.

Stick Man. He'd seen them kissing. Sophie's stomach lurched. Every living soul in Shorten would have been given chapter and verse. A few toddlers might not have received the full in-house briefing…

Anne would know.

Feign illness.

No, just delaying the inevitable.

Jack rested his head on Sophie's lap, wanting reassurance, and Charlotte was in full doe-eyes mode. Good they did empathy but in a few hours they'd be an unhelpful distraction. 'Maud, can you mind the dogs this afternoon?'

Maud folded some linen, didn't glance up. 'Yes, Miss.'

The servants were probably holding a sweepstake. Will the slut from another universe land the son and heir, or be cast into outer darkness?

Sophie skipped breakfast, hid in the gym doing a longer than usual workout, and avoided lunch. But horribly quickly it was time for tea.

Breathe. She could do this. Killed a psychopath, somehow coped with Hugo marrying Clarissa. And after the riot in London, Maud had said Sophie Arundel was as brave as a man. But to face Anne after shamelessly snogging Freddy, against *all* Anne's advice, she'd need to be braver than the average Joe.

In the small drawing room, Miss Parry laid the table in a nanosecond and disappeared.

Anne poured the tea. Miss Parry usually did that.

'Is everything under control?' asked Anne.

Under control? She wouldn't lie to Anne. Anyway, Anne had likely been told every detail. '*Not* under control.'

'Hugo's going to marry Clarissa and you'll marry Freddy,' said Anne. 'You've been indiscreet, Sophie. This will blow over.'

'It will?'

'These things have a way of working out.'

Sophie stared at her lap. Anne had been happily married for thirty years, believed in happy endings, was a dang Happy Endings Role Model. An unexpected tinge of pride surfaced. Stop moping after Hugo, get with the programme. She raised her head.

'You're not the first visitor to be embarrassed like this,' said Anne. 'It's funny, I thought I knew who you'd marry. I just had this feeling. But actually, it was Freddy all along.'

How honest should she be now? 'I'm okay about getting married next year.'

Silence. And it stretched out and out.

'Oh, dear.' Anne's face was white.

Was she about to faint? Sophie jumped up and hauled on the bellpull with unnecessary force.

Miss Parry brought a glass of water and scurried out.

'You're *okay* about marrying Freddy.' Anne took a sip of water, then another one. 'You're in love with Hugo.'

Sophie swallowed. 'He's not in love with me.'

Colour had returned to Anne's cheeks. 'What do you feel for Freddy, *honestly?*'

Creepy, talking about him with his mother. 'We were only friends until I rejected Rupert. After that, we've become closer.'

'I understand. Practical steps.'

Of course, Anne had a plan. Determined and undaunted, she would have been successful in any world.

'I guess we'll be chaperoned,' said Sophie. Even betrothed couples weren't supposed to kiss.

'No chaperone. I hated that when I was engaged. But you *must* be more discreet. Freddy lights up when you walk into a room, Sophie. That won't change. I want him to be happy, and he will be if you marry. You're already close friends. Love will follow.'

Sophie drank her lukewarm tea. She couldn't allow this Hugo obsession to ruin her life, or Freddy's. 'I'm sorry, I was too honest, put you in a terrible position.'

'Nonsense. You didn't tell me, I guessed.' Anne paused. 'And once Freddy sets his mind to something, he won't give up.' Like mother, like son. Anne had fought to marry Richard in the teeth of his late mother's hostility, and maybe because of that, Anne wanted to smooth the way.

'Please don't tell Freddy.'

Anne gave her a look that would have stopped a tiger in mid lunge.

'I should keep calm.'

'Exactly.'

After tea, Sophie collected the dogs and hid in the library, but within minutes Freddy came in and theatrically shut the door.

She stood up, uneasy, despite his mother's assurances. 'Everything can get settled once Hugo's gone to London. A new chapter.'

Freddy stepped towards her and pulled her close. 'Marry me?'

She hadn't expected him to propose so casually. She nodded.

'What about the chap at home?'

'You're my chap now.'

'I suppose I am.' He kissed her, so tenderly she felt tearful.

'I've been saving this.' He took a velvet-covered box from his pocket and opened it, revealing a sparkling solitaire ring.

He slid it onto her finger, fitting perfectly.

She kissed him with renewed urgency, losing herself in the moment and in him.

Freddy mumbled against her mouth, 'We should marry before Hugo leaves.'

'Why?'

He grinned. 'He'll be my best man.'

CHAPTER 27

'It's beautiful.' Maud beamed.

Sophie waved her hand so the ring sparkled in the light from a bedside lamp. The diamond was the size of a large pea. Stones that size at home were only worn by women who'd acquired a bodyguard along with a fiancé. And the ring was a conspicuous reminder: Freddy Forever.

When Sophie called for Hugo that evening, it felt heavy and showy on her finger. His eyes went to her left hand, but he only said, 'I'm glad.'

She walked down the corridor, beyond relieved Hugo hadn't asked questions about the proposal. She'd have lost it.

After everyone was seated for dinner, Freddy announced their engagement. His parents smiled and so did Hugo, and Sophie ignored a pointless barb of regret. The footmen exchanged knowing glances and the butler allowed himself a satisfied nod.

Champagne appeared and, on this special occasion, Mr Crawford and the footmen had fizz too, the footmen drinking as if they'd never tasted it before. Maybe they hadn't?

Richard looked at Anne and proposed a toast. 'The most glamorous visitor of all continues to be my inspiration. Freddy, may Sophie be yours.'

Anne looked embarrassed, Hugo nodded contentedly, and Freddy glowed. Sophie finished her glass of bubbly. She was up for this — seize the moment.

'Miss Arundel, you've *mostly* adapted to our customs.' Richard's eyes twinkled. One of his gentle jokes. 'And we'll—'

A gamekeeper ran in, a shotgun slung across his chest. 'The militia's coming. Five minutes.'

Sophie's insides clenched. *No.*

Richard leapt to his feet and addressed the footmen. 'Tell everyone we've left for the station, caught the London train. Take the dogs downstairs and keep them there. Get rid of any warm food from the table and clear it. Mr Crawford, you're with me.'

Sophie grabbed Charlotte and Jack. Both alert, sensing fear. She handed them over to a footman. Her pistol was in the bedroom, the shotgun and rifle in Lucy's cottage, no time—

Freddy took her arm and half dragged her out of the room after Anne.

In the small drawing room, Richard and the butler were frantically dismantling the linen cupboard and Sophie's heart hammered so hard she thought she'd faint.

'Go quickly,' said Richard, 'but don't slip.'

Anne bent her head and disappeared down the steps, Sophie close behind. Anne sat on an upright chair in the gloom. Freddy, Hugo, and Richard hurried in, Mr Crawford stuffed the linen back and closed the door.

A key turned in the lock.

The boys sat on the floor either side of Sophie, their pale faces strafed in light from cracks in the cupboard door.

Richard knelt at the top of the stairs. He closed a metal panel and pulled a bolt home.

Complete darkness.

Movement. Richard, going to sit beside Anne.

Damp and old dust filled Sophie's nostrils. Keep. Calm. Eyes will adjust. She waved her hands in front of her. Nothing.

Above them, feet tramped and two gunshots rang out, loud and rapid.

The priest hole wasn't a secret. One resentful servant or a careless glance towards the cupboard… Sophie's mouth tasted sour, and her breathing sounded loud in her ears. She was sweating, though the stone she was sitting on was ancient-cold.

Seconds away from all-out panic. She shut her eyes against the blackness, focused on breathing. In out, in out. But she couldn't control her mind: Inkpin's face as the pin slid in. She'd doomed the Laceys, and Hugo. Silent anguished tears wet her face. She dearly wanted to hold Hugo's hand. Keep it together—

A hand reached for hers. Freddy.

Hugo grasped her other hand and more tears prickled.

'Even if there are loads of them, it'll take hours to search the Manor, longer if they check the servants' hall.' Hugo's voice was a low whisper, his breath wine-sweet from dinner.

But her body didn't react to his nearness. In a tomb, dread and fear were stronger than love. Her stomach cramped and she suppressed a gasp. Hugo squeezed her hand and she squeezed back, drawing comfort from his cool skin touching hers.

No noise above their hiding place, but anything could be happening on the far side of the house, or outside. Richard thought the militia wouldn't torch the Manor, but revenge wasn't rational. When smoke seeped into the priest hole, it would be too late to escape.

Take the dogs downstairs and keep them there. If the house got torched, the footmen would bring Charlotte and Jack out—

Think about something else, anything to leave this place. Earliest memory … lying in a pram and far above, leaves fluttering … aged five or six, fighting in the playground, biting in a fight, surprise on the mean girl's face … years later, working out with Lily, learning how to kick … giggling in class with Isha…

How long had they been hiding? Thirty minutes? An hour? No way of knowing—

Bang. Someone hit the outside of the metal panel.

The militia had found her.

Going to die. Weirdly calm.

She couldn't avoid her own end, but she could still save the Laceys and Hugo. She let go of the boys' hands and stood up.

'No.' Hugo gripped Sophie's ankle.

'What are you doing?' hissed Richard.

'Don't move,' whispered Sophie. 'Stay quiet.' The militia might not check inside the priest hole once they were focused on killing her, revenging Inkpin. 'They don't know you're here. I'll distract them.'

Bang.

Sophie wrenched free of Hugo and walked stiffly to where the steps were. Feeling for each tread, she knelt at the last and shot back the bolt.

She slid the panel just enough to step through the gap.

CHAPTER 28

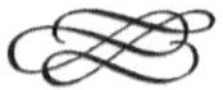

Rough hands grabbed Sophie's shoulders, pulled her out of the cupboard, and the electric light of the drawing room blinded her. A male voice was giving orders, amidst many heavy footsteps. The warmer air smelled of sweat and blood, but Sophie's thoughts were with Hugo and the Laceys. *Please* keep quiet.

Her eyesight adjusted to the light. Armed men dressed like gamekeepers.

Two bodies lay sprawled by the fireplace. One could have been sleeping, the other was stretched across the grate, his arm bent at an unnatural angle.

The militiamen were reporting to a wiry guy with short, salt and pepper hair. Vaguely familiar — from the bakery? He nodded at the man holding her.

Sophie's captor released her and stepped away.

Now they'd shoot her. Preparing herself, she closed her eyes.

A thump and a clattering noise.

'Deal with her first.' The leader's voice was curt, military.

Sophie squared her shoulders and opened her eyes. The

wiry man's attention was on a young man lying on the carpet next to a toppled lamp. Sophie did a double take. Not a boy. Miss Blackmore. Her shirt was sodden red, her face pallid.

They were going to finish her off.

Sophie defiantly scanned the men's faces, shaming them to break eye contact, and then half fell, half sat on the green sofa, floppy with relief. These men weren't dressed *like* gamekeepers. They *were* gamekeepers. And gardeners. She'd seen some of them with Mrs Rawlings two weeks ago in a corridor, memorising the layout of the house.

The wiry man must be Mr Lear, the head gamekeeper. Vaguely familiar because he worked here. *Deal with her first.* He was prioritising Miss Blackmore, ensuring her injury was treated. A young lad pressed a wad of material against Miss Blackmore's shoulder, and she flinched, bit hard on her bottom lip.

Tears of relief ran down Sophie's cheeks. She drew deep breaths, tried to gather her wits, and took in the state of the people around her. A boy, younger than her, had a cut across his temple, bleeding heavily. He wiped his eyes with the back of his hand. Another man nursed his leg, a boy next to him in a daze.

Maud's John gave Sophie a weary nod. Reynolds was beside him, but looked different, dressed in gardener clothes. And everyone was sweaty, as if they'd been working out.

Richard clambered from the cupboard, blinking owlishly, and brushed dust off his trousers. Hugo, Freddy, and Anne staggered out behind him.

'Everybody, please sit down,' said Richard.

Those who had injuries moved onto sofas and chairs, others rested on the floor, but Mr Lear remained standing, as did Hugo and Freddy. Anne sat beside Sophie, took Sophie's hand, and held it tight.

Richard addressed the group. 'Report.'

Mr Lear pointed at the bodies beside the fireplace. 'I dealt with them.'

'One dead, one legged it over the terrace,' said a man by the door.

'We got two.' The man with the injured leg exchanged a relieved look with the boy beside him.

'Three.'

'One.'

'Two.'

A few minutes later, after all the reports were done, Mr Crawford came in. 'Twenty-one militiamen entered the house via the front.'

'So, assuming nobody got in by swimming the moat,' said Freddy, 'seventeen dead and four got away.'

'None of them left through the hall.' The butler mopped his forehead with a large white handkerchief.

Mrs Rawlings walked in. 'Two of the militia are under guard in the kitchen. Injured but not seriously.'

A gamekeeper appeared at the door, holding a modern-looking flashlight.

'Outside?' said Richard.

'Armoury and servants' hall secure. I've seen no militia, but too dark to be certain.'

Lucy came in, followed by Mr Adams and more game-keepers and gardeners.

'We have four fatalities,' said Mr Adams.

'You've checked the upper storeys?' Mr Lear asked him.

'Yes. They didn't get beyond the ground floor.'

'That leaves two unaccounted for,' said Freddy.

'Once the injured militiamen are patched up, escort them out,' said Richard to Mr Adams. 'The drawbridge is still being delivered and installed tomorrow?'

'First thing.'

'The unaccounted militiamen might have swum the moat?' said Mr Lear.

'Or hiding,' said Richard. 'I know everyone's tired, but every able-bodied man should search the ground floor again.'

Without thinking, Sophie stood up to volunteer, and was instantly pulled back into her seat by Anne.

Richard addressed the room. 'Today was really well done. And hopefully, tomorrow, we can put this … incident behind us.'

The next morning, Maud put the tea tray on Sophie's lap and shared a blow-by-blow account of the firefight, as if she'd crept around corners with a shotgun. 'In the large drawing room, Mr Watkins was nearly shot, Miss. He had to throw himself down behind a sofa.' She stroked Charlotte. 'Men are funny, aren't they?'

'How do you mean?'

'This morning, Mr Watkins paced to and fro, wouldn't stop talking about it.' Maud shook her head. 'Almost as if he enjoyed getting shot at.'

'I suppose everyone reacts differently.' She'd not enjoyed hiding in the priest hole. Not. One. Second. Maybe it was harder to wait, powerless, than to do something, anything, even risking your life in a shoot-out? Hopefully, she'd never find out. She finished her tea and gave the dogs some toast. 'Did you get *any* sleep?'

The kitchen servants had stayed overnight in the Manor, but other staff in the servants' hall, including Maud, had locked themselves in.

'I stayed awake, worried sick about Mr Watkins. And worrying about you, Miss.' Maud knew some of the militia had escaped the bakery, could want revenge.

'Lady Lacy helped me undress last night.'

'I didn't mean that, Miss.'

'I know.'

'Mr Crawford should go on the stage.' Maud removed the tray. 'The militia said they were taking over the Manor and calm as anything, he offered them refreshments, told them how the family had gone to London, visiting museums and all sorts.'

Giving the gamekeepers and gardeners vital minutes to spread out inside the house. And the militia came for the Manor, *not* her. A rush of energy, fuelled by relief. 'How did you learn all this?'

'Mr Crawford said what happened over breakfast. You could have heard a pin drop.' The servants ate breakfast at seven, earlier than the family. Maud wrinkled her nose. 'Do you still want to practise your mini-archery?'

'Why?'

'The house is in a right state.'

'We can still access the mini-archery room?'

Maud hesitated. 'I think so.'

'I should practise. Get back to normal.'

But when Sophie walked to the bathroom, the corridor resembled a theme-park haunted house. She hurried along, trying not to notice sticky red patches blotting the carpet and scarlet splatters on the cream walls. Some of the doors had gaps in the wood instead of locks.

Later, when she went with Hugo to breakfast, Richard was waiting in the anteroom.

'May I have a word?' Richard took Sophie aside.

Hugo continued on to the dining room.

'The militia leader asked for you, by name,' Richard whispered, 'demanded that you be found.'

Fear slid over her heart like a shroud, and she froze.

'When Mr Crawford enquired why, he was told, "That's militia business."'

Sophie swallowed. 'Why didn't they tell him?'

'It's just a guess,' said Richard, 'but "Inkpin killed by young lady" wouldn't enhance the late Mr Inkpin's reputation, or the militia's.'

'Mrs Watkins hasn't said a word about this.'

'Mr Crawford was alone in the hall when the militia came in.' Richard lowered his voice further. 'Fortunately, Mr Crawford sensed this was a delicate matter, reported to me privately.'

Now she felt sick.

'I told him the militia must have been incensed when you escaped from the bakery, that Mrs Watkins and her sister raised the alarm, but I also made it clear he shouldn't discuss this with anyone, even Mrs Rawlings.'

Logic check. *She* was the reason the militia chose mid-evening to requisition the Manor, rather than the early hours. They'd presumed she'd be having dinner, would find her in seconds. Far easier than waking up maids to point out her bedroom or searching the house. If they'd come for her overnight, she'd have stood no chance. Shot before she could get out of bed, never mind reach her pistol in the drawer—

'If your involvement in Inkpin's death becomes public knowledge,' said Richard, 'Mr Inkpin Senior will redouble his efforts. Yes, for revenge, but also to save face.'

Sophie raised her chin. 'Operation Scarlet Pimpernel carries on.'

CHAPTER 29

*A*fter breakfast, en route to the gym, Sophie and Maud paused in the hall. The front door and most of the wall had been replaced by the drawbridge. Two footmen laboriously turned a thick iron wheel, winding it closed, and the dogs barked at it, as if it were alive.

Sophie tightened her grip on her heavy embroidered bag. Originally purposed to hold a sampler or book, it now held her pistol during the day, though as with the drawbridge, *horse and bolted* came to mind.

They headed off through an unscathed corridor, but the next had red walls. Queasy, Sophie said, 'You were right. I should have put this off.'

Maud sped up. 'Nearly there.'

Lucy was waiting. 'Short session today.' Her shotgun was slung across her chest, and she had a leather kitbag over her shoulder.

The gym door looked the same as it always did. Once inside, Sophie relocked it.

Lucy unfolded a bedsheet from her kitbag. 'Three

"

gardeners dead and a gamekeeper. Do people *ever* get used to this?'

'I don't know. I couldn't sleep last night, and I thought about a Gandalf quote from *The Fellowship of the Ring*. When bad stuff happens, we can't wish it away. *All we have to decide is what to do with the time that's given us.'*

'Wise words.' Lucy blinked. 'But I hope the Incident was a one-off.'

Richard's name for the deadly shoot-out had stuck.

'Any sign of the two militiamen,' said Sophie, 'that were unaccounted for?'

'No. They must have swum the moat to get away.' Lucy spread the sheet over a table by the window. 'We're burying the bodies in the graveyard, our lads apart from the others. It's the right thing to do, though every digging shift needs a guard.' The estate chapel was well outside the moat.

Sophie straightened the sheet. 'How's Miss Blackmore?'

'Recovering. She's actually buoyed up, and not just with the Laudanum.'

Laudanum was an addictive mixture of alcohol and morphine. The other side effect was blissing out.

'She killed two of the militia before she was shot,' said Lucy. 'The gamekeepers have gone from resenting her, to lauding her to the skies, calling her Annie.'

'Annie?'

'After Annie Oakley, the crack shot in America.'

Sophie hesitated. 'Did you, er, shoot anyone?'

'No. I was in the detail that checked the upper floors. All empty.' Lucy placed her shotgun on the bedsheet, her eyes thoughtful. She took a green can labelled *Bisley Gun Oil* out of her bag. 'You might want to take your ring off.'

Sophie put the ring on the table, well away from the gun and the oil.

'I should have said, congratulations.'

'Thanks.'

'I'll show you my rifle routine next week. It's pretty similar.' Lucy demonstrated how to clean and lubricate the gun with a rag.

Sophie repeated the actions.

Lucy went through pistol cleaning and Sophie carefully copied the steps.

After Sophie re-wrapped the pistol in a tea towel and returned it to her bag, she frowned at her filthy fingernails. 'I'll make sure I wash away the evidence.'

'We don't need to do this in secret. After yesterday, no one would object.'

Inkpin's face popped up in Sophie's mind like a billboard. 'Freddy doesn't approve.' That was surely the honest truth.

'He does realise you won't magically turn into a doormat at the altar?'

A whisper of unease.

'Anne and Richard must have had a different take on things,' said Lucy, 'worked through them.'

Sophie nodded, though their differences had probably always been trivial. Richard had wanted to reform how the estate was run before Anne arrived, and he'd gradually done it, all the while playing a reassuringly familiar Lord of the Manor. And when Anne had changed a convention — allowing women to work after they married — he'd supported her.

Sophie wiggled her shoulders and started her stretching routine for the workout. 'You've got Shorten sussed, you know.'

Lucy raised an eyebrow.

'Your own front door. Your own space. My bedroom door's no match for Maud. She flagged a bit after the bakery, but the Incident hasn't fazed her. Doesn't draw breath between gossiping and nagging.' Maud knocked but sometimes didn't wait for an answer. How would that work when Sophie Arundel was sharing a bedroom with Freddy? Maud might do special training — Maid's Marriage Etiquette? A sudden weariness weighed on her and she stopped stretching. 'The boys seemed fine at breakfast, but I'm wiped out.'

'A drop of rum will perk you up.' Lucy produced a hipflask from her pocket and offered it.

'Hard liquor on tap?'

'Helps with working outside.'

The first taste was medicine, the second … interesting.

While Lucy returned the sheet and oil can to her kitbag, Sophie shared her plan to take over from Hugo in the office.

'People warmed to me working in the gardens,' said Lucy. 'When I made head gardener, there was chuntering but nothing serious. It'll be the same with you.'

Small steps. 'Freddy enjoys analysing data about crops,' said Sophie, 'but not the rest of it. If I get involved, and anything happens to Mr Adams, hopefully Freddy wouldn't fall ill, shouldering all the burden.' She gave the punch bag a precise twisting kick, picturing any obstacles vanishing *poof* in a flash of red smoke.

'Mr Wainwright's an awkward bugger.'

'Who?' Sophie steadied the punchbag.

'The man you found on the estate. If you can persuade Mr Crawford to starve a starving man, helping to run the Manor should be a piece of cake.' Lucy did a flurry of punches.

'Having Freddy there helped.' Sophie drank a little from Lucy's hipflask. 'This is bloody amazing.'

Lucy grinned. 'You'll make a formidable Lady Lacey.'

'An old battle axe.'

'Hardly … perhaps a young battle axe?'

Sophie pretended to set her mouth. 'Oh, I meant to tell you, but with Freddy and the Incident, I clean forgot.' She explained about Janet and Hugo not having the gene, both of them seeing Shorten like Janet's painting.

'Janet said Shorten inspired her, never mentioned that was how she actually saw the colours here.' Lucy frowned. 'Why wouldn't she tell me?'

'I'm guessing she assumed all the visitors saw Shorten as she did. Until we did a colour check in the garage, I assumed Hugo and I saw it the same way.' Sophie threw a punch. 'You think that's wacky.' She summarised what Hugo had said about Janus.

'A real god.' Lucy shook her head and threw another punch. 'Hugo must be excited about London.' Hugo's imminent engagement was catnip for the gossip mill. 'And I'm really pleased about you and Freddy.'

Sophie did a different twisty kick. Her feelings for Hugo were too embarrassing to confide, even to Lucy. 'Marrying Freddy's a big step.'

'You're lucky to have Anne, and now Freddy. When Janet died … no idea how I got through it.'

'Since then, you've never met anyone…' No, like her Hugo obsession, too personal.

But Lucy shrugged, apparently unfazed. 'Nope. Never did.' She executed a confident kick. 'But being on your own gives you freedom. Perhaps my Mostly Happy Ever After?'

'Mostly Happy Ever After sounds good.' Sophie ran on the spot.

'I've never discussed my private life,' said Lucy. 'Better not to.'

'Sound advice,' said Sophie, thinking she should follow it. 'I understand.'

'You don't.' Lucy folded her arms. 'Janet was much more than a friend.'

CHAPTER 30

Sophie stopped running on the spot. Lucy's secret, mundane in England at home, was incredibly dangerous here. 'I'll never say a word. You could go to prison.'

To her surprise, Lucy laughed. 'Social death, yes. Even Anne might not be able to stop me being sacked. But prison, *no*.' She did a focused, clean kick at the punch bag. 'Only illegal if you're male.'

'How bizarre.'

'I knew about this before I came here. Queen Victoria in both universes refused to criminalise gay women because she thought the idea so ridiculous.'

'Really?'

'The court cases in the papers are about gentlemen,' said Lucy, a glint in her eye. 'Never ladies.'

'You might find someone, and I bet nobody would have a clue.'

'You're right. We shared a bedroom in the Manor for weeks when we arrived. But as for second chances, I'm not holding my breath.'

'At home, you can get married now.'

Lucy did another kick. 'That's wonderful.'

Emboldened by Lucy's trust, Sophie said, 'Freddy's lovely, it's just…'

'He's not Hugo.'

She wanted to curl up and hide. If Lucy knew, everyone did.

Sophie took a too-big swig of rum and it went down the wrong way. She snatched her flask from her bag, drank water, and handed back the hipflask. 'I suspected Maud reads my mind. The whole of Shorten must know.'

'They don't. It was only a hunch. When I talked in the summer about the Great War not happening, Hugo's body language was … protective. And your reaction matched up.'

Lucky that Hugo, clever in so many ways, was bone stupid about her. Anne and Lucy had worked it out. Female intuition? 'Could you get me a hipflask?'

'Of course.' Lucy regarded her curiously. 'Are you sure about marrying Freddy? Have you told Hugo how you feel?'

'He's definitely not interested. I fancy Freddy and I think he loves me. Mostly Happy Ever After.' Sophie shot her a poignant smile. 'I'm still getting to know Freddy … he's not as laid back as he appears. And Hugo's a good friend. We have the same off-beat sense of humour.'

'You may be too alike,' said Lucy. 'Would have got bored?'

She hadn't thought of that. Ironic. Until Shorten, she'd assumed they had nothing in common. 'Actually, I'm worried about him. He's not sleeping properly, seems a bit down.'

'Even with marrying Clarissa?'

Sophie punched the bag with her left fist. 'He's homesick.'

'Janet missed her family terribly.'

'Did you meet them?'

'Couldn't. She adored her parents, but if they'd found out about me, she'd have been disowned. They were *very* straight.' Lucy threw a targeted punch. 'University gave Janet freedom, and when we got together, she was so happy. It's wonderful being able to talk about her.'

The right words of comfort eluding her, Sophie patted Lucy's arm, and a new lift idea formed. 'The visitors with the gene might have no close family at home?'

'Your parents are gone, so is my mother. My father's gone too.' Lucy smiled wryly. 'Probably alive but definitely *gone* ... who knows where.'

'And Anne told me she was closer to her nanny than her parents.'

'Alan's around fifty, so was in his thirties when he came through. Perhaps he had no strong blood ties?'

'Could be another part of the puzzle,' said Sophie. 'Wind down?'

Lucy checked her watch. 'I've lost track of time. Grave-yard duty in fifteen minutes.'

They finished their stretching routine, Sophie unlocked the door, Lucy walked briskly away, and Sophie floated towards Maud, wafted by alcohol. The dogs jumped up to greet her, and Sophie fussed until they calmed.

An elderly maid carrying a pile of linen stopped in the corridor. She was thin and short. Her white hair, pulled up in a tight bun, contrasted starkly with dark, old-age shadows under her eyes. 'Miss Arundel?'

'Yes, that's me.' An unwelcome vision of Charlotte bouncing, and this maid being bowled clean over... She grabbed Charlotte's collar.

'Thank you for letting me come here. The Manor's a lovely place.'

It took a second to realise who this was. No, far too old. She couldn't be Mrs Evans' *mother*.

'I'm glad,' Sophie said, finally. This woman shouldn't be

working as a maid. She was obviously very ill. 'How are you, with your heart and everything?'

'Much better since I arrived here, Miss. Much better.'

Sophie smiled. 'Nice to see you but I need to make tracks.'

'Pardon?'

'Sorry, I mean, I have to get changed.'

The old lady went on her way.

Back in her room, Sophie wondered about Mrs Evans' mother. Nearly fifty, so actually forty-something, but she appeared to be seventy, or older. Maybe she'd lived a hard life?

Sophie's own mother was clear and detailed in her memory, even after six years: clear complexion, highlighted blonde hair in a ponytail. Anne's dark hair looked natural but might not be. Had dye been invented yet?

If the revolution panned out like in Russia, Sophie Arundel could be shot or starve to death. Grey hair would be the least of her worries.

In the bathroom, Sophie washed her hands. The gun oil was difficult to shift from her fingernails, and taking apart and reassembling the guns had made her fingers sore. But she had clean weapons, if not the experience to use them.

After a bath and changing into a day dress, Sophie set off to check Richard's latest note. By the library, maids were scrubbing at the walls and carpet, and Sophie acknowledged them before going inside.

The hidden cubby hole contained a scrappy piece of paper. *Barbed wire encircles most of the cottages, deep ditch beyond that. Received machine gun. Put aside another room for ammunition. Orchard felled.* Sophie sighed. Did he have to cut down the orchard?

She finished *A History* sitting by the fire. If Richard's writer ancestor was aware of any secret passages in the Manor, he hadn't shared them.

At noon, she headed to the small drawing room to meet Freddy, her thoughts turning to wedding dresses. Wouldn't be so different here, apart from not showing off her shoulders.

Freddy was already there. When she came in, he closed the door with his foot.

That counted as discreet.

He gathered her into his arms, they kissed intensely, and Freddy's body felt hard against hers. When they finally stopped, she was breathless.

He drew her close again and nuzzled into her neck. 'Do ladies have lots of babies, if they can choose?'

Freddy possessed an insatiable appetite for facts. Hugo must have given him chapter and verse on the pill. 'Most people have two children,' she said, wildly generalising.

'The doctor told Mummy she shouldn't have any more babies. How many would you like?'

His question was perfectly rational. They'd been kissing for a while, so babies were the next stage. Well, almost the next. 'Two girls and two boys.' Always wished she'd had brothers and sisters.

'Do daughters inherit estates in your England if there's no sons?'

Thinking outside the box, or Hugo had been drip-feeding him ideas. 'I'm not sure, but they've changed the rules for the monarchy. The oldest child is crowned, whether they're male or female.' How was that logical? Why not always choose the youngest? Or the one best suited? No, there'd be huge feuds. Similar to Mr Adams' system for accepting relatives ... not perfect, but good enough.

Freddy glanced at his watch. 'From now on, we should meet earlier, in the library where it's quieter.'

She'd have bet the Manor that Hugo knew about their

kissing sessions. Hugo wouldn't barge in before twelve thirty.

Sophie sat primly on the green sofa. Freddy opened the door, sat opposite her with the coffee table between them, and Hugo strode in as if he was late for a board meeting.

Under Hugo's arm was a blue folder. 'New security plan. Your father said we can go through it over a coffee.'

'Righty ho,' said Freddy.

Hugo rang the bellpull and sat down beside Freddy, who gave him a relaxed nod. Freddy knew how to enjoy the moment. In Sophie's mind, a video started up, making out in his Shorten bedroom—

Richard hurried in, his face tense. The boys got to their feet, so Sophie did too.

'You should hear an accurate account *before* you hear a garbled version. Please sit down.' Richard stood by the mantlepiece, his back to the fire.

Miss Parry appeared, poured coffee and left, softly closing the door. 'Mr Crawford will brief the servants,' said Richard. 'The Armstrongs were attacked last night.'

Sophie put her hand to her mouth. They'd visited the Armstrongs. An odd target, just an oversized cottage.

'It was a mob, not a militia,' said Richard. 'Their game-keepers frightened them off, firing into the air. One of the ruffians was hit over the head with a cooking pot. Their cook's a formidable woman, cracked his skull like an egg.'

Freddy winced.

'There's fire damage but nothing major,' said Richard, 'and everyone's essentially all right.'

'What do you mean,' said Sophie, '*essentially?*'

Richard hesitated. 'Alice was assaulted. She's upset, understandably, but she wasn't ... harmed.'

Sophie's heart missed a beat. Richard was downplaying this in line with the Shorten Code. Already emotionally fragile, Alice's first love, a music tutor, had been sent away, deemed 'unsuitable.' This could break her.

She should visit. No, the Armstrongs would want this *really* downplayed. Alice's marriage prospects might be ruined. She should write—

'Anne's invited the Armstrongs to stay,' said Richard, 'until things calm down. Sophie, between you, I'm sure you'll help them settle in.'

'Definitely.' She and Anne could comfort Alice in person.

'Freddy, I want you to review the shift pattern,' said Richard. 'It has to change every day, mustn't be predictable. Start after lunch.'

After Richard left, Sophie's thoughts stayed with the Armstrongs, how they must be feeling, forced from their home.

Hugo rested the folder on his lap, opened it, and selected a pencil from his jacket pocket. 'All the gardeners are now patrolling, but Miss Hemmings believes she can still run the greenhouses. Our obvious weak spot is deliveries from the town. Mrs Slater is our eyes and ears there, so hopefully we'll weed out militia sympathisers.'

'What about trucks being hijacked?' said Sophie.

'Hi what?' said Freddy.

'Sorry,' said Sophie, 'taking over a regular tradesman's van.'

'That's where the extra patrols come in.' Hugo scribbled something in the folder. 'Every vehicle will be searched in the lane.'

'There can't be many sympathisers,' said Freddy, 'not after Mr Miles' murder?'

'The militias are brutal,' said Hugo, 'but once they secure a town, they give out food and pay men to join. Powerful recruitment tool.'

'Where are they getting their money from?' Sophie asked Hugo.

'According to Clarissa, from Russia. If the communists take over, Russia will have a useful ally.'

'Freddy, your parents need a flight plan,' said Sophie.

'A flight plan?' said Freddy, puzzled.

'To leave the country,' said Hugo.

Freddy set his mouth. 'This is my home. I'd rather die.'

CHAPTER 31

The first time Sophie saw the small drawing room where she was sitting now, she'd just walked twenty miles from the portal. She'd been hungry, thirsty — and scared. The drawing room hadn't changed since then, but she had. As weeks turned into months, and she'd realised Anne loved her like a daughter, the Manor had become home. Yet it was only bricks and mortar. However precious and cherished, not worth dying for.

'If push comes to shove,' said Hugo to Freddy, 'we could live with your uncle.' Richard's brother lived in America.

Freddy shook his head.

'And living in New York would be better than dying, I'm fairly sure,' said Sophie, her tone teasing.

'It's always good to have a plan B,' said Hugo, 'but best not to speak about it in front of the servants. Bad for morale.'

Freddy stood up, his face troubled. 'I'll mention it to my parents before lunch.'

After Freddy had left, Hugo got to his feet. 'Let's get some fresh air. The office can wait ten minutes.'

From his tone of voice, he wanted to talk. She really didn't, but she fetched her cape and hat.

Outside, the dogs raced off, Jack staying close to Charlotte, guided by his hearing and sense of smell.

It was colder today but the dogs were cosy in tartan coats. Once Sophie had drawn the simple shape on paper, Maud had sewn the garments that morning, despite her concern for canine 'dignity.'

'Won't catch on for decades.' Hugo turned towards her, his expression indulgent.

Sophie ignored a surprising flutter. She'd expected that to stop after kissing Freddy so thoroughly.

Remembering Freddy's kisses made the Hugo tingling recede. She thought about kickboxing and it faded more. Double distractions were the answer, like pill combos for chronic diseases.

She cast around for something positive. 'If we don't emigrate, we could somehow stop whatever's going to wipe Little Shorten off the map.'

'The university could still be built, but somewhere else.'

She'd be in her fifties by the 1960s. Way too old to wear a mini skirt—

'Is Pete Whatsisface the boyfriend you were missing?'

Pete's surname was Watson, but blessed with movie-star good looks, everyone called him Whatsisface.

'Is this another fact-finding mission for Freddy?' The ring was invisible under her kid glove but felt solid and heavy.

'Freddy asked and I played dumb. You mustn't tell him about Pete.'

'I don't want to start off keeping secrets.' Sophie winced inside. Compared to how she felt about Hugo, Pete was trivial. 'Anyway, Freddy was fine about it, asked if we were engaged. Okay, that was weird.'

Hugo fastened the top button on his coat. 'The word at school was that you dumped him after one weekend.'

Sophie winced. 'We had nothing in common.'

Without warning, Hugo held her shoulders and searched her face. '*Never* tell Freddy you slept with Pete.'

Uncomfortable, she stepped away. 'Freddy loves me. I'll be straight with him.'

'He … won't see you in the same way. It wouldn't matter if he'd kept a string of mistresses before he met you. Yes, it's double standards, but you can't change that — or Freddy.'

She nodded. Freddy hadn't gleefully seduced Betty, thought it shameful. 'Thanks for the heads up, I'll keep schtum.' And on her wedding night, she'd act surprised.

'You and Pete stayed friends?'

'After a week or so, he was really cool about it.' At Hadley, she'd had no interest in Hugo or his girlfriends, but now she was curious. 'Did you date anyone at school?'

An emotion flashed across Hugo's face and was gone. Surprised she'd asked? 'Ekaterina, on the Russian exchange. She was beautiful and bright, but it didn't work out.'

They'd reached the stone bridge or what was left of it — the foundations.

Hugo started back towards the bower.

She kept pace with him. 'Does Freddy share *everything* I do and say with him?'

Hugo shrugged. 'I'm his best friend.'

They were probably giving her kissing marks out of ten. No, Freddy shared, but Hugo wouldn't be interested. She put up the hood of her cloak over her turquoise hat and plumped up her scarf.

'Look, I get that marrying Freddy's a big deal, like Clarissa is for me.'

'When do you move to London?'

'In the summer.' Hugo glanced at her. 'Let's write regularly, not lose touch.'

She wanted to say no, but he'd ask questions she couldn't handle, so she nodded again. Reading his letters and replying would be hard.

They were at the bower, so they sat on the stone seat.

The dogs ran in, their breath white swirls in the air, and lay down, though they'd slept all night and napped till breakfast. Sophie told him about her family theory.

'Interesting.' Hugo took off his fur hat and ruffled his hair. 'I still think the lift is a transport vehicle.'

'But a spaceship that travels between universes … such a crazy idea.'

'More than a portal that only opens for six people?' He traced frost swirls on the sundial with a gloved finger.

'I need to keep an open mind.'

He got to his feet and began pacing. 'You thought the pictures on the lift represented a destination name, like on a bus. But what if it's more like a taxi?'

'Smaller but more expensive.'

'Why aren't you taking this seriously?'

'I am.' Sophie pulled her hat down over her ears. 'Banter helps me think.'

'What if you somehow *called* it, through your state of mind?' Hugo paused pacing. 'Just before we went into the lift, you were thrown to the floor when Charlotte bolted.'

'A miracle I didn't break something.'

'What were you thinking and feeling while you waited for the lift?'

'Out of breath from running, relieved to have found Charlotte.'

Jack yawned and Sophie yawned in sympathy. 'If someone had invited me into a spooky tent in the students' union and said, *Travel to another universe and get trapped there,* I wouldn't have gone for it.'

'Few people would, but what if you called it *subconsciously?*'

'Like a drunk hailing a taxi.'

He shot her an exasperated glance.

'You've been a bit down, but going to London, you've got everything sussed.'

'Honestly, on balance, I'd rather go home.'

'What about Clarissa?'

'I'd miss her, but I also miss my family, my old life.'

Sophie stared at him in surprise. He wasn't in love with Clarissa.

Hugo sat beside her and put his hat on. 'If the government falls, the drawbridge and moat won't save us.'

'So, we emigrate.' Richard probably had it in hand. Mr Pragmatic.

Hugo adjusted his hat, though it was set squarely on his head. 'What if you could call the lift by consciously yearning for home, replicating that emotional energy?'

'The lift won't appear to order,' Sophie said, gently, 'like food on a menu.'

'It wouldn't on a whim.'

'Exactly. I'd have to want to go back *a lot*. A hundred and ten per cent.'

'Can't be more than a hundred per cent.'

'You know what I mean.' She stamped her feet against the cold.

'It has to be a powerful need with no doubts.'

'So, this can't work, can it? Me wanting to stay would scupper it.'

'I reckon you could suppress that.' His voice had a stubborn ring. 'If you focused hard enough.'

'It's a non-starter, Hugo, with how I feel about Anne … and now Freddy.'

He flinched as if she'd hit him. 'You've given up.' He swore.

The word sounded loud and incongruous. He wasn't himself, not thinking straight. 'I'm being realistic.'

'No, you're bailing.' He glared.

She glared too. He was clutching at straws.

He jumped up, swore again, and stomped off, every step clipped and bitter.

CHAPTER 32

Sophie walked slowly back to the house. Hugo was irrationally angry: at her, at Shorten, at everything. He wasn't a bit down. He was depressed. And treatment here would be antiquated, could do more harm than good.

In the hall, Anne was greeting the Armstrongs.

Alice and Ethel were pale and quiet. Not at all how Sophie remembered them.

Over afternoon tea, she and Anne made small talk, but Alice and Ethel just responded with nods.

Probably not a wise idea to directly comfort Alice. Could make things worse.

Before dinner, Sophie didn't call for Hugo and he ignored her during the meal. And that night she slept badly, waking in the early hours, consumed with worry about unfamiliar, angry Hugo.

The next morning, just before nine, there was a knock on the door and Maud opened it.

The dogs greeted Hugo as usual, didn't sense his odd mood. He acknowledged Maud before addressing Sophie. 'Are you up for a chat?'

'Of course.'

Maud put more wood on the fire and left, leaving the door ajar.

Hugo sat awkwardly in the armchair by the fireplace. As it was a Saturday, he wore Shorten Casual, including his favourite sleeveless jumper. Jack settled beside the grate, but Charlotte leaned against Hugo's knees. 'I'm glad the corridors are clean.'

'Me too.' The way to the bathroom was now gore-free.

'I'm sorry about yesterday.' He sighed. 'Sometimes I think it's hopeless too. I should have given you more slack.'

'And I was too negative.' Sophie sat on the bed 'So much has happened, I feel wrung out.'

'Friends?'

She nodded. Better than Angry Hugo, but bittersweet.

'We really need to figure this out.'

Sophie stopped herself shrugging. The trouble is, we're missing basic info. Unknown unknowns, and what we do know we *don't* know, we can't find out.'

'What?'

'Take Anne. Unlikely she'll remember what she was thinking decades ago when she called the lift. Same with Lucy.' Sophie smoothed out the eiderdown beside her. 'Actually, I should ask them.'

'Alan was planning to get himself a nice country pub. Perhaps he was thinking about that before he got in the lift?'

'But all the visitors returned to the lane again,' said Sophie, '*really* wanted to go back, and found nothing.'

'The lane looks the same for miles. The other visitors didn't mark the lift spot, so when they yearned for home, perhaps they weren't close enough?' He leaned forward in the chair. 'And even if they were in the right place, they searched like we did, for physical clues. Weren't *calling* it?'

Sophie trawled her memory and her heart missed a beat. 'Hugo, this is important. Anne was definitely searching. When we arrived, I questioned if she could have mistaken the place and she said, *A room-sized square of light? I couldn't have missed it.*'

'Lucy was searching too.'

'What if we focus on just *us*? We could replicate in the lane our relative positions in the students' union, a few moments before the lift opened? You may not have the gene, but you might be part of the puzzle.'

'And there's something else,' said Hugo, 'but I'm still thinking it through.'

Charlotte ambled across the room and pawed the door.

'Come on,' said Hugo. 'I'm hungry.'

After breakfast, when the boys left for a security briefing, Sophie picked up *The Times* where Richard had left it and put it under her arm. She hurried to the library and collected a note dated the previous day. *Manor security complete, including barbed wire, but I hear the army's been infiltrated. I've written to James in New York, asked if we can visit.*

Yes, Mr Pragmatic. She burned the note.

Sitting in the red chair, she unfolded the newspaper and nearly dropped it. On the front page was a stark headline: *Mr Albert Inkpin assassinated.* The article was brief, with no photo. *Mr Inkpin was shot as he addressed a rally in Hyde Park. Despite members of the public giving chase, the perpetrator is still at large...*

Richard had read the paper over breakfast, shown no reaction to this at all.

This surely meant she was safer? Relief, quickly followed by guilt. The man had been murdered in cold blood.

Charlotte nuzzled into her legs and Sophie put the paper aside. 'Let's go, time to meet Hugo.' She collected her hat and cape from her room.

Hugo was already on the terrace in his long coat and fur hat, facing the garden. He turned, and they walked together onto the lawn. He summarised Mr Adams' briefing, Sophie nodded at appropriate points, and looked beyond the moat. 'Can't see any barbed wire.'

'It's further out, and all around the drive.'

'Alice and Ethel are in a state.' They'd hardly left their rooms except for meals.

'We may never know what actually happened.'

For no apparent reason, thinking about kickboxing moves and kissing Freddy stopped working, and Sophie's body set off on a suicidal, intense Hugo-road trip, out of control and speeding up, making her breathless. She needed another strategy, and fast...

Pretend he's not real, like a Princess Leia hologram.

Charlotte raced in her natty jacket and Jack was snug in his, staying close to Sophie. 'Short walk today. Not feeling brilliant.'

'Another migraine?'

'No, just knackered.'

In the bower, the stone seat was shiny with frost, but Sophie sat down anyway.

'When it's this cold, I miss my skiing clothes.' Hugo sat beside her and jammed his hat further over his ears. 'Even in Colorado, I was fine.'

Not interested. The hologram thing was working. 'I enjoyed the skiing trip with school.'

'You fell off the button lift.'

'Yes, didn't enjoy that.' His memory was awesome. That

skiing trip had been years ago. Expensive extras had stopped abruptly after her parents' death. Aunty Wendy's income had barely stretched to taking Sophie in.

'Freddy told me you'd like four children,' said Hugo.

'Er, yes.' Sophie shifted in her seat. She'd hoped that conversation had been intimate enough to stay private.

'You'll need to be firm with him. Make sure you space out pregnancies.' He looked at the sundial.

What a bizarre conversation. 'The doctor warned Anne not to have any more babies, and she didn't.'

He nodded.

Yes, Freddy had told him that too.

'I've tried to speak to him about consent issues but I'm getting nowhere.'

Freddy had been adamant that Hugo shouldn't know about Betty. Might be why, when Hugo talked about consent, he'd fobbed him off?

'They have supplies here,' said Hugo, 'I'm fairly sure. Not as effective as modern ones, but better than nothing.'

'Supplies?'

'Condoms,' said Hugo. 'One of the running jokes Alex and I had … plenty of supplies, no girlfriends.'

Alex had been his best friend at Hadley.

Sophie thought back to Pete, how she'd gone on the pill when he'd shown an interest. When was the pill invented? 1960s?

'I'm just saying,' said Hugo, 'don't let him railroad you.'

He did care for her, in a horrid platonic way. How many boys would have thought about this? The hologram fiction glitched, letting in the familiar, hollow feeling.

'I could have another word with him.' Hugo was still staring at the sundial.

What was it with that sundial? It wasn't as if it changed every day into a different shape or wacky colour, and in sunless November, it couldn't tell the time. She wiggled her feet against the cold. 'No, I'll talk to him.'

~

Half an hour before lunch, Freddy hastily shut the library door and pulled Sophie close.

When she finally managed to pull away, she was hot and bothered. 'We should have a proper talk.'

'Oh.' He made a face.

'It won't take long.' They needed to be on the same page about a lot of stuff, or at least the same songbook.

Freddy sat in the black chair and Sophie outlined the deal with supplies, using them unless they both wanted a baby.

'I agree,' said Freddy. 'And supplies is a good word.'

Betty had made that easy.

He got to his feet for more kissing, but Sophie pushed him gently into the chair. 'Where I grew up, ladies are more independent. They have their own adventures—'

'*Alice in Wonderland.*'

'Okay...'

'Mummy read it to me when I was little. She said Alice was a hero like a man.'

Thank You Anne.

'I love that story,' said Freddy. 'Did you know that Lewis Caroll was a mathematics lecturer at Oxford?'

'In my world too, but the point is, like Alice, I'll make my own decisions after we're married.'

'Alice was a child, not a married woman.'

With a mother born in the 1960s and a father born in the 1870s, it wasn't surprising Freddy was confused. 'Alice wouldn't have had a complete personality change when she became an adult, would she?'

'I suppose not.'

'And we'll be a team.'

'There'll only be two of us.' Freddy's brow creased, maybe envisaging a Rupert-style arrangement.

'What I mean is, we'll be equal partners, as we were in the servants' hall. Supporting each other.'

His face cleared.

'I get we have to *act* conventional,' said Sophie, 'with you as the notional head of the household. But like your father's notionally in charge of the estate—'

'Notionally?'

'And your mother's notionally in charge of the house … what really happens is your parents decide important stuff together, as we will.'

'I'm not sure that's right,' said Freddy.

'Okay, a silly example, you want to wear pink trousers. I'll be honest and tell you they look terrible. I want to wear a dress that doesn't flatter me, you'll be honest and tell me.'

'Yes.'

'But if you *really* want to wear pink trousers after talking it through, you should, because it's your decision. And if I *really* want to wear the unflattering dress, I will.'

'What if it were … immodest?'

This was hard work. 'You won't be the boss of me and I won't be the boss of you.' She hurried on. 'If I had a migraine, you wouldn't jump on me and vice versa.'

'By jump, you mean…'

'Yes.'

Freddy frowned, a proper frown that included his forehead and extended to biting his lip. 'But you have to obey me. That's part of the marriage service.'

'It's just a convention, Freddy. It's not meant literally. And you … love—'

'I love you dearly.'

She swallowed, surprised by his honesty. And she loved him, just wasn't *in* love with him. Not yet. 'I love you too.'

He smiled, an open glad smile.

'I wouldn't hurt you by making you do intimate things you didn't consent to,' she said in a rush. 'And you wouldn't make me.'

'Even when we're married … Hugo was talking about this, but—'

'I thought you'd understand.'

Freddy frowned again.

Okay, he didn't equate what happened with Betty with consent issues within marriage.

'So, you won't intend to obey me,' said Freddy, 'when you promise before God?'

About this, she should be honest. 'I won't, any more than you'll obey me. But it'll be our secret.' Sort of honest. 'And God's.'

Freddy stared at the floor.

'Suppose you went insane, ordered me to stab myself or jump off a cliff?'

He looked up. 'It can't be unconditional.'

'Exactly. And we're bound to disagree about some things.'

'We can decide on what's best at the time.' He stood up and kissed her, and Sophie relaxed.

Small steps.

CHAPTER 33

That evening, in the small drawing room, Anne said, 'Is Hugo all right? He hardly said a word over dinner.'

No need to worry her. Anne couldn't help with this. Nobody could. 'It's finally sinking in that he can't get home.' Sophie finished her coffee.

'Time is a great healer.'

Those words were too familiar and, anyway, not true. Her parents' faces appeared in her mind before slowly fading. 'Can you remember what you were thinking, waiting for the lift?'

Anne shook her head. 'Too long ago.'

The next day, neither Freddy nor Anne were at breakfast, having a Sunday lie-in, as the Laceys had stopped attending church. Too predictable. Easy targets.

For Anne, churchgoing had been part of her work. Chatting after the service, she picked up early if estate families were having problems. If life ever returned to normal, once Sophie Arundel married Freddy, she'd have to go.

After the meal, in the anteroom, Sophie whispered to Richard, 'I suppose it's good for me that Inkpin Senior's dead. Lucky.'

'I don't think luck had anything to do with it.'

'You know who did it?'

'Not *who*,' said Richard, 'but it was well planned.'

'Someone from the War Office?'

'I wouldn't want to speculate.'

Hugo came in from the dining room and Richard shot her a satisfied smile before walking off.

'I've thought through that idea I was mulling over,' said Hugo. 'Talk in the small drawing room?'

Sophie nodded, although increasingly, she dreaded being alone with him.

Only a hologram.

She left the drawing room door ajar and sat opposite him by the fire. Jack settled by the grate, but Charlotte stood by Hugo who'd sat down on the green sofa. She licked his hand and he put his arm around her.

Sophie looked away. Envying Charlotte. What a saddo.

'Do you think Charlotte and Jack have souls?'

'Sorry?'

He repeated the question.

'If we have souls, so do they.' Jack started quietly snoring. 'You've a dog at home. No brainer.'

Hugo pushed his hand through his hair, making his fringe stand up, and the familiar gesture stalled the hologram fiction. Despite a table between them, Sophie's skin began to heat, like a bomb that could go *boom* at any moment.

Only a hologram. Focus.

'Okay, the next issue's more tricky. Do dogs have free will?'

Where was he going with this? 'The jury's out on free will but if we've got it, other animals have too.'

'The latest research suggests genes determine more than we ever imagined.'

No idea how that was relevant to the lift puzzle, but she went with it. 'Charlotte doesn't just act on instinct when she's hungry or tired. She thinks, feels love, and fear, and pain, but can't explain that in English.'

'Because babies can't talk, people used to believe they didn't feel pain.' Hugo ruffled Charlotte's head. 'The belief was so entrenched, even in the 1970s doctors were operating without anaesthetic.'

Sophie winced. 'Our vet said dogs recognise the same number of words as a three-year-old child. And Charlotte and Jack cuddle up to me when I've no food, so it's not cupboard love.'

'Or they've evolved to make us care for them.'

'Only like we've adapted to be social to survive. That doesn't stop us genuinely loving people, or animals.'

'You said yesterday that even without the gene, I could be part of the puzzle. What if *all* the visitors are?' Hugo met her eyes. 'Including Charlotte.'

'Okay...'

'I'm serious.'

Sophie frowned. She was connected to Charlotte with an invisible umbilical cord, but of course they were separate, sentient beings. *Stupid* that she'd overlooked Charlotte. 'She's a visitor too.'

'We'll never know what she was thinking before we left.' Hugo wasn't smiling.

But Sophie's breath hitched, reliving the moment in the students' union when she'd spotted Charlotte *by the lifts*. She gave a half-whistle. 'I know.'

She jumped to her feet. 'Charlotte's not *part* of the lift

puzzle, Hugo. She's why we're here.' She took a deep, calming breath. '*Charlotte* called the lift. Before I did … *if* I did. That's why she bolted. There was no other dog or cat or discarded food nearby. After the novelty wore off, she hated the noise and crowds at the university. She was miserable, wanted to leave … to travel.'

'You can't be sure.'

'I am. Her body language is open, usually clear.'

'Charlotte must have seen the lift as a different shade of grey.'

'Actually, doggie black and white vision's a myth. Charlotte's always loved children's TV. I assumed it was the childish voices, not the primary colours, but I Googled it. As well as grey shades, she sees dark and light blues, and yellows.'

'And gold's yellow.' Hugo glanced down at Charlotte who was nuzzling his legs. 'But to call the lift, she'd need the gene, and for the lift builders to have passed that on to her—'

'Sexual reproduction … aliens and dogs.' Sophie sat down again. '*Gross.*'

'Not sure why that's more icky than aliens and humans, but it might have happened without sex, like plants or starfish?' He exhaled. 'Perhaps the gene was passed on at a time of the earliest mammals, before dogs and humans developed separately? Or before that? Or it could have been a freak coincidence, the same gene evolving twice—'

'However it happened,' said Sophie, her brain starting to fry, 'you just happened to be with us.'

'You're one clever dog.' He patted Charlotte.

'No, Hugo, she's wonderful, but she's just a regular dog, with hopes and moods and feelings.' Sophie nodded to herself. 'And like the human visitors with the gene, Charlotte has no close family at home. Her siblings were adopted far and wide, and her parents passed away last year. Her second mother — me — came here with her.'

Charlotte was now half asleep, leaning against Hugo's legs. 'And also like the humans, Charlotte *subconsciously* opened the portal.'

'Accidental travellers.'

'If the lift was built for beings to visit universes using thought, perhaps a complex mix of factors isn't needed? Simply a determination to travel?'

'It can't be that easy,' said Sophie, resisting a scary, excited feeling.

'And the ship uses the travellers' wishes and emotions as rocket fuel.'

'You've been giving this some thought.'

'Every day.'

'With Charlotte, it all adds up,' said Sophie. 'She loved her day trips, exploring gardens of local stately homes, so the idea of Shorten was familiar.'

'But if Charlotte called it through her state of mind, to get back—'

'She'll never call it. She has Jack, eats sausages and bacon, has fabulous walks, and doesn't know this is a different world.'

'And we can't explain.'

The dogs were now snoring weirdly in time, in a breathy duet.

'Explains why the trips to the lane were a bust,' said Hugo. 'You weren't calling it and Charlotte snoozed in the car.'

'Content. No desire to go anywhere.' Sophie stared into the fire. 'We should go down the lane, leave Charlotte here, miles from the lift, and I'll try to yearn for home.'

'Perhaps what worked last time is more likely to work again?' Hugo tapped his fingers on the arm of the couch. 'We shouldn't leave Charlotte. I'm sure we can somehow distract her by the lift.'

'My fake yearning for home would have to cancel out her real wish to stay. Why make it more complicated?'

'We should *all* travel,' said Hugo. 'Three out, three back.'

He spoke with such feeling that Sophie frowned in surprise. 'You know that won't happen. I'm happy here.'

'What about Isha and your aunt?'

'Isha's a wonderful friend and I love Aunty Wendy, but it's not the same as close family. Or starting one.' She checked her watch and got to her feet. 'The gym calls. I need to think about this.'

Hugo stood up too. 'I'm going for a very long walk.'

Alerted by the word 'walk' the dogs woke up, keen and expectant, and followed Sophie into the corridor.

Down the passage, a tall footman walked around a corner and was lost to sight.

'Why are all footmen tall?' Sophie asked Hugo.

'Tall *and* good-looking. They add to the ambience of the dining room.'

'Ambience … is that really a thing?'

'Definitely. And when you marry Freddy, you should personally oversee recruitment.' His expression was deadpan.

Was he serious?

He winked.

Not serious. She giggled.

In the gym, Lucy executed an impressive turnaround kick.

'You could do competitions,' said Sophie. 'Seriously.'

'I'd much rather practise with you, with nobody gawping.'

'Girly time is precious.' Sophie steadied the punchbag.

'Can you remember what you were thinking before you stepped into the lift?'

Lucy considered. 'Nope.'

Sophie explained Hugo's 'calling' theory.

'Yearning for home? If it was that easy, every visitor would have scarpered within hours.'

'But we've another theory too, a more specific one, to get Hugo home.'

'You haven't thought this through,' said Lucy. 'Never seeing him again … it still hurts remembering Janet.'

'Janet *loved* you. It's different.'

'You have a point. No point flogging a dead horse.'

'Horrible expression, but yes.' Sophie delivered a series of punches, alternating fists.

'You're being weirdly calm, about Hugo I mean.'

'It's taken a while. When he told me about Clarissa, I was in bits.'

Lucy frowned. 'I'm sorry.' While she punched and kicked, Sophie told her about Charlotte.

'*Really* way-out theory.'

'Hugo thinks we could somehow "distract" her by the lift.' Sophie did a quotes gesture.

'You know, there might be a way.' Lucy steadied the bag. 'A dog's sense of smell is incredibly powerful, right? They live through their noses. If a scent nearby was strong and interesting enough, that might do the trick.'

'Block out how much she loves Shorten and Jack, and never wants to leave?' Sophie rocked back on her heels. 'Would need to be awesome.'

'What's Charlotte's favourite food?'

'Bacon.'

'I can easily rustle up bacon sandwiches from the kitchen,' said Lucy. 'I regularly order snacks for the gardeners.'

'Could work … but an abuse of trust.'

'There'd be no lasting harm to Charlotte.' Lucy stretched, starting her wind down routine. 'But if you're going to do this, make it soon, before Hugo's engagement. If he did get home, that would be easier on Clarissa.'

'Richard won't lend us Reynolds. We'll have to steal a car.'

Lucy's eyes widened. 'I hadn't thought of that.'

'I'll return it in one piece, but Freddy will be *appalled*.'

'You'll need a bolt cutter to open the garage.' Lucy shot her a conspiratorial smile. 'I'll get you one.'

Sophie gave Lucy a long hug.

'What was that for?'

'Lots of things, not just your cunning Charlotte plan.'

'It probably won't work,' said Lucy. 'Oh, I nearly forgot.' She delved into her leather kitbag and gave Sophie a hipflask.

Sophie unscrewed the top and inhaled. 'Wonderful.'

CHAPTER 34

Before dinner that evening, Maud chattered as she laboriously fastened Sophie's corset and formal evening dress. 'A big change, Miss, Mr Watkins moving to London with Mr Harrington.'

'Hmm?' Sophie glanced at her reflection in the long mirror. A girl from another age. With the Armstrongs staying, the full Monty was obligatory: elaborate gown and evening gloves past the elbow. But if the Armstrongs stayed long enough, they'd change from guests into residents, and Anne would allow dinner tea dresses.

Maud stepped back to check Sophie's dress buttons were neatly closed. 'Gentlemen get used to their valets.'

And Sophie was used to Maud. Selfish Sophie wanted Maud to stay, but Rational Sophie knew her duty. Devoted spouses shouldn't be separated. 'Of course, you must go too.'

'The trouble is, Miss, valets are allocated single rooms.'

'Could you rent a flat?'

'They're terrible expensive.' Maud brushed her hands on her skirt. 'Might be better to stay here, meet up when we can.'

After Maud left, Sophie sat at the dressing table and patted her hair, trying to make the artfully styled bun less puffed up. 1980s huge, it reminded her of a photo from childhood, her mother posing in a jacket with exaggerated padded shoulders, young and happy, her hairstyle a miracle of blow-drying and fearsome spray. Sophie sniffed. Would her parents be born in the 1960s here, maybe *not* die in 2011? She wouldn't be around by then, but she'd discounted leaving them a letter. Unless they were completely different people, they'd say, 'It's God's will.'

Sophie checked her watch. Five minutes early. She gave her hair a last pat before knocking on Hugo's door. As she waited for it to open, she repeated under her breath, 'Only a hologram.'

The dogs rushed in, Sophie followed, and choosing privacy over reputation, she shut the door. 'Lucy's come up with a plan to distract Charlotte.'

'Okay.' Hugo stood up from his desk.

Sophie outlined the bacon idea.

'Okay,' he said, as if the hologram had stuck.

She missed the old Hugo. He'd rarely been lost for words.

He walked over to the fire and warmed his hands. 'We're so emotionally bound to the people here, calling the lift may be impossible. How ironic is that?'

'A lot has changed in four months.'

'We steal the car, go down the lane ASAP.' He sat wearily on the bed.

'I'm up for breaking and entering, and I'll take the rap. Freddy will forgive me.'

'He'd forgive you pretty much anything.'

She'd suspected that was true, but it was strange to hear Hugo confirm it so flatly. 'Yearning for home...' She sat in the chair. 'I'll need to practise.'

'We shouldn't delay. It's the frog in the saucepan thing. If you place a frog into water and slowly turn up the heat, the frog won't be alarmed, eventually boils to death. If you put a frog in hot water, it'll jump out. I don't think anyone has actually done the experiment—'

'I hope not. Horrific.'

'It's an analogy, Sophie. We're the frogs.'

He absorbed and analysed facts like a quantum computer, knew about stuff she'd never heard of. His brain was a universe by itself.

Once she'd seen his true colours, maybe she'd always have fallen for him? No, Hugo waiting for the lift in the students' union hadn't been fate. A bizarre accident... Her concentration dipped and the hologram pretence collapsed like a cheap privacy curtain. She needed a distraction. Practical planning. 'We should go before the scullery maids start work.'

'Before dawn.'

She focused. Resurrect the hologram.

Nothing.

Pathetic mental discipline. 'Calling the lift for you will be hard, might not work.'

Hugo swallowed. 'All you can do is try.'

He didn't believe she could call it, any more than she did.

In the anteroom, Sophie accepted an aperitif. At home, only elderly ladies drank sweet sherry. Which was sad as it was mighty fine.

Over dinner, Hugo analysed bowling styles from a village cricket match in the summer, almost like his old self. 'You should visit every year for the match,' said Freddy.

'Absolutely.' Hugo turned to Anne. 'You'd be all right with that?'

'Of course.'

Hugo might be desperate to open the portal, but he was also a consummate performer, could be a poker player or a spy. When he left for London, she'd wave from the Manor steps. Standing on a cold train platform would make her eyes run.

Freddy was listening to Hugo but looking at her. Freddy's lips curved in secret recognition, reminding Sophie of their kisses. The footmen's expressions didn't waver, but they'd got the gist. Hugo hadn't noticed. Neither had the Armstrongs, or Anne who was talking to Richard.

Alice was staring into her wine glass as if it contained a hidden message. As usual, she and Ethel hadn't said a word the entire evening.

Sophie finished her slice of quiche and nodded to the footman to refill her glass. Anne caught her eye and Sophie acknowledged the signal.

Not a good idea to get smashed.

The next morning before elevenses, Sophie met Freddy in the library. Despite the fire, it was chilly, but she wasn't cold for long. Freddy kissed her, and she urgently responded, wanting more. Conscious of Hugo's warning about Pete though, she wasn't going to push. In Freddy's eyes, she'd been locked away in a tower, only for him.

Finally, she pulled away.

'I'm counting the hours until we're married.'

She'd explode if they carried on just kissing. Weirdly, she felt the same with Hugo, *without* the kissing. Nothing she could do about Hugo, but she'd been wrong to put off Freddy.

Not behaving as she would at home was becoming too difficult. A TV documentary about sadistic nuns in a mother and baby institution replayed in her head. No pleasure was worth that fate. Act smart. 'If we married before Christmas, we could open our stockings together?'

Freddy grinned from ear to ear.

~

Two days later, in the anteroom after lunch, Hugo took Sophie aside.

'Lucy's given me a bolt cutter,' said Sophie. 'Safely hidden in my room.'

He seemed distracted. 'This was delivered by hand last night.' He pulled an envelope from his pocket.

The handwriting was familiar. *Mr Hugo Harrington and Miss Sophie Arundel* written in dark blue ink.

A new anonymous note. Her stomach dropped.

'Come on.'

Sophie accompanied him with the dogs down the passage into his room. She closed the door, took the envelope, and sat down heavily in his chair to read the note inside. IF YOU OPEN THE LIFT, YOU DIE. FINAL WARNING.

Unease slid like a worm around her guts.

Hugo perched on the edge of the bed. 'Why have they started again?'

'Lucy wouldn't have breathed a word.' Sophie clapped her hand over her mouth. 'I mentioned to Betty and Will that you were homesick.'

'Who?'

'The family from The Crooked Gate,' said Sophie. 'But that was weeks ago.'

'And *missing* home isn't the same as knowing how to get there.'

Sophie put the note into the envelope, out of sight.

'Whoever it is,' said Hugo, 'they're persistent.'

'But not *consistent*. The first note in July was delivered straight after we discussed visitor dates. We received the second note the day after your gene theory. This arrives *three* days after we talked about Charlotte.'

'If the writer's here in the Manor, dropping a note on the front door mat's easy … they pick their moment.'

'But no one has a motive.' Sophie hesitated. If Hugo got home, John would lose his valet job, be demoted. 'Except John.'

'I trust him,' said Hugo flatly. 'It's not him.'

'With the drawbridge up, if the writer's in the village or Shorten town, they'd have to hide the letter in a food or wine delivery, arrange for someone in the house to extract it.'

'They'd have to write to their contact first,' said Hugo. 'Too complicated.'

'Or a servant overhears us and posts the info to the writer.'

'The writer posts this note and envelope back, *inside* another envelope, and their informant leaves this on the mat.' Hugo exhaled. 'Would explain the delay.'

'But Mrs Rawlings would have recognised the handwriting.' She dealt with all the mail, had seen the previous notes.

'The writer must have used different ink on the outer envelope, changed the writing.' Hugo got to his feet, his eyes on her face, and for a mad moment Sophie imagined him embracing her, falling onto the bed behind him.

Get a grip.

'After we discussed Charlotte,' said Hugo, 'that footman in the corridor… *He* overheard us.' Hearing her name, Charlotte stirred in her sleep by the grate, streaks in her brown fur shining silver in the firelight.

'Maud's heard nothing. Why wouldn't he mention our new theory downstairs?'

'Because people would ask why he was in this part of the house.'

'You're right,' said Sophie. 'Only the maids come down here, to change the linen.' Unease was growing. 'It must be him.'

'Did you see his face?'

'No, just his uniform.'

'There's only three footmen,' said Hugo. 'Two, plus a spare.'

'Fair-haired guy, good cheekbone guy, and the one with freckles. But anyone can steal a uniform.'

'No, everyone knows everyone else.' Hugo frowned. 'It *has* to be a footman. The writer's paying him…'

'Or using blackmail.'

'We keep this to ourselves,' said Hugo. 'No need to worry the Laceys.'

'Pretending to give up worked before. Let's delay going down the lane. Such a wacky idea with Charlotte, we should say it was a joke.'

'No.' Hugo set his mouth.

'But why?'

'They're only letters,' said Hugo. 'And we'll be armed.'

As they walked to breakfast the next morning, Hugo said, 'Once Richard was relaxed last night with his whisky and cigar, I took a risk.'

'How do you mean?' Sophie watched the dogs charge ahead to the dining room.

'I told him about the Charlotte plan.'

Sophie stopped walking. 'You did *what?*'

'I figured the idea's so ludicrous, he wouldn't worry about Anne leaving.' Hugo didn't look contrite. 'Reynolds is taking us tomorrow.'

Disbelief fought with fury. 'That risk wasn't yours to take.' Her words came out as a hiss. 'What happened to *We're in this together?*'

'I'm sorry.' He pretended to look sheepish. 'Freddy thinks the idea's silly but doesn't want you to even try.'

Stealing a car would have been an adrenaline rush with no downside — wouldn't have changed Freddy's feelings for her or how Clarissa felt about Hugo. But this way was easier.

'Now you're not driving, we might get there in one piece.'

He was teasing, like he used to. The old Hugo was in there. Somewhere.

'All of this may be pointless.' He adjusted his tie. 'And I wouldn't want John demoted.'

'Maud's worried he'll get a single room when you marry Clarissa, that she won't be able to go with him.'

'John hasn't asked, and I haven't thought through the details, but Clarissa's buying a house in Eaton Square. A double room will be easy to sort.'

'Richard will have told Anne I'm going to try calling the lift,' said Sophie. 'Just in case I get lucky with that, I'll check with her about John.'

Anne wasn't at breakfast, so Sophie waited a few hours before seeking her out.

In the large drawing room, Anne was at the piano, playing Beethoven's *Moonlight Sonata*, including the fiddly bits.

The dogs ambled about until Anne finished. Recently, Anne had been spending more time in here. Sophie pushed away the thought that Anne knew exactly what she and Freddy did in the other drawing room and the library.

'I didn't realise you played the piano.' Sophie smiled at her.

'I find it therapeutic.'

Sophie nodded. Normally at this time, she'd be in the gym. 'Would you mind joining me for coffee?'

'All right.'

They went to the warmer small drawing room. Miss Parry was summoned, poured coffee and left.

Anne watched Charlotte, settling by the fire. 'The idea that she called the lift and guided it here … certainly imaginative.' Anne's lips twitched.

'It's kind of Richard to lend us Reynolds.'

'This isn't a prison, Sophie.'

Actually, it was. Had been from the beginning. Richard had only acquiesced now because he was convinced their idea wouldn't work, and the patrols were such an impressive deterrent — armed men in ten second-hand cars.

Their prison had become a fortress. Not an improvement.

'I wish you weren't going.' If Anne had her way, she'd never let Sophie Arundel out of her sight.

'Hugo still wants to go home. I'd like to give him that chance.'

'Freddy would miss him.' Anne put her cup and saucer on the table with particular care. 'And if *you* left—'

'I'm not going anywhere. Trying to call the lift is for Hugo. Not me.'

'I don't believe you.' Anne's voice was flat, certain. 'You'd never see him again.'

Sophie's nerves tensed but Anne had got this wrong. 'Hugo will only ever see me as a friend.' She set her mouth. 'I won't leave you, and I'll never leave Freddy.'

Looking relieved, Anne picked up her cup.

Sophie *hated* upsetting Anne. So glad she didn't know about Inkpin. Focus on something else. Unlikely lift scenario. 'If the portal did appear, the situation with Clarissa would be awkward.'

'They're not officially engaged, but yes.'

'I thought I could write, explaining Hugo's been really homesick.'

Anne nodded.

'Mr Watkins would be demoted.'

'He would, but there'd be other opportunities,' said Anne. 'Much more likely, he'll be off to London with Hugo.'

~

Later that morning, when Sophie mentioned the portal plan, Maud couldn't keep a straight face. 'Not sure Charlotte thinks about anything, Miss, except food.'

After lunch, Sophie joined Hugo on a brisk walk with Freddy — away from any servants' ears — to properly explain the road trip.

As the dogs bounded across the frosty grass, Freddy's full mouth gradually pressed into an ever-narrower line. 'I know you miss your family,' he said to Hugo. This was the Shorten Code on full throttle, but Freddy looked awkward, hurt.

Sophie squeezed Freddy's hand. 'It's different for me,' she said. 'My parents died a while ago.'

Freddy's brown eyes widened.

Good, Hugo hadn't blabbed.

'The chances of calling the lift are minuscule.' Hugo's tone was an odd mixture of confidence and apology.

Freddy glanced at him. 'You wouldn't be trying if there was no chance.'

He was holding her hand too tightly, but his tone was measured. Sophie's respect for him shifted up another notch.

'I hope it doesn't work,' said Freddy, 'but I'm still curious.'

Hugo shook his head. 'Your interest in the portal could mess this up, Freddy. Only me, Sophie and Charlotte should go. As far as possible, we should replicate the original journey. I'm taking my shorts, T-shirt and hoodie, and my phone.'

'What about Reynolds?' said Sophie. 'Won't him being there be a problem?'

'I've already talked to him. He's not interested in the lift.' Hugo's voice cracked. Underneath the bravado, he was as upset as Freddy.

'I suppose you have to test the theory,' said Freddy, addressing Hugo, 'or it will nag at you.'

Hugo hugged him. It was a normal male hug, but Freddy

froze. After a long moment, Freddy released Sophie's hand and hugged Hugo back.

They all resumed walking, as if the hug hadn't happened, and Freddy held Sophie's hand again.

'I telephoned the vicar,' said Freddy. 'It takes three months to read the banns.'

Three months. She'd lose it before then.

'I applied for a special licence,' added Freddy. 'Much quicker.'

She gave him her grade-one smile and Freddy put his arms around her shoulders. 'My darling girl.'

Hugo was trudging behind them, hands deep in his coat pockets. He'd enjoy being Freddy's best man, make a witty speech.

Sophie pulled her hat down to cover more of her ears. 'I don't want a big party.'

Freddy grinned and kissed her briefly on the mouth. 'Just family.'

Hugo gave them a mock salute, turned on his heel, and strode towards the office.

'I need to amend the patrol schedule again. See you this evening.' Freddy hurried after Hugo.

Sophie watched them until they disappeared beyond the alley. She'd slammed her foot on the accelerator, so why did marrying feel unreal?

Lucy was by the terrace, taking cuttings from a dark green shrub. She stopped as Sophie approached.

'Reynolds is driving you down the lane tomorrow.' Lucy dropped the cuttings into a wicker basket.

Maud had spread the word downstairs. 'The kitchens are supplying bacon sandwiches.'

'We could meet at the gym in the afternoon,' said Lucy. 'At three?'

'Sounds good, and I'll give you back the bolt cutter.'

Sophie headed to the library to find *The Prisoner of Zenda* and lose herself in Rupert's favourite story — happy ending guaranteed.

~

Over dinner, Freddy announced they'd marry before Christmas. The footmen smirked, Hugo, Richard and Mr Crawford nodded, Mr and Mrs Armstrong's faces registered polite surprise, and for the first time since they'd arrived, Ethel and Alice smiled.

'I'm glad,' said Ethel. 'How exciting.'

But Anne did a double take. 'I can't organise a wedding in five weeks.'

'We thought an unfussy service and family meal,' said Freddy.

Anne exhaled and Sophie felt awkward. Should have given Anne a heads up.

'What about your dress?' Anne asked Sophie.

'I could wear my new tea dress. It's cream, so almost white.'

'Would be unlucky, even if we had it bleached. Freddy's seen you in it.' Anne looked at her husband who gave a slight nod. 'You could wear mine? I only wore it once. A bit old-fashioned but should fit.'

'That would be wonderful.' A warm, belonging feeling enveloped her, and Sophie relished the moment.

After the meal, as she left the dining room, the butler caught her eye. 'Miss Arundel, can I have a word?'

Crap. Mr Crawford never spoke to her. Must have messed up.

'Mr Wainwright is still with us. I thought you'd like to know.'

Only a week since Stick Man had been brought into the

servants' hall. 'I'm not sure if he'll completely recover, but that's encouraging.' Hopefully, the butler hadn't noticed her panicked reaction.

Mrs Armstrong and her daughters retired, leaving Anne and Sophie to have coffee in the small drawing room.

Anne walked over to the fireplace. 'You've achieved in six months what took me decades.'

Charlotte lay down beside the grate by Anne's feet. 'Mr Crawford's respect.'

Anne kissed Sophie on the cheek and Sophie kissed her back. She'd missed social kissing, like with Isha.

'Are you ready for tomorrow?'

'I'll be glad when it's over.'

'You're dreading saying goodbye.' Anne's tone was calm, matter of fact.

'If the lift appears, I'll get in the car with Charlotte and ask Reynolds to drive off. *Not* watch Hugo get in.'

That night, Sophie dreamed about the lift opening into mine shafts, and the dogs lost or in danger, and she woke with a weary reluctance.

She retrieved her roomy shoulder bag from the wardrobe and rifled through it: dead phone, useless purse, useless key to the tower block and other junk.

And Charlotte's fluorescent jacket. That disguise had enabled Charlotte to blend in at the university, posing as a service dog. Aunty Wendy had Parkinson's disease, couldn't mind Charlotte, and kennels had been unaffordable. The jacket should stay in the bag. Charlotte would be warmer in her tartan coat.

Perhaps what worked last time is more likely to work again? Replicating the scenario when they'd come through the portal might boost the chances of it appearing, but they couldn't replicate everything. She couldn't wear the same knickers. In the first week here, hung up to dry after she'd washed them, they'd been trashed by Charlotte. Sophie couldn't wear her jeans either, shrunk by the Manor laundry.

She stepped into white Bermuda shorts — Shorten

knickers — and selected an under-bodice. Her wired bra from home wasn't as comfortable. 'I'll pack my old bra and shirt, and wear the cream tea dress.'

Maud's lips thinned.

'Under my cloak, nobody will know I'm not wearing a corset and day gown.' No way was she standing for hours in the cold in the full Monty.

Maud's lips thinned more, meaning, 'We'll know.' She folded the shirt into the bag with the bra, and found Sophie's black cardigan from home in a drawer.

Sophie packed her child-sized jeans.

After breakfast, Maud reluctantly helped Sophie change out of a formal gown into the tea dress, and Sophie put on the cardigan. She slipped into her cape and collected her hat, scarf, and gloves.

On the drive, the air tasted iron cold, but the sky was clear. The Laceys and Jack saw them off, with Mr Crawford and Mrs Rawlings, as was usual when guests left, even if they'd return within hours.

At the end of the drive were two gamekeepers, waiting to open the ornamental gates to let them out. On top of the gates was barbed wire like bared metal teeth, and more wire snaked along the drystone wall that fronted the rest of the drive.

'Guns?' Sophie asked Richard.

'In the car, just in case.'

Parked by the green car was a battered grey vehicle. One man was behind the wheel, another in the front passenger seat holding a rifle, and a third armed man was in the back. Armed men in another car completed the convoy.

Hugo carried a sturdy brown leather bag with carrying

handles. Richard shook hands with him, and Anne gave Sophie a fierce hug.

After Freddy kissed Sophie on the cheek, he glanced nervously at his father, but Richard was smiling, probably remembering courting Anne.

'I'll be here, waiting for you,' said Freddy.

Sophie hugged him. 'Yes.'

Jack started howling and Charlotte wouldn't move. No amount of lead-pulling and coaxing made any difference. Finally, Reynolds handed Sophie a paper bag of still-warm bacon sandwiches from the boot.

Sophie clambered into the back of the green car, and lured by bacon, Charlotte jumped in. Sophie held onto her while Hugo sat in the front passenger seat and Reynolds returned the food to the boot. Charlotte hadn't been given any breakfast apart from water. A crucial part of Lucy's plan.

The cars drove off and the fortified gates closed behind them.

Hugo held a rifle on his lap and so did Sophie, drawing comfort from the weight and feel of the weapon. They sped up and a bracing wind tore over the windscreen and the car's half-height doors.

'You've left your watch and ring in the house?' shouted Hugo, over the buffeting wind.

'Sorry,' she yelled. 'I forgot.' And her hair was up in its usual bun. She rubbed her eyes that were stinging from the wind. 'I've brought all the stuff from home.'

'I'm not wearing my shorts.' Hugo jammed down his hat to his eyebrows. 'Obviously.' He pulled up his scarf, covering his mouth.

Sophie wiggled her toes inside her walking boots, glad she'd worn thick socks.

A few minutes later, the cars escorting them slowed,

turned around and drove off. Reynolds raised his hand in a lazy salute and speeded up again.

'They're not coming all the way?' yelled Sophie to Hugo.

'The militia want the Manor.' His words were just discernible over the wind. 'We've no idea how long this will take. They can't lose two patrol cars. Every few hours, they'll drive five miles out to meet us.' He gestured at the deserted lane. 'Forget the militia. Focus on the lift.'

Sophie patted Charlotte who was turning restlessly on the seat. Soon her canine brain would be fixated on bacon while her mistress tried to call the lift.

Was she summoning a machine or a god? Sophie leaned forward. 'Reynolds, this may take a while.'

He glanced at her in his rear-view mirror. 'Right you are, Miss.' His expression was bland, but she wasn't fooled. He thought they were nuts.

Despite his stated nonchalance about the militia, Hugo kept his eyes on the road, particularly when they rounded a bend. Sophie kept half an eye, holding onto Charlotte. But they reached the Janus stone without seeing a soul.

Hugo got out and laid his rifle across the rear seat, and Sophie did the same. Hugo walked towards where the lift had opened and stopped on the edge of the verge, replicating where he'd waited for it in the students' union, but then stepped back onto the tarmac.

Sensible. Ensuring the lift didn't land on top of him.

Reynolds gave Sophie the sandwiches, and with Charlotte on the lead, Sophie headed to the 'fairy entrance' at the base of the oak. Yes, it was silly, but touching it might bring her luck?

It wasn't there.

She looked at the Janus stone, and at the tree again.

Hugo frowned. 'What's wrong?'

'This isn't the right place.' She told him about the tree.

Hugo went to the stone and examined it. 'It's been moved. The bottom's scraped.'

'This has to be the anonymous note writer, to keep us away from the lift spot. Who else would go to all that effort?' She shivered. 'Let's find my tree. I'll go on, you go back. Look for a hole at the bottom of the trunk facing the road.' She walked slowly with Charlotte, examining every tree.

'Found it.' Hugo emerged from the bend.

Sophie hurried with him down the road. And there it was. The oval hole like a doorway.

With Reynolds' help, they wrestled the stone into the car. Reynolds turned the car around and drove to the fairy tree.

After they'd put the stone in place, Hugo said, 'Good thing you realised.'

'Those scrapes … it's been dragged the whole way. Whoever did this doesn't have a car.'

'Most people here don't. Doesn't narrow down the suspects.'

Sophie scanned the empty lane, pushing down a nervy, uneasy feeling. 'All good now.' She bent down to touch the fairy door, then walked across the verge opposite the lift spot, ending up beside the tall hedge. Not as far as they'd been from the lift when Charlotte had bolted, but it would have to do.

Hugo resumed his stance in front of the lift and Reynolds returned to the car, no doubt hoping they'd quickly tire of chasing shadows.

Sophie stamped her feet. Already going numb. She opened the food bag but held it close so Charlotte couldn't grab it. Charlotte's nose twitched. The scent of bacon was pungent, and for Charlotte, that was magnified, hopefully blocking every rational thought.

And Sophie had a plan to fool the lift. Memories had stopped her losing it in the priest hole, so she reasoned reliving happy times before Shorten might camouflage her desire to stay — and Charlotte's.

She focused. Charlotte splashing in a paddling pool in summer … in winter, racing in the snow.

Sophie fed Charlotte a sandwich, kept the bag open but out of reach, and concentrated: Charlotte on a beach in Cornwall, fleeing from the waves and shaking, drenching her and Aunty Wendy, Charlotte sniffing fallen leaves in autumn, Charlotte dozing in the shade on a long hot day…

Not ready to give up, even if this took hours. Hugo's best shot. Maybe his only one.

Flexing her fingers against the cold, Sophie gave Charlotte another sandwich, and focused: Charlotte as a puppy, nipping at Sophie's fingers, Charlotte running in the garden with a stick, longer than her whole puppy body, Charlotte asleep by the fire, legs twitching…

The here and now Charlotte was sitting with her front legs straight out, like anchors, ignoring her mistress and the tantalising bacon. Reynolds had switched off the engine and was noisily adjusting something under the bonnet.

Concentrate.

Despite the icy grass, Sophie knelt, part-dreaming, part-hallucinating, almost in a trance. Living the memories, again and again, until she lost track of time.

A blast of harsher, colder air stung her face, jerking her awake.

Charlotte was in the same pose but staring at gold doors struggling to open. A grinding sound echoed loud in the country quiet, metal on metal, and a clang rang out.

Sophie blinked, unsure whether the force of her wanting hadn't conjured up a mirage, shimmering in and out. The boxy lift shape was hardly there, had taken on the colours and textures of the evergreen bay hedge and skeletal trees.

The doors had completely slid back but weren't outside the structure … no shaft or haulage mechanism. *Not* a real lift.

And except for the brightly lit interior, the transport vehicle — or whatever it was — would have been invisible. A small chandelier hung from the ceiling. Droplet-shaped crystals, prettily arranged in tiers, floated amidst three silver branches curving upwards, cradling tented bulbs that starkly illuminated the inside walls: swirls of different wood grains, darkest ebony to light birch.

Sophie got to her feet on stiff legs and exhaled, sending pale vapour into the air. Charlotte was seriously stubborn, but Sophie Arundel had done it. Incredible. 'Hugo.'

He glanced at her, his gaze questioning, and turned towards the lift. His mouth dropped open.

Reynolds scanned the lane and resumed his work under the bonnet. If it was invisible to Reynolds, how come Hugo could see it?

Hugo pulled the scarf off his face, strode past Reynolds and leaned into the car. He picked up Sophie's bag and his, and marched towards the lift, his expression set, determined.

The stuff she'd originally brought through the portal, he'd drop it nearer the lift, reinforcing the fiction that she wanted to travel. Clever.

Sophie's breathing fluttered, uneven, shallow…

Don't watch Hugo get in.

CHAPTER 37

*I*ntending to do the right thing was difficult. Doing it was far harder. Sophie stared at her boots and forced her legs to move. Go to the car.

Charlotte was pulling towards Reynolds, so Sophie let go her lead.

'Time to go.' Hugo was standing between her and the car.

Sophie looked at the lift. He'd left her bag *inside,* with his.

Hugo met her eyes. 'Three in, three back.'

'No. You don't need us. It's for the best.' She hurried to the other side of the car, her heart beating loud in her ears. He'd thought she and Charlotte were crucial, but the lift was here—

Charlotte snarled. Then a cracking noise, like a branch breaking.

The next moment, Hugo was lying lifeless on the verge, his face bloody, and Alan Parkes was standing over his body.

Charlotte leapt up and mauled Alan's arm, her jaws deep in his flesh through his coat. Alan swore and swung from side to side, fighting to throw her off.

Oh god. Where was Reynolds? Sophie wheeled round,

dropping the sandwiches. Another man was banging Reynolds' head against the bonnet with sickening force.

Will Mason, Betty's brother.

Sophie froze in horror.

With his free arm, Alan made a jabbing motion. Charlotte yelped, loosening her grip on him, and he kicked her. She launched into the air and dropped, shuddering, a few feet away. Sophie's heart lurched. *No.*

Alan shifted his attention to Sophie. 'You're not going anywhere. Not today. Not ever.'

Fear pooled in her guts. He strode towards her, past Reynolds wrestling with Will, and Sophie scurried backwards, keeping the car between them, desperately trying to focus.

They circled in matching steps, a horrible dance. He'd killed Hugo and Charlotte and would kill her. Why? Don't think about that.

Survive.

Her rifle wasn't far. Just had to lean into the car … no, before she fired, Alan would grab it. Better off kicking or punching and running. She'd done a marathon in her last term at school. Twenty miles was doable, and she'd meet a Manor patrol in fifteen.

Sophie ripped off her gloves, hat, and scarf, and slipped off her cloak. Floor-length, would get in the way. The tea dress was shorter, the skirt wide enough for kicking.

Alan paused and gaped at her.

Needed to warm up. Fast. She ran on the spot, assessing him. He was only a little taller, but much heavier. She didn't go into a regular competition stance, wanted to keep the element of surprise, but made sure she was balanced.

Blank out Hugo and Charlotte. Focus on Alan. Intent and calm, but she was fitter and faster—

He lunged, a knife in his right hand.

She dodged left past the blade, swivelled, and kicked out with her left leg at his wrist. The knife tumbled and his mouth twisted in shock. Her right fist hit his jaw in an explosive punch, jolting his head back. She followed with a left hook and her ring ripped into his cheek.

His weight advantage … don't reach for the knife, get in too close.

Alan reeled but recovered and lunged again. Sophie was ready. She feinted to her right and kicked him in the groin. Muscles crunched under her boot, and he crumpled.

She kicked him in the head as he lay there. Not a sporting kick, but this wasn't a game. She drew deep, whimpering breaths, the sub-zero air searing her lungs.

Reynolds had rallied and was hitting Will with a metal bar. Will slid down against the car, his forehead a mushy pulp smearing red along the green paint. Reynolds dropped the bar and it bounced by his shoes.

A wrench. He must have been using that on the car. Sophie dragged Will's body clear and opened the driver's door. 'The Manor. *Now.*'

Reynolds came out of his trance. He leaned in and adjusted the brake. 'The engine's cold.' He fiddled with a button below the bonnet and turned over the crank. Bending into the driver's seat again, he pulled out a knob and clicked a key on the dashboard.

Hurry.

Going to the front, Reynolds tugged at the button, flicked the crank from left to right, and the engine started. 'You can't rush her, or she won't start at all.' Reynolds jumped in and slammed his door.

A grunt. Alan struggled unsteadily to his feet.

She stared in disbelief. He'd been out cold.

Her rifle. She wrenched open the car door, but in a

second, Alan seized her from behind, pulled her around, and punched her so hard she saw stars.

She screamed, 'Reynolds *go.*' Escape, be a witness.

Reynolds put his foot down, swerved around the Janus stone, but Parkes sprinted, trying to grab the wheel over the half-height door. The car sped up, Alan slipped, and he fell over, shouting and cursing.

Sophie hauled herself up. Her jaw was a ball of pain and blood swamped her mouth. Warm, metallic-thick.

Thirty minutes before Reynolds met a patrol, another thirty before help arrived. Play for time. 'You won't get away with this,' she jeered, her voice surprisingly confident. 'This isn't home, ten years in prison and cups of tea. You'll *hang.*'

'Aren't you the feisty one?' A flap of skin hung off his cheek like a blood-stained flyer, but he seemed unconcerned.

The lift was open. If she ran inside, the doors might shut? Could buy a lot more time.

She sprinted, past Charlotte's body and Hugo's, but Alan was close, his breathing a dogged panting in the winter stillness.

Sophie was almost at the threshold when he threw himself at her. His momentum pitched her forward and she met the frozen ground with a whack. Alan's weight pinned her arms and legs, and the reek of him engulfed her in a putrid fog.

He grabbed her neck and squeezed. 'Over in a jiffy.'

Need more time. As her throat constricted, she forced out, 'You could have a bit of fun first?'

'I'm doing this because I have to. I'm not a rapist.' His hands tightened.

Pain.

∼

Far away, something changed.

The weight on top of Sophie lifted and so did the grip on her neck. She took an automatic, shearing breath, her throat so raw she gagged. Dots of light danced in her vision. She was on her back, the cold earth pressing through her dress, the smell of winter, crisp, clean…

Had Reynolds returned, pulled Alan off? Or was she dead? No, in too much pain to be dead. She drew another burning breath that turned into a gasp and sat up.

Hugo. He was kneeling, his eyes glazed, his face and hand bloody.

She got to her feet, hauled him up, and he swayed. Close by was a wheezing sound, steady as a drum beat. Alan sat on the verge, shaking his head.

Sophie pushed Hugo behind her, and he almost fell over.

The tiny lights were still dancing across her vision. 'We get in the lift. *Escape.*' Every word was a razor stripping her throat.

'Yes.' Hugo picked up Charlotte and panting with effort, stumbled over the threshold.

He'd retrieved her … Sophie's breath hitched as she rushed into the lift.

Hugo laid Charlotte on the floor, and leaned against the rear wall, barely able to stand. Sophie turned around. Outside, Alan was on his feet, brandishing the knife, his lips drawn back in a snarl.

Sophie desperately hit a chunky wooden button to close the doors. Nothing. She backed further in.

'You're no match for me.' Alan's voice was hoarse, certain.

'I can kick,' Hugo whispered. 'Give me a minute.'

They didn't have a minute. 'Don't move. I need some room.'

Alan advanced, his blade glinting. As he reached the threshold, Sophie executed a focused turnabout kick and her boot slammed into his stomach. The same instant, a harsh rattling noise started up.

Alan doubled over but in a heartbeat he moved again, his knife arm ready.

A slicing noise, efficient and clinical. The lift doors shut, and the blade bounced with a clatter on the floor. Attached to the knife was Alan's quivering hand.

Severed at the wrist.

CHAPTER 38

Sophie threw up and the pain in her throat spiked. Her vomit covered Alan's severed hand and a vile stench engulfed the lift.

Hugo lay across Charlotte, one hand in a loose, half clench. His nose was bent and broken and swollen. 'She's not dead.'

Sophie knelt beside Charlotte. She was breathing, but a deep cut in her shoulder was bleeding out. Sophie grabbed the shirt from her bag and tore off a strip to cover the wound. Wrapping it over Charlotte's shoulder and under a front paw, Sophie tied it securely, and she cradled her precious friend, her sobs magnified in the enclosed space, echoing off the walls.

Finally cried out, Sophie registered Hugo's injuries anew, and drew an agonising, shaky breath.

'I assumed it was a militiaman. Only realised who it was when I hit him.'

'Thank you,' she said in a hoarse whisper.

'Alan ... *why?*'

'No idea.' She took another burning breath, wishing she

could heal Charlotte just by wanting. Her throat spasmed, and she put her fingers to her neck.

'Gene theory needs more work.'

'Do you really want to talk about this, *now?*' She swallowed. That made it worse.

'Talking's good.' He touched his smashed nose. 'Distracts me from the pain.'

'Hurts if I speak,' she croaked, pointing at her neck. Throbbing turned into stabbing.

'I'll do the talking.' Hugo's voice was thick, nasal. 'Alan called the lift before, must have the gene. Why didn't it let him in?' He opened his holdall and gave her a flask.

Water slipped down her throat: unbelievably soothing. The gamekeepers would be outside soon. Alan wouldn't stick around — unless he'd bled to death.

'If this machine uses emotions and thoughts as fuel, perhaps it senses evil intent, is programmed to help the good guys?' Hugo rested his head against the wall. 'A sentient lifeboat.'

'Alan's not evil,' Sophie said, as softly as possible.

'Could have fooled me.'

'When he was strangling...' She swallowed again and regretted it. 'I suggested he have fun, to buy time, and he said, "I'm not a rapist." Sounded affronted.'

'While he was murdering you.'

'I know, surreal.' She stroked Charlotte, hoped Charlotte could feel it and be comforted.

'Alan saw two pictures on the lift in the students' union. A mansion on fire and a road that forked.'

'Or a river.' Another blissful gulp of water.

'What if the pictures aren't destinations? What if they represent the *choices* each visitor makes? Alan deciding to kill us — he chose the wrong fork in the road?'

'But he could be ill, paranoid,' said Sophie, 'didn't *choose* to attack us.'

'He sent the notes.'

'Whatever his deal, if he survives, I'll see him brought to justice.' She had to swallow, and her throat spasmed. When it stopped, she drank more water.

Hugo glanced at Charlotte. 'She's in a bad way.'

Fresh grief rose up in a terrible wave. Sophie wiped her eyes. 'Reynolds killed Will.'

'The guy from the pub?'

'Will attacked him when Alan punched you.'

'But why?'

'No clue.'

Hugo sighed. 'It took ages to call the lift.'

'I was doing it for you, Charlotte *really* didn't want to, and bacon mind-control is unreliable.'

'When you stood up and said my name, it wasn't there. Then it outlined, detail by detail.'

Sophie swigged water.

'Where's the hand?'

'Under my vomit.' The stench wasn't as strong now.

'There's no vomit, Sophie, and no hand. Just the knife.'

The knife was unremarkable. A wooden handle with a serrated blade, shiny and clean. She scanned the pristine floor. Translucent-cream and underneath, as wide as the lift, a purple, glowing cobweb, rhythmically pulsing.

'You remember Charlotte's accident?'

Sophie's brain had turned to mush. 'No.'

'Her peeing in the lift.'

When the lift had opened in the lane, faced with standing in pee or leaving, they'd chosen the latter.

'No trace of it,' said Hugo. 'Perhaps this machine or whatever it is, disposes of waste?'

'Pee, vomit, body parts... Logical, I guess. Binning stuff

that poses a threat of disease.' She shuddered. 'Won't ever forget that hand.'

She forced herself to stand and examine the doors, running her fingers over the centre. Not the slightest crack, as if it had only ever been a wall. 'I'll focus on Shorten, get out.' Her raspy voice was fractured, like speech on a poor phone line.

'About that—'

The lift tilted, as abruptly as a car on a roller coaster dropping over the edge, and Sophie smashed into the doors that were now the floor. The doors were iron hard, and pain shot through her shoulder. Hugo and the bags flew past, something shiny missed her by inches, landing with a clang, and Charlotte was on top of her, a floppy deadweight.

Sophie nudged Charlotte aside and shoved Alan's knife into her bag, blade-first. She closed it and grasped the straps. Hugo gripped his bag just as the doors-floor tipped sideways and up, and they all dropped, hitting a different unyielding wall.

The lift rolled forward, turned completely over, and Sophie curled to protect Charlotte, scrunching up her eyes as the lift moved faster and the interior blurred.

Endless minutes passed before they came to a gentle stop, like the last step in a ballet.

'Are you in one piece?' Hugo's face was rigid with fear.

Dread was draining her of hope and energy, but she gritted her teeth. 'You'd pay good money for this at a theme park.' She'd meant to sound flippant and calm, but her rasping voice jarred in the silence.

'Those fancy rails. Wondered what they were for.'

She followed his gaze to curved bars on each side, made from polished oak.

Charlotte's lead was still attached to her collar. Sophie

unclipped it, put it over the bar, and secured it around Charlotte's middle.

Gripping the bar, she leaned over Charlotte, bracing for the next roll, while Hugo held onto the other rail. Lit by the overhead chandelier, he looked theatrically battered.

'That light fitting's an illusion,' said Sophie. 'Real glass would have shattered.'

'Doesn't matter. Concentrate on getting to the twenty-first century. Give Charlotte a fighting chance.'

Yes, a vet scan and surgery might save her.

'Fix on something pleasant, specific to you,' said Hugo, 'or we could end up in a horrific version of home.'

'What do you mean?'

'Analysing the visitor dates, we talked about it.'

Immersed in calling the lift, she'd forgotten about infinite numbers of universes. Charlotte was silent on her lap. What if she was beyond saving? Dread morphed into panic. 'It must be easier to turn back. Maybe we haven't moved yet?' Freddy would be beside himself.

'With all this spiralling? It's too late, Sophie. Home, *please*.'

The fear in his face mirrored her own. In the summer, Hugo had speculated that the lift ran on subatomic software. Random, unpredictable...

Sophie shut her eyes. Stay calm and *remember*. A lazy barbeque, lying on the grass as her parents talked and laughed.

The lift silently barrelled again, over and over.

Eventually, it slowed and stopped. How long had they been in here? Felt like hours. Sophie checked her watch: 12.15. 'What does your watch say?'

'12.15.'

Both watches had broken. Or was time suspended?

Sophie took stock. Charlotte's jacket had provided protection for her during the barrelling, but it was now tropically hot and humid. Sophie unclipped the lead, removed the jacket, and hauled off her own cardigan.

Hugo sat beside his rail, his dark trousers and red T-shirt reflected in a mirrored ceiling, but rippled and distorted. His discarded coat, scarf, and sleeveless jumper, and Charlotte's tartan jacket and Sophie's black cardigan, were all warped reflections too, dark contrasts with Sophie's cream dress.

Apart from a brass plate that secured the chandelier, the ceiling was nearly all glass, or an illusion of it, encircled by gold petals, suggestive of the sun's rays or a flower.

Hugo covered his mouth and coughed red flecks onto his palm. His cheeks were as swollen as his nose, black and violet bruises mingling with dried blood.

'How are you feeling?'

'Tired.' He lay down, his arm cushioning his head, eyes closed, his breathing oddly peaceful as if he'd been asleep for hours. And the lift had somehow expanded. Plenty of room to sleep.

If they got home, would she have to pinch Hugo awake? She might have to drag him out with Charlotte? She could do that, even with her knackered shoulder and throat.

The air was sweltering, muggy and still. Sophie wiped her brow and tried to imagine a breeze. Instead, she pictured Freddy in the lane, confronted with Will's body and blood on the verge.

The lift tilted, just a little, adjusting course.

Concentrate. Perfect afternoons in the sun-dappled garden with Aunty Wendy—

Scuffling, akin to Charlotte's paws skidding on a smooth surface. Hugo was flailing in his sleep. Sophie held his hand to reassure him, and he went rag-doll floppy.

She was struggling to breathe. Trapped in a sealed box, hurtling to an unknown destination. A new surge of dread rose up, together with an overwhelming urge to sleep, and she lay on the floor. It was flat but springy, like rubber. And wonderfully cool. She kissed Charlotte's forehead. 'I love you.'

Keeping Charlotte close, Sophie rested her head on Hugo's chest and his eyes flickered open. He should have been surprised, but he put his arm around her, casually, as if he did that every day. Not erotic or romantic.

Comforting.

Sophie's shoulder was sore, but her throat was bearable, a dull ache, and her jaw didn't hurt at all. Hugo's heartbeat was slow, and Sophie's breathing slowed too, matching his rhythm. His nearness no longer torture.

Solace.

Her thoughts turned to Anne and Freddy. No, keep with childhood memories. The lift interior and her childhood garden merged, out of focus and smudged. It split into two young faces, looking in opposite directions. Janus…

She slept.

CHAPTER 39

*R*attling.

Lift doors slowly, noisily opening.

Sophie was dreaming. Doors needed servicing. Where did the lift go when they weren't in it?

Communal noise ... disembodied chatter.

'We're here.' Hugo's voice.

Sophie opened her eyes. Beyond the lift was the students' union. She stood up, willing it to be true. Modern, busy ... *real*. She sagged with relief. Couldn't have coped with a different universe.

And Charlotte was on her feet, snuffling about the lift. '*Yes.*' Sophie punched the air, and her shout resonated, sang off the walls. She swallowed. Her throat felt fine. She wiggled her shoulder. That felt fine too.

Hugo had on his jumper and coat. He draped his scarf around his neck and nonchalantly picked up his bag, as if their bus had reached a regular stop. Had the lift somehow drugged him to forget what had happened? And his face... No blood, no bruising, and his nose was straight. She blinked. Impossible—

Hugo sauntered into the crowded hall.

Sophie slipped on her cardigan, stuffed Charlotte's jacket into the roomy bag, and clipped Charlotte's lead to her collar. Slinging the bag strap over her shoulder, Sophie stepped over the threshold, but Charlotte stayed put. 'You need to see a vet.'

Sophie yelled to Hugo, 'Need help here.'

Hugo turned and frowned, but strolled back, and between them, they dragged Charlotte out. Once clear of the lift, Charlotte calmed.

Hugo walked off towards the students' union exit. A dark-skinned girl in a short denim dress stopped in her tracks and removed her headphones, her eyes on Hugo. Beside her, a skinny boy with messy blond hair gawped.

Sophie ran to catch up with Hugo. 'What is *wrong* with you?'

He eyed her, puzzled, as if he was half asleep.

'I don't know how, but your nose is completely better. How's your hand?'

He flexed his fingers. 'Not hurting.'

Charlotte pushed against Sophie's legs, trying to tell her something, and Sophie looked back. A girl dressed in an emerald Indian sari was stepping into the lift.

'No,' shouted Sophie, but the doors were already rattling shut.

Hugo turned slowly around as if seeing the students' union for the first time. 'Look.' He pointed.

On the wall was an official-looking poster with old school photos of her and Hugo. *MISSING* said the headline, with a police phone number. The paper was laminated but tatty.

The vast, packed hall had gone silent, and everyone in it was stock still, staring at them. A cleaner had paused sweeping debris on the floor, his gaze fixed on Hugo as he muttered into his phone. The only other sounds were whispering and fingers tapping on phones.

Hugo was wired now, definitely awake. 'We must get out.'

What was he saying? Hysteria bubbled up and her brain raced. This *wasn't* their world. She'd been so relieved about Charlotte and getting here, she hadn't noticed what was obvious. All these creepy watching people…

'Come on.' Hugo's tone was urgent.

'Let's run to the lift, call it again. Charlotte will help. She wants to go back.'

'No. We need to lie low, stop attracting attention.'

He grabbed her arm and she let him hurry her towards the exit. Charlotte was growling, pulling on the lead towards the lift, and it took all Sophie's strength to tug her along.

Near the door was a convenience shop. A boy glanced up from the till and stared. 'You all right, mate?'

'Fine,' said Hugo.

'Haven't seen you in a while.' The boy tapped on his phone.

'Do you know him?' asked Sophie.

'Never seen him before.'

The students in the hall were still whispering and watching, and the eerie muttering followed them to the exit. Hugo hastily opened the door, and they walked into darkness.

Cold air and sleet hit Sophie in the face, but she hardly noticed because a police car screeched to a halt, blue lights flashing and siren on full wail.

The siren stopped and a policeman got out. 'Stay where you are.'

Sophie's teeth started to chatter from the sudden cold, the shock of the lights and the siren, and sensing her reaction, Charlotte jumped up and tried to eat her lead. Struggling to compose herself, Sophie patted Charlotte's already damp head and made her sit.

The policeman watched them, talking on the phone, his British police uniform silhouetted in the pulsing blue lights. Hugo put his arm through Sophie's and pulled her close, and she realised she was shaking.

'We should go inside,' said Sophie, 'find another way out.'

'How would we find an exit?' His voice cracked. 'The people in there wouldn't help us.'

'Stay where you are,' the officer repeated. 'If you attempt to leave, you will be stopped.'

He didn't seem to be armed but it was difficult to be sure. The police lights in the dark reduced and distorted shapes.

Regret and fear coursed through her. She should have focused on a person or event unique to home... But how could you predict in advance what would be slightly or a lot different? Keep. Calm. She'd kept it together in the bakery and the priest hole, she could do the same here. Wherever *here* was.

Her hair was soaked, as was her cardigan and dress. Sirens sounded in the distance and light flashes lit up behind her. Students pressed against windows, phones held high, snapping, recording. Fear hollowed out her guts. They knew to keep inside, knew what was going to happen.

More police cars raced towards them and stopped, forming a half circle, cutting off escape routes. The sirens switched off but the lights stayed on.

'Mr Harrington, is there any third party in the vicinity who could harm you or police officers?' A new male voice.

'No,' said Hugo, his pale face overlaid by the blinking blue lights.

'Are you here under duress?'

'I'm here of my own free will,' said Hugo, 'and nobody is making me do anything, except you. What's going on?'

Five men with rifles, military, not police, walked in front of the cars and took aim.

CHAPTER 40

It was the end of a half-term holiday when Sophie last saw her parents. As she'd waved goodbye at the station, her mind was already full of school: kickboxing, new lessons, seeing Isha. She could still remember the diesel smell of the platform, greasy and sharp, the rough wool of her school coat, the crisp autumn air on her face.

A fortnight later, her parents were dead. One moment, breathing and thinking and planning. The next moment—

Hugo held her hand, his touch dragging her into the present. In seconds, this would be over. Would she meet her parents? Hug them?

'Put up your hands where we can see them.' The man's voice was abrupt.

They raised their hands.

'If you disobey any instructions or try to leave, these men will fire.'

The men with the rifles … calm body language, focused. They'd done this before. Sophie's mouth dried.

'Put your bags on the ground. Slowly.'

Hugo set down his bag, and Sophie slipped the strap from

her shoulder and placed her bag by her feet. She took tiny steps until Charlotte was behind her. Having somehow survived Alan, Charlotte couldn't die now—

'Mr Harrington, take off your coat and jumper, and your companion needs to remove her cardigan.'

Hugo complied, and while Sophie peeled off her sodden cardigan, an old news story from Africa filled her head: teenagers locked in explosive vests, remote controls in the hands of mad adults…

They thought they were suicide bombers.

Charlotte was trembling, leaning against Sophie's legs.

'Empty your bags.'

Again, they complied, shaking out the contents.

By the firing squad, two policemen stood by the original officer. Another man in dark overalls emerged from between the cars, holding a large black labrador by its collar.

'The dog is going to approach you,' said the policeman who'd told them to take off their coats. 'When he does, do not move.'

They couldn't move. Nowhere to go.

'And you must control *your* dog.'

Sophie turned, gripped Charlotte's collar, and said firmly, 'Down.'

The man released the labrador and Sophie's brain changed what she was seeing into slow motion. 'Down,' she repeated. 'Please, *down*.' She pushed, so Charlotte lay almost flat. Charlotte was growling as well as trembling. How long would Charlotte let her do this? Protecting her was Charlotte's strongest instinct. Sophie fell to her knees, using her body weight to keep Charlotte still.

The labrador was in front of them.

He sniffed the cardigan and the contents of her bag on the ground, before snuffling so close Sophie could smell his hot breath. The labrador gave Charlotte a cursory sniff and Charlotte tensed like a curled spring.

The dog moved on to Hugo, and Sophie sagged, but kept her grip on Charlotte.

After examining Hugo and his belongings, the labrador raised his head and ran to his handler. Sophie cautiously let go of Charlotte's collar, and stood up, holding her lead. Charlotte stood up too, shook herself and regarded Sophie reproachfully, saying she could have bested that police dog, *if* she'd chosen to. But it was bluster.

The dog and handler had disappeared, but the men were still pointing their rifles.

Calm, slow breaths.

'Empty your pockets.'

Sophie turned her skirt pockets inside out and Hugo did the same with his trousers.

The two policemen walked cautiously towards them. Their uniforms were identical, and it was only when they drew closer that Sophie realised one of them was female.

'This won't take long,' said the female officer, addressing Sophie. 'I need to check you're not wearing anything untoward.'

Untoward? She was wearing huge, old-fashioned draw-ers. For an insane moment, she nearly giggled with hysteria.

The officer patted Sophie's stomach, chest and legs, looked up and froze. 'What's that in your hair?'

'Only hairpins and scrunched up paper.' The woman's expression didn't change, so Sophie added, 'It makes my hair fuller at the back.'

The officer turned and strode back to the cars. Her companion stopped searching Hugo and retreated too.

'Take out a hairpin. Very. Slowly,' ordered the female officer.

Sophie extracted a pin and held it up. 'And this is a ball of paper.' She pulled one out.

'Take out another pin.'

Sophie complied.

After talking on her phone, the woman returned and patted Sophie's hair. She strode away and shouted 'clear.' The policeman searching Hugo yelled 'clear' too and said in a normal tone, 'Repack your bags.'

They started packing, and as Sophie stuffed discarded pins and paper into her bag, she wanted to scream. They shouldn't have risked it. Hugo would have had a good life with Clarissa.

Cold and wet, they finished packing.

The firing squad hadn't moved, their rifles as steady as their eyes. But then they swivelled as one, trained their sights beyond the police cars to the campus entrance. Relief flooded through Sophie, so powerful and all-encompassing, she nearly dropped to her knees again.

A different police officer, older and heavily built, strolled over to them. 'Sorry about that,' he announced, in a pleasant northern accent, addressing Hugo. 'I'm Inspector Moore. Please put your coat and jumpers on. You'll understand, sir, nowadays, can't be too careful.'

Hugo nodded. 'This is about my father.'

'It's more to do with you, sir, but I take your meaning. I've received instructions to escort you and the young lady to London.'

Sophie pulled Charlotte close.

The inspector smiled. 'And the hound.'

They picked up their clothes and bags and plodded after the inspector, passing the bright blue lights and the firing squad who were cradling their rifles and chatting. Just a regular day at the office. And Hugo seemed calmer. What was that about his father?

They approached a black four-by-four and dropped their bags in the boot as the inspector asked. He gestured for them to get in the back and another officer got in the front passenger seat.

With numb fingers, Sophie struggled to fasten the middle seatbelt around Charlotte and to fasten her own.

'The journey's about four hours,' said the inspector, as they drove away.

Charlotte settled herself on the leather seat, seemingly content, but her internal injuries could kill her in the next few hours — or days. Were there vet scanners here? Pets might be routinely mistreated? No. The inspector's smile at Charlotte had been genuine.

Sophie glanced at Hugo and the old longing returned, taunting her. Right. Only temporarily extinguished by Alan, a terrifying lift, and a firing squad.

Beyond the car windows, there were no streetlamps, just unrelenting dark. Tears of frustration and self-pity ran down her face and as if in sympathy, rain streamed down the window in careering lines. Sophie wiped her eyes. Fish for more info and escape.

She leaned forward and deployed her best, Hadley-posh accent. 'Can I ask what all that was about, at the university?' Her polite manner was also reassuring. Not criminals. Not a threat. Would have worked at home.

The inspector cleared his throat, embarrassed. 'You could have been wearing suicide vests, Miss, or had bombs in the bags. I have a duty to protect my officers and the public. You've been missing for months with no information regarding your whereabouts. You could have been murdered, or kidnapped and brainwashed.'

'I see,' said Sophie.

The police radio crackled, and the officers talked about football. Life went on, in every universe.

Charlotte began turning around on the seat.

'Is it possible to stop for my dog?'

'No reason why not,' said the inspector.

They stopped at a service station, and everyone got out except the inspector. The other policeman stood by the car watching them, one hand under his jacket. He was armed, but soon they'd be locked inside a police station.

As Charlotte busied herself in the rain and dark, Sophie whispered, 'We need to escape *now*.'

CHAPTER 41

How many versions of home were there?

She'd likely only landed in this one by the skin of her teeth. Those poison-pen letters might not have been from Alan, but from an unknown, experienced visitor. Getting Hugo back may always have been a doomed quest.

Charlotte nudged Sophie's legs, ready to leave the service station verge and return to the dry, warm car.

'We *don't* need to escape,' said Hugo.

'It's our only opportunity. This isn't our world.'

'It is. I'm sure.' Hugo glanced at the officer watching them. 'Keep schtum about Shorten. People will think we're bonkers.'

'So, we need a cover story.' She considered. 'We fell madly in love but had anxiety and stress and dropped out of Uni. Didn't use money, just bartered for things.'

'Who's going to believe that?'

'It's more believable than the truth,' said Sophie. 'Hippy travellers took us in. We stayed in caravans and foraged for food.'

'Completely off the radar.'

'Exactly,' said Sophie. 'What was that about your father?'

'He's a politician.'

'I thought your parents were farmers. You said you could manage the estate.'

'My *grand*parents are farmers.'

'Oh.'

'Dad's in the Cabinet. We have state-of-the-art security at home and armed protection around the clock. Surreal at first, but you get used to it.'

Sophie wasn't surprised. Her school fees had been paid by a scholarship, but the other students' parents had been wealthy, paid the full whack. And she'd been into animal rights, taken little interest in mainstream politics.

A layer of tension lifted. Explained the reaction in the students' union. The media circus would have been relentless. Only a hermit wouldn't have recognised Hugo.

Back in the car, Sophie shivered, again wet and cold. The police would want to interview them. Might be a while before she could travel to Shorten.

'I can guess what happened when we dropped off the map,' Hugo whispered. 'I've no history of rebellion, kicking the system. The security guys assumed we'd been kidnapped… My parents must have been going through hell.'

Sophie couldn't remember his mother and father at Hadley's leaving ball. 'Why didn't you mention your father's job before?'

'Why would I? What he does for a living wasn't relevant to anything.'

Sophie leaned against the headrest and tried to sleep, but the remaining hairpins and rats were prickly. She took them out, stored them in her pockets, then felt slovenly with her hair down.

Eventually, she dozed. Anne came out onto a dreamy Manor terrace. 'All will be well. Go for a swim with Freddy.'

An instant later, Sophie was larking with Freddy in the moat. He kissed her in his slow, gentle way and they floated on their backs, holding hands. The water was clean and cool, and a summer sun was warm on her face. Freddy nudged her arm.

'Nearly there.' Hugo's voice cut through the dream.

Sophie registered the police officers and remembered. Sensing the end of the journey, Charlotte was staring out the window at streetlamps and a deserted urban road.

The police station wouldn't be fun.

Metal gates loomed up and opened with slow, electric precision. They turned into a circular drive and security lights clicked on, illuminating a square Georgian house. Two policemen stood beside a red front door.

'What's this?' Sophie whispered to Hugo.

'Home.'

Sophie hauled herself out of the car with Charlotte, who started bouncing. Struggling to control her, Sophie glimpsed an elegant woman in jeans and a short fawn jacket running out of the house. The woman hugged Hugo and didn't let go. She wept into his chest, her short dark hair awry, and he embraced her, murmuring, 'I'm alright. It's alright.'

Finally, she extracted herself. 'You better have a good explanation for this.' Her voice was stern, but her heart wasn't in it. She registered Sophie. 'Where are my manners? Fiona Harrington.'

'Sophie Arundel. Hello.'

Charlotte bounced up at Hugo's mother and Sophie wearily pulled her away. 'Sorry, she's over excited.'

'Aren't we all?' said Fiona, who'd recovered her composure. 'Come on, time to face the music.'

Sophie retrieved her bag from the boot, Hugo got his, and the unmarked police car drove off. They trooped into the house, one of the officers by the door patted Charlotte as she padded by, and in a spacious hall, Hugo dropped his bag on an upright chair.

An older, grey-haired version of Hugo stepped towards them, casually dressed in navy chinos and a cream open-necked shirt.

'Hello,' Hugo said, sheepishly. He took off his coat and scarf and hung them on a rack.

'Glad to see you in one piece.' Mr Harrington hugged Hugo, then smiled at Sophie, but it seemed like an effort. 'Edward Harrington.'

'Sophie Arundel. Nice to meet you. I know this is rude, but could I use your phone? To call my aunt, tell her I'm okay?'

'Of course.' Hugo's father went over to a side table and passed her a handset.

She punched in the digits. There was no mobile signal where Aunty Wendy lived, so Sophie knew the landline number by heart. After two rings, it clicked into an answering machine. 'It's me,' said Sophie in a rush. 'I've been in a bad place but I'm fine. I'm *really* sorry I couldn't call you. Speak tomorrow.'

She replaced the phone in its cradle, hoping against hope that the stress of this hadn't made her aunt's Parkinson's Disease worse, that she wasn't in a nursing home … or dead.

Sophie hung her bag on the rack and followed Hugo into a smart drawing room, not so different from Shorten. She perched on a couch beside Hugo, keeping Charlotte on the floor.

Charlotte's ears pricked up. Another dog was howling and barking.

'I put George in the music room,' said Hugo's father. 'With Sophie's dog, we thought it might be a bit much, given the circumstances.'

'It'll be fine,' said Hugo.

'I'm not sure,' Sophie said, but Edward had already opened a door.

A golden labrador bounded in and launched himself at Hugo. Charlotte didn't move, watching. George licked Hugo's face with focused thoroughness, until Hugo could push him off and scratch behind his ears. 'Sorry I was away so long.' George abruptly noticed Charlotte.

Sophie gripped the lead as George trotted towards Charlotte and sniffed, his tail wagging. Charlotte raised her head disdainfully, but George persisted and, due to indifference, exhaustion, or a change of mind, Charlotte did a token tail wag.

Edward was pacing, in a Hugo way, occasionally pausing by a large sash window, as if he'd glimpsed a pageant or an unusual animal. 'Mum's sorting tea and sandwiches with Pamela.'

A few minutes later, Fiona came in with a laden tea tray, followed by a plump woman carrying a tray of chunky sandwiches. Everything was rapidly set out on a large coffee table.

Hugo stood up and hugged the plump lady. 'Sophie, this is Pamela Beeching. A family friend.'

Pamela gave Sophie a curt nod. Okay, Pamela didn't approve of her, or Charlotte, or both. But she could be imagining it. She was beyond stressed. So was Pamela.

George stared longingly at the sandwiches and Pamela dragged him out of the room.

'May I use your bathroom, please?' Sophie suddenly *really* needed to get away, compose herself.

'Of course,' said Fiona.

Hugo held Charlotte's lead, and Sophie followed his mother down a corridor.

Alone in the small cloakroom, Sophie shut the door and frowned at a mirror above the sink. Maud had combed through Sophie's hair with her usual care this morning, or was that yesterday? Now it was a dishevelled, tangled mess. But by the time Freddy saw her again, she'd be restored. Normal.

She touched her jaw where Alan had punched her. Not even the beginning of a bruise. The lack of physical evidence from the fight — and the barrelling lift — nagged at her, made it all seem less real.

Sophie rested her hands on the sink, and the cold, sterile porcelain helped her gather her wits. *Believe* the travellers lie. Edward was a successful politician. Wouldn't be easily fooled.

Back in the drawing room, Hugo was eating, drinking tea, and feeding Charlotte.

And after tea and an egg sandwich, Sophie felt stronger.

'So,' said Edward, 'are you going to tell us where you've been?'

Faced with his father's intent stare, Hugo said nothing, so Sophie looked Edward in the eye and laid out the cover story, adding convincing details: shabby ponies and happy, scruffy children.

'Travellers?' said Hugo's mother. '*Gypsies?*'

'I don't think so,' said Sophie. Keep it vague. 'They were kind and had the same ... philosophy.'

'That's beautiful lace on your dress,' said Fiona, addressing Sophie.

'The travellers are like the Amish in America. Women dress modestly.'

Hugo's mother shook her head. 'You were in a *cult?*'

'No, they're spiritual, but not ... weird. Hippies.' Tea calmed the nerves. Sophie reached for her half-empty mug and the diamonds in her watch and ring glittered in the artificial light.

Fiona gasped. 'You're *engaged?*'

In mid swallow, Sophie's tea went down the wrong way and she spluttered.

'Right, we've got the picture,' said Edward. 'You're both okay, that's the main thing. I'll ask the police and security people to close the case.'

'You're done in,' said Fiona, abruptly. 'Everything will seem clearer in the morning, I'm sure. I've made up a bed on the first floor for Sophie.'

'Thank you.' She'd feel better, after a long, long sleep.

CHAPTER 42

After taking Charlotte out onto some grass, Sophie fetched her bag from the hall and led Charlotte upstairs.

Sophie's room was furnished in a guest bedroomy way, but there was an elegant, free-standing mirror, spookily similar to the one in Shorten, and an ensuite shower that looked *wonderful*.

But she couldn't take a shower, unfastening the dress by herself was impossible. She was institutionalised, like an escaped criminal. Wouldn't ask Hugo's mother or disapproving Pamela ... she'd sleep in her dress.

She peeled off her damp cardigan, emptied the rats and pins from her pockets into the bag, and sat in a button back armchair to ease off her boots and socks. Charlotte was already asleep on the bed. 'You were a hero today.'

A knock and the door opened. Hugo was clutching an electric toothbrush, still in its wrapping. 'It's charged and there are new brush heads in the bathroom.' He left it by the bed.

'Thanks.' A wondrous device. She'd take it to Shorten. Should be able to make it work.

'The lift must have healed me.' He touched his nose. 'As if it never happened. Incredible.'

'Charlotte seems completely better, but a vet should check her out, just in case.'

'I'll make an appointment.' Hugo fished a charging lead out of his pocket. 'This might revive your phone.' He put it on a bedside table. 'I'm going to sit with Mum for a bit. She's upset.'

'Um, I can't get undressed. All the buttons are on the back.'

He nodded. 'I'll sort them.'

She stood up and turned around in a rush, her face heating. He started from the dress collar and worked down, his fingers unhurried, deft. Her insides flip-flopped. If gods were real, Loki would be laughing his head off. Maybe there was a trickster god?

'All done.' Hugo shot her a brief smile and left, closing the door behind him.

She'd missed that smile. If the lift did physical healing, had it done mental healing too?

Sophie stepped out of the damp gown, hung it on a fitted wardrobe door to dry, and took off her watch. Her reflection in the standalone mirror was a forlorn shipwreck of a girl, her white bodice and knee-length drawers clinging to her skin.

Resisting the urge to lie down, she plugged in her phone, undressed, and brushed her teeth with the electric brush. Fabulous.

The shower was even more fabulous. She washed her hair with a posh shampoo, piled in moisturising conditioner and lingered, luxuriating in the fierce hot water. After the shower, she found a comb in her bag, mostly detangled her hair, and put her underwear on. In a strange house, damp undies trumped going commando.

In a warm bedroom, snug under a duvet, she should have been asleep in seconds. But Hugo's house was too quiet. In the Manor before dawn, there'd always been the murmur of domestic sounds: scullery maids in the public rooms, cleaning grates, adding fresh wood, whispering, gossiping...

Sophie adjusted a pillow under her neck and switched on a bedside radio, hoping music would send her to sleep. *'It's six thirty, time for the news headlines.'*

The voice carried on but Sophie didn't hear, lost in longed-for sleep.

Sophie woke to a rustle of curtains opening and a clink noise.

'Thought you'd appreciate something familiar,' said Hugo's voice. 'Tea and toast.'

Still half-asleep, Sophie sat up. 'Thanks for this.'

Hugo lowered a tray onto her lap. Under his arm was a lurid pink dressing gown that jarred with his jeans, pale blue shirt and Shorten pullover. 'Charlotte seems perky but she wasn't interested in breakfast. I took her out at eight.'

'What time is it?'

'Just gone eleven.'

Charlotte's eyes were on the toast. Sophie drank her tea, fed Charlotte half a slice and ate the rest.

Sophie moved the tray off her lap and glanced at her dead phone. Four months ago, she'd been a social media addict. Now, thanks to parallel universe rehab, entirely cured.

'It's working, but it was bleeping. I didn't want it waking you up.'

Hugo watching her sleeping... She pushed away a

poignant, vulnerable sensation and switched on her phone. *Friday 12 January.* She stared at it dully. '2018. We've missed Christmas.' In the context of getting here in one piece, why was missing Christmas important?

'Everything's the same.' He sat in the armchair and yawned. 'Same old news.'

Messages were stacking up, but Aunty Wendy didn't text. Three missed calls overnight. Sophie tapped in the number and her aunt answered.

'You're okay?' Sophie blurted.

'Surprisingly,' said her aunt, 'given the circumstances.'

'I love you.'

'I love you too, but the last few months have been … difficult.'

Sophie welled up. 'It's complicated. Can I call again this afternoon?'

'You'd better.'

'I promise.' After Sophie hung up, she drew a long, relieved breath. She'd call Isha today, but no point in wading through the mountain of messages. Would be in a different universe tomorrow. She put the phone aside.

Hugo offered her the pink dressing gown. 'Isobel's, to tide you over.'

His sister's. Hugo had three, all flown the nest. Sophie accepted the dressing gown with a smile and got out of bed.

Beyond the window there was lawn, winter-bare trees, and drenched flowers. A large garden for London, but nothing like Shorten. She touched the double-glazing that fronted the window. They really were back.

'You could start an exciting trend in music videos.'

'What?'

'Instead of wearing as little as possible, you could twerk but in old-fashioned underwear.'

'Very funny.' She quickly pulled on the dressing gown and

walked over to the wardrobe. How could she fasten her dress? This was ridiculous. 'I'll buy normal clothes for the journey.'

'You should order online.'

'Planning to. Express delivery.' Traipsing around a mall didn't appeal. 'I know it's a pain, but could you do up my dress?'

'No problem.' He sounded bored, not put out.

She shucked off the dressing gown, slipped the gown on, and tried not to think or feel. Her underwear was almost dry. So was the dress.

When he'd finished, he settled in the armchair and crossed his legs. Pale sunlight danced on his dark hair and the grey and navy pattern of his Shorten pullover.

'You haven't any other jumpers?'

'I prefer this. It's more flexible than a regular pullover.'

'It's very dated.'

'Says the girl in period costume.'

Had a point. She sat on the bed and out of habit, put on her watch, still stuck on 12:15. 'How's your mother?'

'Recovering herself. We face-timed my sisters.'

'Where do they live?' Sophie stroked Charlotte, dozing beside her.

'Isobel's in Scotland, Alice is in California and Juliet's in Washington. They came over when we vanished but couldn't stay forever.'

Consequences from their adventure had spread across continents, traumatised people she'd never met.

Hugo stood up. 'Brunch after the vets?'

'Brunch … haven't heard that word in a while. I'll be there in a minute.'

After Hugo disappeared downstairs, Sophie went to the loo and combed her hair, but as she pulled on her boots, Charlotte leaped off the bed and eyed her reproachfully.

'Don't worry. You'll see Jack again soon.'

On the ground floor at the rear of the house was a kitchen, a modern extension. A high ceiling and modern French windows created an impression of space and light, but the kitchen was cosy and practical, with Shaker cupboards and a traditional Aga cooker.

Hugo pressed a screen icon on a red coffee machine. 'Espresso, cappuccino or latte?'

'Too much choice,' said Sophie.

'There isn't an option for can't decide. Perhaps there should be?'

She giggled. 'Latte, please.'

He touched another icon, and the machine hissed.

She'd miss his sense of humour. If her debit card worked, she'd buy a notebook at the station and write down everything about him. Then as long as she lived, she'd never forget.

By the coffee machine on a granite worktop was Hugo's Shorten notebook, a pencil, and a dog-eared textbook: *Epistemology and Moral Philosophy for A level*. She pointed. 'Easy read?'

'No.' He handed her a mug of coffee. 'I didn't choose to disappear.' He moved another mug to the machine and pressed a different icon. 'But I feel terrible, knowing what I've put my family through.'

The need to embrace him, comfort him, was almost overwhelming, but she made herself sit at the far end of a wooden table. 'Where are your parents?'

'At work, even after being up most of the night.'

'Really? How come?'

'Dad's got some secret intelligence emergency. He's

briefing the Cabinet this morning, and my mother's got a high profile case she can't delegate. She's a commercial solicitor.'

Sophie sniffed the dark, rich scent from her mug, but after swallowing some, she set the mug down. 'This tastes ... odd.'

'It's the steamed milk.'

A cautious sip. 'You're right, but this is how I like it. You learned a lot in Shorten.'

He plonked his mug on the table. 'Would you pass the coffee test?'

'You have too much milk and two sugars.'

'We did drink a load of coffee.' He placed a water bowl on the hardwood floor and removed a can from the fridge. 'This is what Charlotte rejected. It's regular, not veggie.'

Charlotte was standing by the French windows. Almost all glass, they took up an entire wall.

'Regular's fine,' said Sophie. 'She's holding out for bacon and sausages.' Veggie dog food had been a Sophie indulgence, not a Charlotte one. 'She'll give in eventually.'

Hugo emptied the dog food into another bowl and put it on the floor, but Charlotte didn't move from the window.

'Who chose the mugs?' Sophie's featured a cute dog doing yoga. So did Hugo's.

'Mrs B.'

'Who?'

'Mrs Beeching, Pamela. Sorry, I've called her that since I was little.'

'Aunty Wendy has the exact same mugs. That is so weird.'

Hugo shrugged. 'Probably a factory in China churning out millions, so not much of a coincidence.' He sat down at the table opposite her.

Freddy's words about Betty surfaced. *Making a connection between two, three or even four events, and on that basis reaching a conclusion ... is foolish.* 'Coincidence is tricky in maths. Well, according to Freddy.' Saying his name out loud felt jarring, as if the syllables had torn something. A ripple in reality—

'He asked me all these questions about the latest theories.' Hugo stared into his coffee. 'When I couldn't give him coherent answers, he realised I was clueless and got frustrated. He was convinced maths and science were key to understanding the lift.'

'He's like you in that way. Doesn't understand why other people can't grasp what he finds easy.'

Hugo frowned. 'I don't think that's true.'

George scampered in, enticed by the dog food on the floor. Charlotte was still beside the French windows, showing no interest in George — or eating. Hugo got to his feet and picked up the bowl. 'I can't blame her for holding out for human food.' He covered it with cling film and stashed it in the fridge.

'I wonder if I'd be veggie if I was reincarnated as a dog?'

'You should Google it,' said Hugo. 'I bet someone remembers being an animal in a past life.'

'I'm *so* going to do that.' She savoured his teasing. It would stop soon enough.

Hugo glanced at a clock on the wall and hastily finished his coffee. 'The vets is a five-minute walk.'

The vet touched the screen. 'She's absolutely fine. No blood that shouldn't be there.'

'Are you sure?' asked Sophie.

The vet nodded. 'You said she was kicked?'

'Yes,' said Sophie. 'Very hard. And stabbed. It happened yesterday.'

The vet knelt beside Charlotte. 'This scar tissue is weeks old.'

'Maybe I muddled up where she was injured?' said Sophie, though she hadn't.

At the counter, the bill was a shock, but Sophie had her student loan, and the loan company didn't collect in Shorten.

'You'd think,' said Hugo, as they left, 'that once we went missing, the bank would have stopped our cards.'

'Geared up for odd patterns, not zero spending?'

'Or perhaps the police were hoping our kidnapper would use them, give them a location trace.'

Sophie strolled with him, cosy in one of his jackets, past upmarket homes and into a park. She unclipped the lead, and Charlotte zoomed off, bounding around rowan trees and across heathland. 'If the lift somehow disposes of waste, it might also clean and treat injuries? Your nose and hand were definitely broken.'

He flexed his fingers. 'Bonkers, but makes sense.'

Sophie turned her mind to Shorten. She'd stock up on tampons, painkillers, antiperspirant, shampoo, conditioner, and the pill. And she'd tell the doctor the truth. That she was planning an expedition somewhere seriously dodgy…

CHAPTER 43

In the kitchen, George bounded up to Charlotte, but she ignored him, walking over to stare at the garden.

Hugo tapped his phone. 'Here's how our disappearance was reported.'

Sophie had half forgotten how modern newspapers were laid out — colour photos and less dense text. *The son of Edward Harrington, missing since September last year, has been found safe and well in Derby. Another student, Sophie Arundel, was also unharmed.* 'Derby? Where did that come from? And I thought the article would be bigger?'

'*Found safe,* is far less interesting than *abducted by fanatics.*' Hugo tapped his phone again and handed it to her. 'Two days after we left.'

The photo of a younger Hugo from the police poster covered half the front page. *Foreign Secretary's Son Missing. Former public schoolboy, Hugo Harrington, hasn't been seen since Monday. If a targeted kidnapping, this marks a new development in the war against terror. Security for high profile figures and their families is under review...*

'This is bad,' said Hugo. 'Misled the security people and might give terrorists ideas, get children really kidnapped.'

'You look like a child in this picture.'

'It's from year ten.' He dropped bread into a toaster and switched on the coffee machine. 'They wouldn't have found much on social media. When Dad was promoted, a lot was deleted.'

Next to the picture of Hugo was the smaller photo of Sophie — her younger self. 'Charlotte has a higher profile than me.' She gave him his phone. 'I'll go get mine.' If Aunty Wendy rang, or Isha, she should answer.

When she returned to the kitchen, Hugo had put out plates and cutlery, and toast, butter, and marmalade.

She sat at the table and took a slice of toast. 'Shorten's converted me to marmalade.'

'And me.' Hugo handed her a coffee and picked up his.

He looked different in modern clothes. Not as mysterious. The familiar yearning taunted her. Don't think about it.

Hugo sat down and spread marmalade on his toast. 'There's one thing I don't understand.'

'Just one thing?'

He shot her a tired smile. 'Last September, we walked into the lift at eleven and when the doors opened in Shorten, it was about the same time. We left yesterday after breakfast, but here it was dark.'

'We were in there a *long* time,' said Sophie. 'And if Charlotte's scar is weeks old, either the lift somehow speeds up time, accelerates healing ... or we were in there for *weeks*.'

'Your apple.'

'Sorry?'

'Four months ago, that first ride in the lift lasted for what seemed seconds, but your apple had gone mouldy.'

She'd bought it that morning, but it had turned fluffy with green putrid bits.

'Takes a while for fruit to go off.' Hugo cut his toast in half.

'Maybe it was coincidence that we arrived in Shorten at the same time we'd left?'

'But if we were in there for so long, for both crossings, how come we weren't dehydrated, hungry?' He rubbed his chin. 'I didn't need a shave. Perhaps it insulates sentient travellers?'

'Would explain why our phones died,' said Sophie. 'I wonder why after the first trip your watch carried on working?'

He peered at the watch's face on his wrist. 'This might just require winding.' He wound it up. 'Yes.'

Hugo's watch had been his great, great grandfather's. An antique. Sophie's watch was an antique too, but only in 2018. Once she was in Shorten, Freddy's gift would be brand new again. She wound up the art deco watch and grinned.

'Perhaps my watch still worked after the first crossing because we were in there for days, rather than weeks.' Hugo shook his head. 'I don't remember leaving the lift in the students' union yesterday, or anything about the crossing.'

'I remember it all,' said Sophie. 'Down to the gene? After the lift stopped spinning, it got horribly hot, and you and Charlotte were fast asleep.'

'Could it have put us into a coma, to heal us?'

'Makes sense.' She touched her neck, remembering. 'My throat was really sore, and I'd banged my shoulder, but nothing serious.'

'Again, bonkers but logical,' said Hugo. 'And why did it turn over like that?'

'If it's powered by emotions, I'm surprised it didn't explode, the way I was feeling.'

'I wouldn't ride that lift, not for anything.' He looked

pensive. 'Sorry, I know you're set on doing that. I should be more positive.'

Sophie finished her coffee. Focus on practical stuff. She felt strangely clear-headed. Probably the caffeine. 'My suitcase might be with my aunt, but it could be with the police. If it is, could you help her collect it? I'll give you her contact details and the password for my laptop.'

He nodded.

'I'm leaving my house in Buckinghamshire to my aunt.' Her parents' life insurance had paid off the mortgage, and when Aunty Wendy had taken Sophie in, the property's rental income had really helped. And in Buckinghamshire, even small properties were valuable. 'I'll write an old-fashioned letter, have it witnessed by two people, so it's legit.'

'I knew GCSE law would prove useful.' He was trying for flippant but failing.

'Would you be happy to be executor?'

'I guess.'

'In seven years, I'll be presumed dead.'

Hugo swallowed. 'You've thought this through.'

'You know me, prefer to be in control, tie up loose ends...' Okay, her attempt at flippant was pants.

'Talking of loose ends, we should Google Alan.' Hugo hastily tapped his phone, keen to move on from inheritance planning. 'Not too many Alan Parkes...' He gave a soft whistle and showed her the screen. 'Definitely him.'

Sophie looked at the bad mugshot and caption. *Wanted for questioning about a one-punch murder in Deptford. Last seen in August 1994.* 'What's a one-punch murder?'

'A person's punched, falls, cracks their head and dies from that, rather than the punch.'

'That's why he assumed you were dead, Hugo.' She shivered. 'He'd done it before.' Should fetch her cardigan. It was colder here than upstairs.

'He went into the lift in August 1994, or just after,' said Hugo, 'not in October as he said in Shorten. Explains why his dates didn't match the other visitors.'

What had Alan said to Betty? *Scientists hoped to open a safe route to the future.* 'Alan thought if we permanently opened up the portal, the police would track him down.'

'He must have been working at the university under a false name.'

'But in Shorten, he had no need to,' said Sophie. 'Best bolthole ever.'

'Until we showed up.'

'It was a near run thing…'

'Understatement.'

Sophie described how she'd given ludicrous understatement a name.

'The Shorten Code … when you get back, don't tell anyone. They'd be offended.'

'I only mentioned it to Lucy. I wonder how long before you lose that?'

'Probably not long,' said Hugo. 'It only works if everyone gets it. There was a battle in the Great War and our boys were in dire straits. We told the Yanks the situation was a bit sticky. They didn't think it was serious, so didn't show up. Everyone died.'

'That's horrible.'

'Will attacking Reynolds… What was in it for him?'

'Alan must have made up some baloney, how the lift would destroy their life, the pub—'

Pamela bustled in with bulging shopping bags. 'How does bacon and eggs sound?'

'Sounds excellent, Mrs B,' said Hugo, standing up to help.

Sophie got to her feet, feeling awkward in her ankle-length silk dress.

'We'll take care of this,' said Pamela, looking indulgently at Hugo. 'He's well trained.'

Hugo stashed butter and cheese in the fridge. This was a side of him she'd never seen. Domesticated Hugo. 'Can you cook?' Sophie asked him.

'Not really.'

'You do a passable spaghetti bolognese.' Pamela put a sliced loaf in a bread bin. 'What about you, Sophie?'

'Definitely *not* a domestic goddess.'

'Oh, dear,' said Pamela, 'one of you needs to learn or it'll be a lifetime of takeaways.'

She'd bought the whirlwind romance fiction, so might believe the travellers hogwash too?

Pamela lifted a lid on the Aga and placed a frying pan on a cooking plate.

'Sophie's going to stay a few days.' Hugo stacked rice and pasta in a cupboard.

Pamela dropped a scoop of butter into the pan. 'That will be nice.'

'Actually,' said Sophie, sitting down, 'I should probably—'

'You need a proper rest before you leave.' Hugo set out glasses of fresh orange juice.

No. Staying even one more day would drag out this stupid yearning.

George wagged his tail, watching Pamela transfer bacon slices into the sizzling pan.

'Pamela, would you mind if I give some bacon to my dog?' Sophie drank her juice.

'Not at all.'

'Sophie's veggie,' said Hugo.

Pamela nodded vaguely. 'We can have quiche tonight.'

'Thank you.' Pamela had decided she liked her now. If this adventure had turned out differently, they might have become friends. And quiche would be fine, if samey. For months, she'd eaten it for lunch *and* dinner. When she got back, she'd ask Anne to sort a different recipe, with hot peppers or broccoli.

On a whim, Sophie Googled *The Prisoner of Zenda*. She'd enjoyed the first chapter in Shorten. Her eye caught a plot summary — and the ending. *The king is rescued and restored to his throne, but the lovers, trapped by duty, must part.*

She plonked the phone on the table, face down, illogically shaken that the novel had no happy ending here.

Only a story.

She picked up a lifestyle magazine from a wicker basket near her chair, hoping to distract herself in the glossy pages. Millions of people were interested in sofas and curtains. Maybe once she married Freddy, she'd be interested too?

Pamela looked over at Charlotte, who was still standing at the window, despite the lure of cooking bacon. 'Your dog seems to be waiting for someone.'

Charlotte thought she wasn't far from the Manor. 'She's missing another dog.' Sophie walked over and ruffled Charlotte's head.

'Double espresso, Mrs B?' Hugo was by the coffee machine.

'Yes, please.'

Hugo made Pamela's coffee, gave Sophie a latte, and prepared another. Pamela plated up two helpings of bacon, fried eggs, and sautéed mushrooms.

'This looks yummy,' said Sophie, sitting down. 'Aren't you having any?'

Pamela patted her ample hips. 'Diet day. I had yoghurt for breakfast.'

Outside, sleet was falling. Sophie moved her chair closer to the Aga and enjoyed her meal, leaving the bacon. Hugo ate with his phone propped up against the marmalade jar, reading something.

'I'm taking George for a walk. He needs the exercise, whatever the weather.' Pamela attached a lead to George's collar. 'Sophie, I can take your dog?'

'That's very kind of you but she's fine here.' Like her, Charlotte was upset. Needed to stay close.

Pamela left with a happy George, who bounced along, looking forward to exploring and jumping in puddles.

Time to call Aunty Wendy. On her phone, Sophie prepared on a notes app what she planned to say, then rang. She went through the cover story and the pretend romance with Hugo, related the truthful romance with Freddy, and added that there was no wi-fi and no phones.

Her aunt snorted. 'A love triangle … and trust you to go from atheism to a cult.' She paused. 'The church has been supportive but the last few months have been quite hard.' Aunty Wendy had developed her own version of the Shorten Code.

Deep breath. 'I'm going back, to be with Freddy.'
Silence.
'Are you sure?' Her aunt sounded upset now.
'Freddy's special, and I'll be safe.'

CHAPTER 44

'I love you.' Aunty Wendy ended the call.

Sophie blinked and felt sick, and fought to compose herself. Hugo was staring at his screen, pretending not to listen.

With a heavy heart, Sophie signed into her social media account and clicked on a link: *Find Sophie*. Isha and Aunty Wendy stood beside a huge poster at the university entrance. They'd spent months trying to find her. Overwhelmed with gratitude, she showed Hugo.

He glanced up. 'It's humbling. My family and friends did the same for me.'

'Do you reckon your parents bought the traveller thing?'

'In the absence of any other explanation.' He got to his feet and collected their empty mugs. 'More coffee?'

'No, I'm good.' She'd overdosed on caffeine. Needed to doze in the guestroom this afternoon, rest up before the lift. But in the meantime, their cover story needed work. 'Your friends won't buy our romcom lie.'

'Alex did. I've already messaged him.' Hugo transferred

his plate and the mugs into the dishwasher and sat down. 'I'll call him later.'

His attention was on his phone again and Sophie studied him under her lashes. His freshly shaven jaw, long dark eyelashes, taking her time… This was stupid. Masochistic.

She thought back to the school leaving ball. Hugo had left his friends and sought her out, and Isha had mused that he liked her, so might believe the romance fiction…

As if on cue, Sophie's phone rang. Jarring. Unfamiliar. She hit the green button.

'Is it really you?' Isha's voice was too high, stressed.

'Yes,' said Sophie, 'I don't know where to start.'

'The beginning's usually a good idea.'

This was going to be hard. Isha knew her better than Aunty Wendy. Sophie repeated the travellers' hogwash and talked about Freddy. 'Um, before Freddy, me and Hugo got together—'

Isha hooted with laughter, though it sounded strained.

'I was right,' said Isha, still laughing.

'I'm *so* sorry we put everyone through this, but once we were there, we couldn't use our phones. Leaving all that behind was part of their philosophy.'

'Hey, I've seen those documentaries.' Isha was typing. 'It's Saturday tomorrow. Where are you? I'll be there.'

'The thing is, tomorrow I'm going back … to Freddy.'

Silence. And it lasted longer than when she'd told her aunt.

'I hope,' said Isha, finally, 'that this Freddy guy's worth it.'

'He is.' The words were confident but in her mind swirled a whisper. *Is he?*

Hugo's eyes were still tethered to his screen. They were in the same room, but he was somewhere else.

'Will I *ever* see you again?' Now Isha sounded angry.

Sophie hesitated. 'Probably not.'

'Can you at least write an old-fashioned letter once a year?'

'That would be against their guidelines too.' She wiped her eyes. 'I love you.'

'I love you too. Stay safe.' Isha's voice broke before she disconnected.

Sophie swallowed down tears.

To distract herself, she ordered clothes in a frenzy: jeans, tops, socks, bras and loads more knickers. 'What's the postal address here?'

Hugo recited it.

The package would arrive before one tomorrow. She wouldn't rock the boat in the Manor by wearing jeans in public, but she could in private.

'We should send out a joint message,' said Hugo, 'thanking everybody.' He didn't look up. 'I'll do that now.'

'Is there a doctors' surgery and pharmacy nearby?'

'Hmm?'

'I thought I'd stock up on painkillers and the pill.'

'Wimbledon High Street's not far but you won't get a surgery appointment today.' He showed her his phone.

We sincerely apologise for all the heartache and trouble we've caused. A huge thank you to everyone who tried to find us. We'll explain everything soon. Hugo and Sophie.

'The right tone,' said Sophie, 'but it feels wrong, leaving you to field questions.'

Hugo shrugged, sent the message, and scrolled on his phone.

He was behaving as if Shorten hadn't happened. And that was downright odd. She was seeing this England through a detached, sharper lens. Ordinary. Safe. She chewed her lip, imagining the lift opening in a war zone or prison world. Even if she arrived safely, there'd be more stuff like the bakery and the Incident. 'I'm a bit nervous about Shorten.'

Hugo dragged his eyes from his screen.

'The revolution.'

Hugo put down his phone. 'We need to talk.'

'What's there to talk about?'

'Freddy was shaken up after the bakery.'

'He seemed fine.'

'He wasn't,' said Hugo. 'And for us, Shorten could easily have been so different.'

'How do you mean?'

'If Anne hadn't come through all those years ago, if we hadn't been taken in, I reckon we'd have joined the militia — just to eat.'

'We'd have been shot or hung.'

'Hanged,' corrected Hugo, his lips twitching.

'How can you joke about it?'

'It's safely in the past.' His mouth twisted into a grim smile. 'And a different universe.'

It would never be a joke for her. Freddy and Hugo were *civilised*. In that way they were identical, despite growing up in different worlds. But what they'd done at the bakery must have changed them, sliced through their characters with blunt scissors. 'If I'd realised Freddy was upset, we could have talked about it.'

'He'd have hated that,' said Hugo. 'It's a man thing, behaving as though you're fine when you're not. Freddy coped better after the Incident. Perhaps you become used to seeing dead bodies?'

'Disturbing idea.'

'I was surprised the bakery didn't affect you as badly, but I'm glad.'

She sighed. 'Hugo, of course it affected me. I was doing a Freddy.' She rubbed her eyes. 'Anyway, we shouldn't talk about it, defy Mr Crawford. Even here.'

Hugo stood up, sat on the chair beside her and covered

her fingers with his.

Faint tingling and perverse comfort mingled. She gently withdrew her hand.

'The bakery … I know how you escaped.'

The words hung in the air like a noose. She pushed down panic. He meant her hiding in the rubbish.

'Maud told John and he told me, *before* Crawford read the riot act.' Hugo's tone was carefully casual. 'A bit garbled but I got the gist.'

He'd known about Inkpin all along. That's why he'd held her hand after the bakery. *No.* 'He shot Robert Miles and I had seconds before his mates appeared. It was horrific.'

'You don't have to justify it, Sophie. I understand.'

'You do?'

'Context is crucial. It was pre-emptive self-defence, and you had to improvise.' He gave her a half nod, as Richard had when he'd heard her out. 'Once I'd agreed to defend the town, I killed five people, perhaps more.'

'You shot them from a distance. It's not the same.'

'I know. Are you still having nightmares?'

'About Robert, not killing Inkpin.'

'I didn't have nightmares last night but in Shorten I dreamed a lot about the bakery. Lying in the road, surrounded by dead children. Tiny children.'

She clasped her hands. 'I dreamt you knew about Inkpin, and so did Freddy, and Freddy shot me.'

'Right.'

Freddy. 'You didn't tell Freddy!' She heard the alarm in her own voice. 'I want him to think I'm normal, not…'

'Inkpin's pin-wielding nemesis.' Hugo winced at his own poor taste joke. 'I didn't tell Freddy — or anyone. You *are* normal, Sophie, but *never* tell Freddy. He might not get it.'

'He wouldn't. He thinks I'm *practically perfect in every way.*'

The vet had written that in Charlotte's notes after her scan, a quote from the movie, *Mary Poppins*.

The scent of Hugo's aftershave, newly cut grass wrapped in sunshine, cut through her thoughts. Too close. She left her seat by the table, hurried to the French windows, and pretended to adjust Charlotte's collar. Outside, the sleet had softened into rain.

'I realised you were struggling when you sought out Richard,' said Hugo, his tone matter of fact. 'And that you needed to keep a *very* low profile.'

She stilled, remembering what he'd said at the evacuation drill. *We've got this.* 'You knew Richard was secretly briefing me.'

'I suspected.' He sighed. 'Inkpin's picture on the front page of *The Times*. A big deal.'

She faced him. Miss Kemble had been there when Inkpin had introduced himself, must have told Maud his name, so of course she'd told John, who'd told Hugo.

'Inkpin Senior being assassinated,' said Hugo. 'An even bigger deal.'

'I think the government had something to do with that. Richard knew more than he let on.'

'After dinner, he'd sometimes tell stories from his days in the War Office. But they were careful stories. The War Office may have been a cover story.'

'For what?'

'Another department,' said Hugo, 'that later became MI5.'

Richard had been a spy...

'I Googled Inkpin, and only found Inkpin Senior.' Hugo picked up his phone and tapped. 'Here.'

She went over to him and took his phone. The man in a sepia photo looked like a mild type of person, an academic or philosopher. *Albert Inkpin, 1884 - 1944. First General Secretary of the Communist Party of Great Britain. Head of the Friends of Soviet Russia organisation, a position he retained until his death...*

Sophie put Hugo's phone on the table and sat down, well away from him. 'So here, Inkpin Senior wasn't assassinated.'

'In our world, he was a conscientious objector, believed war harmed the working classes. A pacifist.'

'His son wasn't,' said Sophie. 'Well, in Shorten.'

'Richard was clever, all of us hiding in the priest hole. They'd never have believed you'd gone to London on your own.'

Could only hope she wouldn't have to hide there again—

'Stoicism.' Hugo folded his arms, as if he'd found the answer to the ultimate question. 'I've been thinking about what I learned. Never understood it before.'

'No idea what you're talking about.'

'When you can't change a situation, it helps to just accept what's happening. Before I failed my exams, most of what I wanted fell into my lap. At Shorten, that didn't happen.'

What rubbish. He'd been fine. When he'd told her about Clarissa ... if there were a stoic competition, she'd win hands down. Okay, maybe not. Feigning a migraine and throwing up wasn't stoical. But Shorten had changed her too. After a lifetime avoiding public speaking, she'd spoken in the servants' hall, and by the time Freddy asked to kiss her, she'd considered what to do — *before* letting him.

Hugo clasped his hands behind his head. 'We've seen proof of parallel universes. How cool is that?'

'There are more things in heaven and earth Horatio than are dreamt of in your philosophy.' Showing off. One of her favourite quotes — from Hamlet. She'd regretted not doing drama at Hadley. In Shorten, she'd organise a Christmas play. Not Shakespeare. Something simple.

'I've forgotten most of the lines, but I remember that one.' Hugo had played Hamlet in their final year.

Showing off with him had always been hard, but it was the challenge that made it fun. His look of surprise, translated as, 'I didn't expect her to say that.'

He snatched up his phone and tapped rapidly. 'It's all here, Sophie. What we didn't figure out.'

'Like?'

'For a start, what happened to Little Shorten.' He read aloud. '*In 1941, after a raid on Derby, a German bomb destroyed the local pub and half the houses. The surviving inhabitants drifted away, and the village remained a forlorn pile of rubble until the university was built in 1963.*'

'That sucks. Maybe the village won't be bombed in the other universe?'

'Would be nice.' Hugo scrolled. 'The younger child in this photo. Is it Maud?' He held up the screen: two little girls in white pinafore dresses, sat on a bench in Little Shorten.

'It *is* Maud, with her sister, and that photo's in the students' union. I meant to tell you.'

Maud here had already lived her life. Did she survive two world wars? Marry John? He would have been about thirteen in 1918. Too young to fight and die.

On her phone, Sophie Googled *Maud Watkins born 1900s*. A Maud Watkins had died in 1986 in a nursing home, but there was no photo. Might not be her. For whatever reason, the other Maud's life had left few footprints in the sand.

This was creeping her out. The real Maud was young and very much alive, and when she arrived in Shorten, Sophie would hug her until she popped.

Hugo tapped on his phone again. 'Do you know Anne's maiden name?'

Anne had mentioned it. 'Cochrane, Campbell, no … Cameron.'

'We should Google her and Lucy. They'll be unexplained disappearances, cold cases.'

'We could,' said Sophie, 'but we can't tell the police they're okay. We'd be sectioned.'

'Fair point.' He gave his phone another tap. 'There it is. Shorten Manor. Open to the public but looks the same. Before you go, how about we visit?'

'Hugo, I *really* don't want to. Everyone will be dead or never been born.' She stood up abruptly, the legs of the chair scraping on the floor.

She rushed upstairs to her room and Charlotte came with her.

'We're going now. Before I bottle it.'

In the guest bedroom ensuite, Sophie splashed her face with cold water, pulled on her cardigan and picked up her bag.

Downstairs, she dropped the bag by the coat rack. Shame about the pill, and the clothes she'd ordered, but she'd make do. She unhooked Charlotte's lead from the rack and strode into the kitchen.

Charlotte had already dashed ahead to the French windows, resumed sentry duty, and Hugo hadn't moved from the table, still scrolling on his phone. 'I didn't think you could store so many messages.'

Sophie left her phone by the coffee machine and opened Hugo's Shorten notebook. With the pencil, she wrote down six numbers. 'If people keep texting, feel free to use my phone to fend off questions.'

He glanced up. 'Thanks.'

'The passcode's in your notebook, on the first page.' Sophie went over to Charlotte and cuddled her. 'Let's go.'

'I know she's missing Jack,' said Hugo, 'but this morning, when you were all tucked up, your face in the pillow, the instant she realised I was there, she leapt off the bed all happy.'

The vulnerable feeling was back, entangled with the stupid yearning. 'She trusts you.' Sophie's plate of bacon was still on the table. She hurriedly took it and held it out, but Charlotte turned her head away. 'She associates bacon with Alan and the lift.'

'Understandable.' Hugo frowned. 'People must have called the police seconds after we left the portal. For a very long twenty minutes in the rain, I believed we were in a dystopian world.'

'When did you realise we weren't?'

'After the military guys stood down. And the police were polite, didn't beat us up.'

'Can't be many places where police would beat up a Cabinet Minister's son,' said Sophie. 'Bad cops pick on powerless people.'

Hugo yawned. 'That's a bit bleak.' He looked as knackered as she was.

'I should have realised when I saw the posters. We'd gone missing from here, so of course this was home.'

'Actually,' said Hugo, 'I'm not sure about that. There could be other universes where we've disappeared. Other versions of us who've landed in Shorten or somewhere else.'

'This is making my brain hurt.'

'If things go south at the Manor and you need to escape with Charlotte, deploy sausages.'

Sophie pushed away mad thoughts about evacuating everyone in the Manor and the village. 'I thought black pudding.'

'Sound choice.' He bit his lip. 'We don't properly understand how it works. It's not a given that Charlotte can help call it.'

'I wish you had the gene. Three of us longing for Shorten could have called the lift in record time.'

He shrugged. 'I can't face going back to the university, even for a day.'

The lift hadn't mentally healed him. 'You're abandoning your degree?'

'Living by the portal, wondering whether you'd made it to the right Shorten. Recipe for a nervous breakdown. I'll get a job instead.'

'If the lift doesn't appear, I'll join an animal charity,' said Sophie. 'Or one for girls. Carry on the work I did with Anne.'

'I can see the logic, and you enjoyed the Lady Bountiful stuff in the end.'

'It wouldn't be that, more feminist activism,' said Sophie. 'With a dog-friendly company.'

'Would reduce your options.'

'Charlotte's non-negotiable.'

'Why am I not surprised?'

If the lift was a bust, she'd want a clean break from Hugo. But she wouldn't do weird platonic ghosting. He'd be baffled, worried. She'd gradually text less, not answer messages … the hollow yearning morphed into misery.

Hugo tried to tempt Charlotte with dog food, but she stayed with Sophie by the window. He returned the dog food to the fridge and scraped Charlotte's bacon into a recycling bin, his body language tense and awkward.

Had his nonchalance been an act? Sophie attached the lead to Charlotte's collar. 'Which way to the nearest tube station?'

'Turn left. It's not far.' He stacked her plate in the dishwasher.

Charlotte trotted with Sophie towards the hall then stopped, conflicted, her eyes on Hugo.

'Jack will be lost without you.' And Freddy would be distraught. 'We can't stay.'

'I'd like to sort something before you leave. It won't take long.' Hugo closed the dishwasher. 'If I'd travelled by myself, I don't think I'd have got home. Coming back with you and Charlotte was always the plan.'

'It wasn't.'

'Honestly, it was.'

He was teasing, and she responded in kind. 'You'd have had to drag me in.'

'I did briefly fantasise about knocking you out and carrying you.'

Surprising. 'I can't imagine you doing that.'

'You'd have kicked me to the ground and sat on me.'

'Maybe.'

'And, keeping with reality,' said Hugo, 'if I'd avoided your kicks and punches and knocked you unconscious, your thoughts couldn't have guided us here.'

'True.'

'Plan A wasn't kidnapping you.'

Plan A? He seemed serious. What had he said before Alan showed up? *Three in, three out.* And carrying the bags to the lift, his expression had been resolute, stubborn. She was missing something. 'Why didn't you remind me that you could land in the wrong universe *before* I called the lift?'

'If I had, would you have tricked Charlotte?'

'No.'

'Figured as much.' His face was like Charlotte's when she'd misbehaved: a conflicted mix of guilt and petulance. 'And if I'd mentioned it once the lift appeared?'

She paused by the kitchen door, remembering the effort it had taken to walk to the car. 'I wouldn't have let you get in.'

'Who knows where I'd have ended up?' said Hugo. 'I wouldn't have needed much persuading.'

Charlotte lay down by a cupboard, making settling noises, and Sophie frowned. She had the gene. So had Charlotte. Don't dwell on what could go wrong.

'There was a plan B,' said Hugo.

'Okay, spill.'

'It's academic now.'

Strange to think they'd both had plans. He'd had A and B. She'd only had A: Get Hugo Home. Note to self: never apply for a job in planning.

'You look good in the old-fashioned underwear.'

'What?'

'I'm just saying.'

'Can't see it catching on,' said Sophie. 'And since when was it appropriate to talk about my underwear?'

'Obviously not in Shorten. Would have been an outrageous remark.'

She checked and double-checked. Anyone else and it would have been obvious. A misguided butterfly fluttered in her stomach. That ship had sailed.

'We make a good team.'

More stupid butterflies. What was he doing? Actually, a better question was *why*? The last thing she needed was a casual fling… Who was she kidding? 'Hugo, I'm confused.' He seemed serious but might be teasing again. 'You don't like me, not like that.'

'Says who?'

'*You*, in Shorten.'

'That was there,' said Hugo. 'You don't understand.'

She did. Sex without commitment was the 'something' he wanted to sort. 'Don't bother dressing it up, Hugo. You want sex.' He must have been frustrated in Shorten. Visiting Clarissa in 1920s London, constrained by convention, he hadn't even kissed her.

'This isn't about sex,' said Hugo, his eyes earnest.

Sophie raised her eyebrows.

'Okay, sex comes into it but it's more complicated.'

Sex comes into it. If she slept with him today, tomorrow she'd be a contender for the Most Messed Up competition, but she could work through that. She took in his intense, set expression. Hugo did nothing without engaging his brain. He'd have supplies or buy some, and she'd have a precious memory to take to her grave.

'In Shorten, it couldn't have worked.' Hugo folded his arms.

Yes, clear what plan B had been. He didn't feel like she did, but as with most boys, Hugo had a one-track mind. And they were friends. Close friends. Adding benefits to that friendship — once — wouldn't change his feelings, or her determination to return to the Manor, *or* confuse the lift. And Freddy would never know. Gossip didn't travel between universes.

She dropped Charlotte's lead and walked towards him.

'I've always had a thing about you. In chapel at school, I watched the sun dancing on your hair. A distraction from endless prayers.'

She remembered the endless prayers. He'd made the other stuff up to persuade her into bed. He stood stock still as she stepped closer, seemed mesmerised.

This would be sex, not making love. She ignored the warning voice in her brain and kissed him cautiously on the mouth. He responded with such intensity that her whole body pulsed with energy, but a second later, he lifted his lips from hers, rested his hands on her shoulders and took a half-step back, staring at her as if she'd appeared from a magic mirror.

'Don't stop.' She put on her best doe eyes.

'You feel the same.' It was half a statement, half an accusation.

Yes, he'd been frustrated. 'Shorten *was* a sex-free zone.'

Now he looked surprised. 'What about Freddy?'

'He'll never find out and … once we're married, that will be it. I won't have had a normal sex life before settling down—'

'I get that.' He dropped his hands from her shoulders. 'But I'm not sleeping with you weeks before you marry Freddy.' His mouth twisted. 'I won't do that.'

She'd misunderstood.

He'd been teasing after all.

CHAPTER 46

In Sophie's last year at Hadley, when Pete had shown an interest, she'd been flattered, and though she'd found him boring, it was her first romance, so she'd gone with it.

Eventually, she'd dumped him. Nicely, giving him the old 'needing her own space' excuse, but she'd ended it far too late. Her inexperience and curiosity had hurt him, and she still felt guilty.

Sophie rested her hands on the top of a kitchen chair and took in Hugo's set expression. He'd led her on, only to push her away, and there was no remorse there. Depression or not, this wasn't his first rodeo—

'I shouldn't have started flirting,' said Hugo. 'I told you, there's stuff we need to sort.'

Resisting an urge to slap him, Sophie looked down, sour rejection twisting her guts. But the way he'd kissed her. If he didn't fancy her, *really* fancy her, she was a walrus.

'You only had half the picture in Shorten.'

Thanks to Maud's ear for gossip, anything Sophie Arundel didn't know was trivial.

'You're definitely set on going back?'

'Yes.'

He walked to the far end of the table. 'Because of Anne and you're in love with Freddy.'

'Yes, because of Anne. And I promised Freddy. I'm not in love with him, but I fancy him, and he's kind and clever and sweet.'

'*Sweet.*' He dragged his fingers through his hair. 'But you fancy me too?'

After pushing her away, he expected an answer? She countered with a question. 'I thought, when you kissed me … did I get that wrong?'

'No,' said Hugo. 'I'm *so* glad I didn't realise this before.'

'Realise what?'

'That you fancied me.'

Understatement.

'I needed to marry Clarissa,' said Hugo, 'and you needed to marry Freddy. We'd both have had the resources to protect ourselves — or leave the country.'

Bizarre. She'd reasoned by marrying Freddy, she could protect Hugo better. Nothing like a chat with your best mate... Might be a blessing he'd been teasing. Friends with benefits could have nagged at her, hurt her relationship with Freddy. She took the lead and pulled, but Charlotte didn't move. 'What's going on with you?'

Sophie dragged her into the hall.

Charlotte looked back at Hugo who was standing in the kitchen doorway, then up at Sophie, meaning, 'Sort this.'

Okay, from their tone of voice and body language, Charlotte knew she and Hugo were at odds. But this was beyond sorting. Sophie took her bag from the coat rack and slung the strap so it was secure across her chest, but at the same moment, Charlotte wrenched the lead from Sophie's grip and rushed over to Hugo.

He sighed. 'For what it's worth, I feel guilty about Clarissa.'

'I'll try and soften the blow, tell her you were homesick, couldn't adapt,' said Sophie. 'Come on, Charlotte.'

Charlotte raised her head, her stubborn face on.

'Clarissa was great fun,' said Hugo.

'She *loves* you.'

'I'm not sure about that. We were both outsiders, so we clicked, and given the circumstances, a no brainer.'

'Would you ever have married me?' Her voice was miraculously casual.

'No.'

His certainty was a kick to the stomach. 'Thanks for that. I wouldn't want to get ideas above my station.'

He opened his mouth but didn't reply.

Sophie walked back and grabbed Charlotte's lead.

'Look, there's stuff you don't know.'

'You're in bits, Hugo. It's been a hell of a trip and I've got another one.' She was losing it. 'If you've crucial info, just tell me.'

'If I hadn't married Clarissa, whoever I married would have been the estate manager's wife, lived in the tied cottage.'

'Rent free. I know.'

'You wouldn't have been happy,' said Hugo, 'married to the estate manager.'

'What's with this estate manager thing? If we'd got hammered and hitched in a drunken haze, I'd have married *you*, not a job description.'

'I'm serious, Sophie.'

'So am I.' Sophie pulled on Charlotte's lead, but Charlotte's attention was fixed on Hugo.

He set his mouth. 'You'd have resented not being in the big house.'

'Oh, so now I'm a snob?'

'You couldn't have ended up with me.'

He made it sound like a prize in a tacky game show. 'Being a snob, not wanting to be Mrs Estate Manager … it's complete crap.'

'I know you pretty well.'

'You don't.' Whatever he was doing or why, she was at the end of her tether.

'Please hear me out, before you disappear.'

Sophie hesitated. More info could head off landing in a nightmare world.

'Last night, when I was undoing your dress, I realised why I'd travelled without the gene.'

His fingers on her buttons… Sophie inwardly winced. 'You just happened to be there.'

Hugo shook his head. 'Once I'd double-checked the logic, it was obvious. The lift is powered by thought and emotion. Janet and Lucy were close friends.'

'Yes.' Sophie wouldn't break Lucy's confidence and tell him how close.

'As with me, if the bond's strong enough, it trumps DNA or mood.'

'Hugo, when we got in the lift at Uni, we hardly knew each other. *No* bond. That doesn't work.'

'It does. I Googled Janus. One of his statues symbolised the number of days in a year, showing his mastery over time.'

'Okay…'

'The lift didn't see us linked in the past or the present,' said Hugo, 'but did see us linked in the future. Whoever built it could see beyond linear time.'

'Too complicated.'

'Bear with me, think about it.'

She put the bag down, buttoned up her cardigan, and sat on the chair by the front door. Thinking was easier sitting down.

When they'd arrived in Shorten, Hugo had quoted Einstein: *The past, present and future exist simultaneously. Time isn't linear, we only think it is.* And she'd called the lift in the lane not by yearning in the present, but with memories ... the past.

The delicate hands on her watch inexorably clicked forward, like the clock in the headmistress' study. Tick tock. She exhaled, pushed away the familiar wood polish smell. If the lift could analyse her brain, right this second, what would it see through her eyes? Hugo's hall? No. Hadley's headmistress, her face strained. 'An accident ... *So* sorry.'

That time, that place, was always with her. She'd never accepted her parents were gone, and in her mind, she'd never left that room. Or that moment.

If the lift understood English, it would say, *You Live Here*.

For Sophie Arundel, the past was an integral part of the present and the future. And although at school they'd hardly spoken, she realised now ... despite her flawed assumptions, she'd always been *aware* of Hugo: physically, when he'd entered a room, and in a noisy crowd, easily distinguished his voice.

Always. There.

'A mad idea,' said Sophie, 'but you were my Shorten BFF, so it fits.'

'I didn't see the lift until you said my name. Perhaps you reinforced our link, gave me visual clearance?' He gestured to the tatty paperback by the coffee machine. 'I looked through Isobel's old philosophy book this morning.'

His sister must be as smart as him.

'It's quite possible we have free will, that *we* make decisions, but our choices are also inevitable because of our genes, and who knows what else.'

Unpack that? 'How is that relevant?'

'It was fate that we found the Manor.'

'Fate's the secular equivalent of "God's will," Hugo. I'm not a fan.' Janet and Andrew, and Robert who'd died with his pie, would have been arbitrarily snuffed out. '*Nothing is inevitable until it happens* is a much better idea.'

'I feel the same, but it's the final piece of the puzzle. We called the lift like a taxi.'

'And carrying on the analogy,' said Sophie, 'like an Uber, it had already logged in the journey.'

'Not really. The lift had *always* known.'

Sophie shivered. She fastened the top button on her cardigan.

'Perhaps it's not the traditional "fate." The lift saw us together in some universes but not in others.'

Right. He was going through the motions to fit his theory: sad, misguided, and for her, pointlessly cruel. 'So, you theorised about star-crossed lovers and started flirting.'

'I'm not in thrall to the lift, Sophie, acting out what it knows. I've wanted us to get together … for years.'

Years. At Hadley? Why was he doing this? His actions and words in Shorten, consistent to a fault: pleased she'd stopped dithering about Freddy, his satisfied nod when Freddy announced their engagement. But now it was Flirt, Reject, Snob and Lift Theory Tease. The old Hugo didn't hurt people because he could.

A selfless, brave girl would stick around, ensure he got help until he recovered, or didn't. And all the while, he'd never feel like she did.

Sophie stood up, slung the bag strap across her chest again, picked up the lead and dragged Charlotte towards the front door, Charlotte's bottom sliding inelegantly along the polished floor.

'I appreciate you're unwell.' Finish this. She'd never see him again. 'I fell for you, head over heels.'

He looked stunned. One last surprise.

'I'd have done anything to be with you. *Anything.*'

'Why didn't you tell me?' He seemed angry. 'All those times we talked in my room—'

'You'd have laughed your head off.'

'You think I *enjoyed* knowing you were kissing Freddy, *marrying* him. It took masochism to new heights.'

His vehemence surprised her, but what he thought he remembered was fiction. The slightest hint in Shorten and she'd have kissed him senseless.

Charlotte was still resisting but they were nearly at the door. 'You're depressed. It's messing with your mind. Get professional help.'

He ran past her and put his arms out like a scarecrow.

'Seriously?'

'I haven't been straight with you but I'm not ill.' He exhaled slowly. 'I made a promise to Freddy, but I'll break it.'

This was new.

Charlotte slipped her collar and hurled herself at Hugo. She kissed him full on the mouth and he ruffled her head.

Using Charlotte's love was a cheap trick.

But Sophie's hopeless longing was a weight, deadening her brain. 'Five minutes.'

CHAPTER 47

Hugo sat at the kitchen table, his head in his hands.

'You were concerned about Rupert, nagging me to marry Freddy, remember?' Sophie's voice was measured. 'If you'd wanted me, you'd have said so, kissed me.' She sat down on the nearest chair. 'I wouldn't have encouraged Freddy—'

'You didn't encourage Freddy.' Hugo raised his head. 'You could have sworn at him or hit him or ignored him. Would have made zero difference.'

Right, not getting through. 'Freddy only recently got serious. That's how it was.' Sophie refastened the collar on Charlotte, tightened it up a notch, but unclipped her lead.

'*Here*'s how it was. Freddy was smitten from the moment he met you. He was a ticking bomb with no off switch. I can't tell you how often he talked about your hair, or your smile, or the way you talk. The day after we arrived at the Manor, he said, *I'm going to marry Miss Arundel.*' Hugo's mouth tightened. 'He wasn't joking.'

He drummed his fingers on the table. 'He was nervous just talking to you, but he was obsessed. That first week, he planned to propose on one knee, in front of his parents and the servants.'

'No...'

'You'd have rejected him out of hand, humiliated him.'

'I'd only met him *days* before.'

'I managed to talk him out of it,' said Hugo. 'But he'd confided in me, trusted me. If I'd told you his intentions, he would have felt betrayed as well as humiliated—'

'We'd have been chucked out.'

'We'd have been destitute.'

Sophie frowned. 'At the beginning, he didn't flirt, showed no interest.'

'He was *beyond* shy, Sophie. He'd never even kissed a girl.'

Okay, Hugo knew nothing about Betty.

'I thought he was deluded, but actually, if you hadn't been forced into the lift by Alan, you'd have been happy.'

'Mostly Happy Ever After.'

Hugo gave her an odd look. 'I guess. The kickboxing and when you grabbed that branch as a weapon, that made him nervous. But he was fascinated. And Rupert focused his mind, pushed him to propose.'

'And the whole time, I was out of the loop.' Sophie stared at him, baffled — and angry.

'He made me swear, Sophie, to keep his confidences secret, help him court you, marry you. I swore on his bible.'

'You're not religious.'

'It was a solemn promise, and I meant to honour it. I knew we might never get home. We were completely dependent on the Laceys and by marrying Freddy, yes, you'd have had security, but you'd also have been loved and cherished, and forged your own path with the estate.' He sighed. 'As I got to know you, keeping my vow became ... difficult.'

Sophie's mind raced. Should she tell him about Betty? Despite the boys being close, Freddy had assumed —

wrongly — that Hugo, more assured and worldly, would be unsympathetic. She should keep her promise.

'He couldn't talk about you to his mother, let alone his father. You were his first love. He agonised for more than a week about Rupert, worrying he'd lost you, but he wouldn't propose until he knew you'd accept. That's why, near the end, he asked me to sound you out.'

'So, Freddy was besotted for a while,' said Sophie. 'Doesn't explain *your* miraculous conversion to my charms.'

'I was trapped.' Hugo met her eyes. 'Freddy talked endlessly about how he adored you, his plans for children, for the estate. If we'd got together, Freddy would have seen it as a calculated betrayal. Unforgivable.' Hugo's lips thinned into a hard line. 'He would have completely lost it.'

'Anne wouldn't have chucked us out.' Sophie's anger had turned into tears, and she blinked, distracted, conflicted. If she stayed, she'd dearly miss Anne, would be betraying her *and* Freddy.

'I don't know how Anne would have reacted, but if Freddy had suspected for a second...'

'He might have thrown a punch—'

'He'd have looked for his shotgun.'

Sophie hesitated, trying to take it in. 'I'm not sure. He was so...'

'Decent? I would have shattered that. Even with a universe between us, I feel horrible.'

A whisper of hope. 'When we spoke about marriage and money, you said it was about survival.'

'It would have been.'

'You'd have married Clarissa?'

'Yes.'

'We were in our own silos, Hugo.' Her brain was humming, re-evaluating memories, changing them. 'We should all have talked, worked things through.'

'Discussed it over elevenses.' He made a scoffing noise. 'The idea that he'd have patted me on the back... *Actually, Freddy, I'm fond of Sophie too. Oh, and by the way, our etiquette's different so we've already slept together. Can we live in one of your cottages?*'

'Obviously, if you'd put it like that—'

'How would you have told him?'

Sophie swallowed. I could love you but I'm *in* love with Hugo. No, Hugo hadn't said he loved her. 'It would have been too difficult. Impossible.'

Freddy was in love with her, but Hugo wanted her. Really wanted her. And he'd tried to tell her without breaking Freddy's confidence, just as she meant to keep Freddy's secret, and Lucy's. Hugo was honourable, not ill. She watched him, not daring to believe it.

'There were moments when I thought you might feel the same, but I couldn't risk you throwing your life away.'

'You didn't trust me.'

'Not with this. You act first and think later.'

'I'd have left the Manor,' said Sophie. 'Gone with you.'

'And we'd have had to steal and beg. The novelty would have worn off fast.'

Hugo's mock salute, turning on his heel after Freddy kissed her, planning to marry before Christmas...

A shedload of guilt was there, under thankfulness and surprise. Like the tide, it would ebb and flow, but the joy of right now was an exuberant street parade, clearing all in its path. 'You were so determined to get home—'

'*With you.*'

Primeval forces were gathering deep inside, making ready. The sensation was so strong, she caught her breath. She didn't have to brave the lift. Tomorrow, or ever. Hugo. What she'd believed was impossible.

He was scrutinising her, as if she might disappear in a puff of smoke.

'This being together thing, it's not because we're in the correct world and I'm in your house?' Her tone wasn't flippant. She needed to be sure.

'So, you'll stay?' He stood up.

She got to her feet. His casual tone didn't fool her. 'Obviously.'

Hugo strode towards her and kissed her, and she responded with a frenetic hunger.

Something was scratching her back.

Hugo mumbled over her lips. 'What's wrong?'

Charlotte was jumping up. For the first time ever, Sophie wished Charlotte would find a hobby. 'I'll distract her.'

Sophie hurried to the bread bin and gave Charlotte two slices, but when Charlotte slid under the table with her treat, Sophie regretted her mean thought, and tried not to think about Jack.

Hugo gathered her close and nuzzled her neck. 'Do you want to hear what Plan B was?'

A delicious shiver, though his mouth was warm on her skin. 'Go on.'

'If the lift appeared, I was going to share how I felt. If you'd still walked away, I'd have been stuffed. You could have told Freddy or written to Clarissa.'

'I *so* wouldn't. Plan B would have worked.'

'But there's no way you'd have left Charlotte behind.' He scanned her face.

Sophie's eyes widened. 'That's why you insisted Charlotte come with us.'

'Might have been.' He trailed kisses on her neck.

'After your engagement news, I pulled a sickie. You must have suspected?'

'I didn't, you'd had migraines at school. And when you

kissed Freddy in the library, I thought, game over.' He was still kissing her neck, tantalisingly slowly. 'The lie about Pete seemed odd, but a few days later you brought forward the wedding.'

He needed to understand she wasn't callous and selfish. 'If Alan hadn't turned up and you'd said… Going with you would have been hard.'

Hugo paused his trail of kisses. 'I promised Freddy you'd return to the Manor, whatever happened.'

'You reassured him when all the while—'

'I had to, or he'd have insisted on coming. And once the lift arrived, I had one shot.'

Thud. Charlotte was pawing at the French windows. 'I'll take her out,' said Sophie, 'or she won't settle.'

Hugo unlocked the door, they stepped into drizzle, and Charlotte circled around, sniffing.

Sophie looped her arms around Hugo's neck and kissed him, and when he responded, *really* responded, her knees buckled. Okay, romance novels, not dramatic licence…

When they drew apart, Sophie rested her head on his shoulder, watching Charlotte speeding towards a sturdy pigeon and, like every occasion before, at the very last second, the pigeon flying to safety.

'You're a good actor,' said Hugo. 'Just now, I was convinced you only wanted a fling.'

'I'm not that good. Lucy realised. So did Anne.'

'You told *Anne?*'

'She guessed,' said Sophie. 'It was … awkward.'

'It must have been excruciating. I don't understand. Why didn't she tell Freddy?'

'You were marrying Clarissa, and once you were out of the picture, she was confident Freddy and I would be happy. I was too.' Sophie looked up at the sky, relishing the cold rain on her face.

'If we'd got together at school, you'd have nagged me to stay home and properly recover from glandular fever. I'd have done my exams the following year, secured my Oxford offer.'

'But I'd have enrolled at the same Uni and Charlotte would still have called the lift.'

'She wouldn't,' said Hugo. 'Mrs B would happily have minded her, and we'd have met up every weekend.' He shot her a wicked grin. 'And not gone out much. I hope you'd never have yearned for another world.'

'In other universes, we might be living that life … different versions of us.'

'Not sure if that's comforting or disturbing.'

The future held endless possibilities, opportunities. Obviously, she'd be spending quite a few hours in Hugo's bedroom… But outside of that, if she couldn't get a job with a charity, she'd volunteer, and in the summer, she'd wear shorts, swim in a bikini and for the rest of her life wear anything she damn well liked.

Reckless and heady, Sophie cherished the moment. She was sailing into harbour, the whisper of hope now a steady breeze.

Charlotte raced into the house, keen to be warm and dry again, and they followed. In the kitchen, Sophie took off her watch and engagement ring, and relief lit up Hugo's face.

'They'll be safe in my bag.' She dashed into the hall and put them in a zipped compartment, her mind buzzing. Hugo's days in Shorten had been a mirror image of hers, a serene glide on the surface, while underneath desperately paddling. But when he saw the lift, he would always have betrayed Freddy. A hard choice, but not finely balanced. Not a real choice at all. And if Hugo was correct about the lift, they'd been fated from birth.

When Sophie had started at Hadley, her mother had sent

her a text message. Initially a source of comfort, then an ironic epitaph: *Trust in God's will to choose the right path*. Gods might not exist, yet maybe for humans — and other animals — none of their choices were theirs? She didn't want to believe that. In an infinite number of universes, there was surely one creature that didn't follow nature and nurture, made an unforeseeable, unique choice?

But she wasn't that creature. Not today.

Back in the kitchen, she stood so close to Hugo that the wool strands on his jumper brushed her cheek. 'I'd always have chosen you.'

'Ten minutes ago, you thought I was ill—'

She kissed him and he held her even closer, his body pressing against her clothes. A deeper tremor of longing was flooding through her, and she murmured against his mouth, 'You'll need to unfasten my buttons.'

'When I was undoing them last night, you were trembling.'

'It was cold.'

'No, it wasn't.'

His lips were on hers again and she reacted with a mad, hungry yearning. He pushed her against a wall, and she arched towards him. Her breathing had gone shallow and shaky. 'It's 2018, we can do anything we want.'

'Now?'

'Definitely *now*.'

'My bedroom's on the second floor.' Hugo took her hand, they ran upstairs, and he opened a door.

He had a king-sized bed. 'Are your intentions honourable?'

'Entirely *dis*honourable.'

Sophie smiled. 'Mine too.'

As Hugo closed the door, Charlotte settled in the corridor. She'd stand guard.

Hugo turned a key in the lock and hauled off his jumper. She tugged her cardigan over her head.

An instant later, Hugo's fingers were fumbling on her dress collar. 'Too many buttons.'

Sophie drew a shuddery breath, excitement making her pleasantly giddy.

A long moment passed, then another. Finally, with a genteel swish, the gown fell to the floor.

EPILOGUE

Three hours later, Sophie was asleep, her head on Hugo's chest, her long blonde hair fanned out like a victory flag.

Faint but shrill on the ground floor, the front doorbell rang, and Sophie stirred. Hugo gave a sleepy sigh, put an arm around her, but didn't wake, his dark hair tousled against the pillow.

Sophie squinted at a bedside radio: 15:47. Hours before his parents finished work.

Ring.

Pamela would answer it.

Hugo still didn't stir, blissfully unbothered by doorbells, and Sophie relaxed, enjoying the touch of his skin, breathing him in. A sleeping prince. *Her* prince.

Against all the odds, she was going to live Happily Ever After. Not a one-night stand or, more accurately, a day-stand. Why didn't people have more day-stands? They were infinitely superior. You weren't tipsy or tired, and you remembered *everything*.

Instinct told her their balloon would never burst. Not with babies, busy jobs or whatever life threw at them.

Ring.

This was beyond annoying. Sophie gently removed Hugo's arm and slid off the bed, standing on her complicated dress, discarded on the floor. She snatched a towelling bathrobe from a hook on the wall and pulled it on. Much too big but would do.

She secured the tie about her waist, unlocked the door, and stepped into the corridor. Charlotte jumped up in excitement, George was there too, and Sophie went downstairs serenaded by stereo barking.

Sophie looked through a peephole at the policeman who'd petted Charlotte. Better open up.

The officer was cradling his rifle. It was narrow and sleek. Alien. This was *her* London, but the picture in her mind and the reality didn't match. Maybe it never had?

'Sorry to bother you, Miss.'

George trotted off into the house, but Charlotte stayed on the doorstep. 'There's a young man by the gate who insists he knows you. He's not on any of our lists. Says his name's Frederick Lacey.'

Sophie's breath caught and she gasped for air. Was she still in Shorten, dreaming? One hell of a dream: X-rated. Once dreams changed, you never got back to the good bits, and when you woke up, you couldn't remember. Typical.

No, this had to be real. Far too much detail... She heard herself say, 'We've known him for ages.'

The policeman gestured to another officer beside the gate, and maddeningly slowly, the heavy gate swung open. Freddy stepped onto the drive and let the policeman search him. He wore a baggy suit and was carrying his winter coat. Didn't look wildly out of place, but over a century, men's suits hadn't changed much.

Close the door.

No. She couldn't shut out Freddy.

He strolled up the drive. 'Sophie, am I glad to see you.'

She made herself smile. 'Ha, me too.'

Charlotte leapt towards him, her tail furiously wagging, and Sophie leaned against the door jamb, her head spinning. She was naked under the bathrobe. If she fainted, Freddy would see exactly what she wasn't wearing. Entwined limbs, slow, exquisite sensation… Breathe.

'My darling girl, are you ill?' Freddy peered at Hugo's bathrobe.

'Caught a nasty bug. You'd better come in.'

On impulse, or out of guilt, she kissed him on the cheek.

She stepped back into the hall and Freddy sauntered past her, looking around like a millennial buying his first flat.

'Go into the drawing room. I'll be down in a few minutes.'

Sophie closed the front door. Actually, she might be dreaming, safe in bed with Hugo, subconscious stuff working itself through. She ran upstairs, deliberately banging her hand on the balustrade. It hurt.

Once in Hugo's room, she locked his door.

He smiled at her. 'What's with all the barking?'

'Freddy's here.'

Hugo's mouth dropped open.

'He's downstairs.'

'You're winding me up.'

'I'm not. Honestly. I've no clue what to do.'

'Let's put some clothes on,' said Hugo. 'Perhaps after this afternoon, *you're* having a breakdown?'

They grinned at each other like naughty children.

Sophie found her underwear and struggled into her dress. As he fastened her buttons, hysteria morphed into panic. 'Shoes, Hugo. I said I'd been sick. You can't be sick too.'

'Agreed.' He put on loafers. 'Even if you are a nutcase, I love you.'

'Good to know.' They were solid, bonded by shared experience and atavistic lust. 'I love you too.' If she *was* dreaming, with true love, she'd wake up. She kissed him, a lingering kiss that made her toes tingle. No. Not dreaming. Anyway, if kisses could free her from an enchanted sleep, she'd have woken a lot earlier…

She followed him out and down the stairs. Okay, if this was a delusion, including Hugo in it hadn't helped.

Freddy stood in the hall, looking up at them with a broad grin. George was snuffling his crisply ironed trousers and Charlotte was zooming, beyond thrilled. Freddy offered his hand and Hugo stepped off the bottom step, gave him a firm handshake.

Sophie paused on the stairs. Breathe. Forget poker and spying, Hugo should be a professional actor. She walked down to Freddy and he tenderly kissed her, and she felt guilty and mean and horrible.

'I'll make tea.' She retreated to the kitchen, switched on the kettle, and hunted through cupboards for a teapot and mugs.

Charlotte had come with her but was now staring towards the hall. Freddy was here, so expecting Jack…

The kettle took forever to boil, and Sophie's stress levels kept climbing. Freddy's old-style money didn't work here. How did he get down to London, let alone find Hugo's house?

And how did he cross universes so fast? Wasn't as if he could hail the next lift and follow them to the exact right universe. She'd concentrated *so* hard, before and during the crossing, and couldn't shake the worry she'd been lucky.

Her hands shook as she poured boiling water into a teapot and as she set the tray, her thoughts became increasingly manic. Freddy must have inherited the gene from Anne, but his knowledge of this world was second-hand, and limited. How could he yearn for it?

He'd yearned for her.

Anne's words danced through her head. *Once Freddy sets his mind to something, he won't give up.* Freddy filled her brain: asking to kiss her, politely, respectfully, *how* he'd kissed her, carefully, urgently, folding her into his arms, close and safe, and his face as he'd slid the ring on her finger, intense, certain. He wanted her, loved her.

If he found out about Hugo, he'd go insane. She rushed into the empty hall. Hugo was talking in the drawing room, his voice casual, normal. She grabbed her bag and put on the watch and ring. It felt wrong. Sour, bad.

Back in the kitchen, she tried to calm down. Think ... serene thoughts. She'd returned safely from the Shorten quest, captured her prince, and seized her Happy Ever After. But this wasn't the end of her journey. She'd hardly started out. Hugo hadn't hesitated when he'd realised Freddy was really here. She could be as brave as Hugo.

She picked up the tray—

Hugo came in and shut the door behind him. 'He's stressed witless from the journey. You should get your ring and watch.'

'Ahead of you.'

'We can distract him.'

'For how long? He's on a mission.'

'He can see thousands of movies,' said Hugo, 'play video games, experience virtual reality. He'll be moved and shocked and amazed.'

Sophie rested the tray on a kitchen surface. 'He can follow *Star Trek* from the very first season.'

'He'll find algorithms and super computers *fascinating*.'

'You're right. It'll be okay.'

'I'll take the tray. Freddy needs to realise that in this benighted world men do domestic chores.' He picked it up. 'All set?'

'Twenty-first century London will be the biggest adventure of his life, and he'll meet loads of sassy girls.' Sophie opened the door. 'Freddy's going to love it.'

~

~

~

IF YOU ENJOYED ESCAPE
LET PEOPLE KNOW

Reviews are the most effective way of building awareness of a book you've enjoyed.

While I love telling people about the *Shorten Chronicles*, honest reviews bring books to the attention of other readers.

If you didn't buy *Escape* from my website, I'd really appreciate it if you'd spend just a few minutes leaving a review (short as you like) where you bought it.

Thank you!

Sophie's adventures continue in **Exile**, the third book of the *Shorten Chronicles*.

Buy the print book direct from Rosalind's website. You'll get the best price *and* support the author.

www.rosalindtate.com

ABOUT THE AUTHOR

Rosalind Tate lives in Gloucestershire, England, and holidays on the Cornish coast. She served in the British military, then worked as a journalist and a lawyer.

Rosalind's enjoys speaking at authors' and readers' conferences, talking about publishing and encouraging new authors. When she's not behind her computer, you can find Rosalind reading her favourite books, walking her dogs, swimming, or watching sci-fi and fantasy shows.

Rosalind has three grown up children, a tolerant husband, and two utterly gorgeous dogs.

ACKNOWLEDGMENTS

To my husband, Ian. Thank you for your patience, support, and sharp, proofreading eyes.

To my mother, who many years ago showed me how to be a writer.

To *Jericho Writers* and my editor, Debi Alper, and my fabulous readers in *Team Charlotte*.

Thank you to our labradoodle, the wonderful Bella. You inspired the *Shorten Chronicles* after all.

And thanks also to Bella's goldendoodle kid sister, for her author guarding skills. She's called … Sophie. *What?* Okay, when we adopted her, I was obsessed with Sophie Arundel, and our energetic puppy has some things in common with her literary human counterpart. She's sassy, runs fast and is far too impulsive.

Finally, Toby deserves a mention. He was our first labradoodle and is no longer with us.

Well, in this world.

Rosalind Tate
Gloucestershire 2021

ESCAPE

BOOK TWO OF THE SHORTEN CHRONICLES

First published in Great Britain in 2021
by TOB Publishing
Copyright © Rosalind Tate 2021
® The Shorten Chronicles is a registered trademark

A catalogue record for this book is available from the British Library: ISBN: 978-1-8380544-6-5

Cover Design: 187 Designz, thecreativitybank.com
Website: dan@authorpop.co, sprkdesign

TOB Publishing

www.rosalindtate.com
rosalind@rosalindtate.com